Shimmy Shimmy Homicide

Shimmy Shimmy Homicide

A Belly Dancing Boomer Mystery

Rima Perlstein Riedel

To Louise,
Thanks for joining
me for my launch.
Rima

Rima S. & David P. Riedel

SHIMMY SHIMMY HOMICIDE

This is a work of fiction. The characters, incidents, and dialog either are products of the author's imagination or are used fictitiously.

Published by Rima S. and David P. Riedel

ISBN 978-1-7374314-0-4

Cover Design by Tamara Womack-Speaks

Dedication

To my Father, Lester, my Mother, Esther and my sister, Jeanio, who I hope are smiling down on me from up above. Miss you all!

To my wonderful husband, David, and in memory of our brave little terrier cross, Patch—our very own Streak, who is somewhere up in doggy heaven terrorizing all the bigger dogs.

And to all my wonderful dance students Past, Present and Future!

Contents

Chapter 1

THEY call it "The City With Village Charm"—and charming, Leicester truly is—with its Victorian houses, cobblestone streets and trees everywhere. A typical sleepy New England town, complete with a lovely manicured green and even a gazebo. But, our lovely hamlet wasn't quite so charming the day I tripped over the corpse on the darkened staircase at the Senior Center . . . .

I was just coming in through the side entrance, followed by my usual mini entourage of dance students. All of us were loaded down with the stuff for class, when I literally tripped over what appeared to be a pile of soggy old clothes. My ladies, who had been right at my heels were taken by surprise, toppling into me. We went down one by one, like a pile of dominoes. Positively surreal! Looking like something out of a Keystone Cops flick, there we lay sprawled in a rather undignified heap at the bottom of the stairs. Fortunately, Henrietta Hirshfeld, Henri for short, a sprightly little septuagenarian, managed to disentangle herself from the pile and help get everyone back on their feet. Finally, after several false starts, accompanied by a serious giggle fest with my students, I was able to right myself. Bending down to retrieve my now flattened and extremely soggy bags, I looked closer to see what I had tripped over. A rheumy eye stared back at me. Stifling a scream and the strong urge to throw up, I felt for a pulse and found none. Quickly backing away, careful not to set off the domino effect again, I turned back to Henri and the other ladies.

Gently nudging them aside, I pointed and said, "Looks like we've got a problem here (talk about a major understatement). It appears someone's had an attack of some sort. I'm afraid it's too late to do anything for this poor guy." Suddenly four pairs of eyes lit up; all varieties of expressions in them, from utter shock to barely disguised excitement, as they crowded around straining to look over my shoulder to catch a glimpse of the gruesome sight.

"Ladies, please head to the elevator downstairs. We have to call the authorities, and they're not going to appreciate our tramping all over the place. Besides, it's freezing cold and damp down here. We don't want to catch pneumonia."

Melisande (Mel for short) Wilson, a twinkling, blue-eyed, curly haired, magenta Miss Marple—the Dame Margaret Rutherford version—yelled out, "Pneumonia! Oh, pooh! Who cares about a little P–neu–monia when there's a dead body right at our feet. Haven't had this much excitement since the big storm twenty-something years ago, when the whole town closed down!"

Charlotte Rae Knowles, our resident "Southern Belle," chimed in. "Ain't that the truth. Ah sure haven't. Not since I married my Yankee soldier boy and moved up North. Boy was my daddy rippin' mad!"

" 'A Yankee!' he shouted. 'Ya couldn't just settle down with a good ol' Southern boy?!' "

"Would'a been our fiftieth anniversary this year, if my Billy Boy hadn't gone and succumbed to that nasty ol' flu a few years back. Who knows, maybe it's murder …?" she finished, licking her lips. Sudden silence followed by a group intake of breath accompanied this statement, then a chorus of moans and groans.

Henrietta turned on her, saying, "Bite your tongue, Charlotte! Don't even think about such a thing! What are you, nuts?! Flu's one thing, but murder …?"

"OK, ladies, we really need to calm down now and get moving. Someone has to get hold of Claudia. NOW! Henrietta, would you please take care of that?"

"Sure Ez! Are you going to be alright staying here by yourself?"

"Got no choice, I've got to put in a call to 911. Besides, someone has to stay with the body until they show …." I gagged. "It might be best for the rest of you to head to the library and wait there. The police may want to talk to us."

As the ladies trudged back down the stairs towards the elevator, I heard our own slightly hearing impaired "Miss Marple" loudly declaring, "Oh boy, does this mean we'll all be grilled by the cops? This is so exciting—just like in a mystery book!"

Behind her, Henri drolly replied, "Yay, just what we needed on a cold snowy day—a murder ...."

As I started to hit my emergency dial, Rosemary Chase, a very youthful sixty-something, dashed in accompanied by a rush of cold, wet, snowy air. She stopped short on seeing me and cried out, "What the h ...? Are you alright, Esme? Is that what I think it is?"

"I am and it is," I said, covering the speaker with my hand as it began to ring.

"Hold on, I'm just calling the police now. Fill you in, in a minute. Yes. Hello, my name is Esmeralda Fine, I'm calling to report an incident at the Senior Center ... an old man lying on the stairs. I think he's dead. What? No, I'm not a doctor, but he doesn't appear to be breathing and his skin is hard and cold to the touch, with a bluish gray tinge," I explained, having accidentally touched his hand when I tripped.

"That's right, side entrance of the Senior Center. Forrest Street. I've already sent a message to the director, Ms. Martin, with one of my students. Me? I'm just one of the dance instructors. No, I don't recognize him in his current state. No, my students are usually women. Yes, I'll wait. Several of my students happened to be with me when I tripped over the man. Yes, you heard right. I literally tripped over him when I came in ... thought it was just an old bundle of clothes at first. Yes it was quite a shock. I've asked my ladies to stay. They'll be in the library. OK. Thanks."

Hanging up I turned my attention to the woman waiting at my side, positively salivating, eyes popping out of curiosity.

"Well, as you've probably figured from my conversation with the police, I was coming into the building with my usual load of stuff, when I tripped over ... that." I told her, pointing to the spot, gagging at the memory. "Some of the girls were helping me, as usual. You can guess the rest. Not a day I'm likely to forget any time soon."

"How about you?" my friend and student inquired. Putting her arm around my shoulders, "Are you OK?"

"Except for a few bruises here and there, when the ladies landed on top of me, I'm fine." Then as a mental picture of the whole ridiculous scene, entered my mind, I began to laugh hysterically, barely able to catch my breath.

"Whoa, girl! You'd better sit down. I believe you've just entered what is laughingly known as the hysterical shock stage. Pardon the pun. Here, sit down," Rosemary said, gently pushing me onto the lowest step as far away from the body as possible in that dark, narrow space.

"You just sit tight while I go and grab you a nice strong cuppa'—I know, lots of milk, no sugar. I'll be right back."

"Thanks, Rosemary. I probably could use one about now. Haven't eaten yet today."

"What else is new?" Rosemary laughed, patting me on the back. Gingerly edging around the body, she sprinted downstairs to the lower level where the elevator is located.

Leaning against the wall, I tried to force my thoughts into some sort of order. It wasn't as if I'd never seen a dead person before. There was just something different about this one … something funny that I couldn't quite put a finger on. I couldn't wait until the police made an appearance—not to mention the Senior Center's director, Claudia Martin. She was definitely not going to be a happy camper. For this to happen now, what with the plans for a new Center being finalized and all the bureaucratic bologna accompanying it, the new year was showing signs of becoming one everyone would love to forget!

Chapter 2

As I sat there in the eerie stillness, with no one for company but a corpse, my thoughts tumbling over one another, kind of like our recent debacle, I heard the sound of sirens approaching. It sounded like they had sent out the troops for this one. Suddenly the door crashed open and this giant of a man strode in followed by one of his assistants, a tall, lanky young man, with flaming red hair and a sprinkling of freckles, who appeared to be barely out of high school let alone a policeman. He in turn was followed by the CSI guys, all covered from head to toe in protective gear, to prevent cross-contamination. The big guy, who resembled a sumo wrestler, extended a massive paw and introduced himself as Lieutenant Ralph Kai. Then he nodded toward the young man. "This is officer James O'Reilly." The lieutenant asked me to repeat my stats, you know: name, address, business, etc. Everything, but my age and body type, thank goodness. I explained that I was there to teach a class this morning. Unfortunately, his next words threw me for a loop.

"Well Mrs. Fine, I think I have the basics for now. Let's continue our conversation elsewhere in the building. This hallway is now designated a potential crime scene. The Forensics people will take over from here. However, I noticed a bathroom as we entered. Before we take our leave, I'm afraid I must ask you to remove the clothes you are wearing and change into the coveralls one of the forensics people will provide. We need to check your clothing and your bags for elimination purposes. With that a young officer led me back down to the bathroom. She handed me what looked like something out of a sci-fi thriller—of course it was at least two sizes to big .... Fortunately the little bathroom had a changing stall and even a shower—which I wasn't allowed to use, in case they found it necessary to heap additional indignities upon my person—I should have paid more attention when watching *CSI* way back when. Tying the matching belt around my waist to keep from tripping yet again—this time over my own two feet, I exited the stall, and she provided me with a large bag into which I tossed all my clothes. The police had already confiscated my numerous tote bags.

Lieutenant Kai was waiting for me when I exited the bathroom. He gallantly took my elbow, helped me negotiate the stairs without getting caught in the overlong overalls. We took the elevator up to the main floor. The lieutenant asked me where there was a room we could talk without interruption. I rattled off several possibilities. Well we can probably use the Rec Therapist's room. Judy's usually off running a program elsewhere in the building. Then there's the social worker, but she may be in with a client ... and there's also the computer room, but that joint's usually jumping."

"Just lead the way, Mrs. Fine."

I showed the detective to the alcove that branches off into the various offices. Glancing through the open door of Judy's office, I noticed she was out. I checked the calendar on her wall to make sure she wouldn't be back for a while. Entering, I motioned him to one of two old, but sturdy metal chairs padded in green vinyl. "Okay, Lieutenant. What else would you like to know?"

"Well, Mrs Fine, you mentioned that you were heading upstairs to a class when you came across the body."

"Try 'tripped over' ...." I shivered again, remembering all too well.

"Alright. You tripped over the body. Then what did you do?"

"Actually, I didn't really *do* anything. You see, a number of my students literally were following on my heels—several of them carrying some of my stuff .... I stopped short and they ran into me—looked like a scene from the Keystone Cops, if you'll pardon the expression. I haul around an awful lot of stuff, as you probably noticed when your officer collected it all."

Lieutenant Kai coughed to cover up his obvious amusement. "Yes, I had noticed ... speaking of which, what do you teach?"

I paused before replying, knowing too well the reaction my announcement would elicit from the rather large detective, when mentioning my occupation.

"Bellyrobics."

"Bellyrobics—what exactly is 'Bellyrobics', if I might ask?" His "coughing fit" becoming more pronounced as I explained.

"Well, I guess you can call it a cross between belly dancing and aerobics—great workout for the ladies. Not usually a class that would attract male students."

He scratched his head, looking at me in what I can only describe as surprise and humorous wonder. I get that a lot, as you can imagine—a sixty-something belly dancer who looks more like a cuddly, albeit "young" looking grandmother which, thankfully, I am.

"Am I correct in thinking that would explain why you didn't initially recognize the victim?

"You are."

"Are you quite sure you've never seen him around or spoken to him before? I would imagine that given the nature of your class, it might attract interested onlookers—especially since many of them have to pass through the auditorium to get to the lunchroom."

"Well, now that you mention it, I might have seen the gentleman in my wanderings. I often stop in the cafeteria and visit with some of the members. The problem is, as I explained to the dispatcher over the phone, I didn't recognize him in his current state. Besides, the fact that the stairwell was so dark and dank, I wouldn't have recognized anybody!"

Detective Kai replied, "I know this must be very difficult for you, but would you mind taking another look?"

"I'll try, but wouldn't it be better if you asked Claudia—Ms. Martin? She knows just about everybody who passes through these doors and where all the bodies are hidden … oops," I murmured firmly clamping my hand over my big mouth. "Sorry. Not quite the thing to say under the circumstances."

"Don't worry. We get that all the time. It's a perfectly natural reaction. Of course, we will be speaking with her too, but since you are the one who, ummm," he coughed again, " 'tripped over the body', I'd really like to get an idea if you recognize him."

Not knowing whether to be insulted or laugh, I chose the middle ground. Smiling rather sardonically, I asked, "Hey, does this mean I might be a suspect? You know, being the first one to find the body and all that?"

Smiling, he said, "Just trying to get a little background information, as you can understand. Since you obviously seem to know the routine, have you had experience in this area before?"

"Yeah, but only in mystery books. I positively inhale them! Fortunately, I've never had first-hand experience, unless you want to count slightly murderous thoughts. I love my job, but when you're dealing with lots of people day in and day out, the politics can get to you sometimes. Hey! I'd better be careful, or you may be tempted to fit me up for a couple of nice 'bracelets'," I chuckled, holding out my wrists.

"Yes. If I were you, I'd be very careful who you share that with, Ms ...."

"That's 'Mrs.' Fine. I worked hard for my M R S status."

"Pardon me—'Mrs.' Fine. As I was saying, it's best not to joke about these things, especially with a homicide detective. Now, if you would just accompany me back to the scene and take a look around. Please let me know if everything appears to be the way you found it when you first entered the building and ... ummm ... came upon the body. And if you could please take another look at the gentleman's face?"

"O ... kay. But you'd better have a bucket handy, just in case."

By the time we got back to the gruesome scene, the CSI people had finished their work. The body had been placed in a bag and taken out through the exit below, ready to be loaded into the waiting ambulance. Yellow tape surrounded the area, waving in the icy wet breeze of the partially open door. The lieutenant took me gently by the elbow and led me over to the body while his young sidekick, Officer O'Reilly, unzipped the bag just enough for me to check out the victim's face.

It was the face of an old man, who had seen and done it all: craggy features, sparse, grizzled white hair, two or three day old stubble and those rheumy brown eyes with unusual silver flecks, just staring into space with a look of shock and pain. His face was twisted and blue with foamy white spittle streaming down the corners of his mouth. I noticed too, that there were signs of vomit on both his face and clothes.

"I hope you've got that bucket ready," I said trying to keep up my bravado. "I'm in danger of heaving any minute now. What's with all the spittle and vomit? Was he poisoned or something?"

Still maintaining a firm grip to keep me from keeling over, the lieutenant gently replied, "You're the mystery buff, You know I can't answer that. The body needs to be sent to the coroner to be autopsied. Now, take it easy and try to tell me if you recognize anything about this man."

"I don't know … there's something about those eyes. I just can't put my finger on it. I may have seen him around, talking with one of my ladies, the social worker, Jeannie Gardner or the usual luncheon regulars. It's really hard to tell in the present situation. The poor man's face is all distorted and twisted in pain. What a horrible way to go!" I cried, shivering and covering my eyes, in an effort to forget the sight. "I can't begin to imagine how much that poor man must have suffered. Me, I can't even handle a twenty-four-hour stomach virus!"

"That's OK, Mrs. Fine, we understand. It's not an easy sight to see, even for the most seasoned cops. Come on, let's just get you away from here and maybe grab you a nice cup of coffee or tea."

"Thanks, Lieutenant. One of my students went to get me something, but she's probably trying to figure out where I ended up."

Even as we spoke, I spotted Rosemary's sweet face peeking through the glass of the door. "As a matter of fact, here she is now, but I'm afraid that my appetite has been destroyed for the duration. I may never eat again, although I could definitely use that cup of tea she's holding up!" Lieutenant Kai signaled to his minion, Officer O'Reilly, to collect it. Waving goodbye, Rosemary mouthed out, "Call me …."

Nodding, I continued where I'd left off with the detective. "I usually don't eat before I dance—not great for rippling don't-cha know?" I could see that the good detective was doing his best to keep from laughing, as I continued. "I usually only drink white tea, green tea or water, when I'm teaching a class and then a bunch of us go out for a nice long lunch … but of course, this is not what you want to hear. I'm afraid that I sometimes suffer from verbal diarrhea—just keeps spilling out when I'm nervous or excited." Taking a deep breath, I forced myself to calm down and try to stem the flow.

"No need to apologize, Mrs. Fine. Death hits people in different ways. Do you think you are ready to continue? Have you had a chance to process what you saw?"

"Oh, yeah! I'm still processing."

"Now that you've taken a closer look, does it strike a familiar note?"

"You mean, other than the fact that he's dead? Sorry. Sorry … still nervous. Yes, now that I think of it … there's something familiar about his eyes—the silver flecks, but I can't quite put a finger on it. I believe I've seen him in the cafeteria and possibly at several open meetings to discuss the new Senior Center. I think he may even have commented, but it could have been someone else who looked like him. I hope this helps you a little. I'm kind of running out of steam and I still need to check on my ladies. See how they're holding up. Do you think we can take a break for a while? You can always find me at my house. I'll even give you a cup of coffee or tea. Got a closet full."

"Yes, I think that we can call it a day for now. Go home and get some rest. Here's my card. Call me anytime, if you remember anything at all which may help with the case. And I hope I don't have to remind you not to pass along anything you may have seen—especially to the press."

"OK. But, please take it easy on my ladies and consider what some of them have to say with a grain of salt."

"Don't worry, we'll be gentle."

I laughed at that. "Yes, but they might not! If you think I'm a rabid mystery buff, wait 'til you meet the likes of Melisande Wilson, Charlotte Rae Knowles and Henrietta Hirshfeld, or Henri, as she's called. Oh ..., and watch out for Flor. She's been with me for over thirty years years—I started young ...." At this, Lieutenant Kai let loose with a booming basso laugh which practically shook the walls.

"I'll try to remember and take it under advisement," he said as he stood up. Snapping his sausage size fingers, he signaled to the boy officer. "O'Reilly, please help this lady out to her car."

"Thanks," I replied, as I shook his out-sized paw. "But first, I have to talk to my ladies then stop at the office. Since this class is a bust, I need to make arrangements for a makeup class." Seeing that the lieutenant was about to issue me another warning, I held up my hand and told him, "I know what you're about to say. 'Don't discuss the case with anyone, especially NOT my ladies or the office staff.' Got it, Chief!" I said making a mock salute. Once again, he let loose with that booming laugh and I definitely detected a slight gleam in those sharp, squinchy, little bear-like eyes.

"And don't you forget it!" he said as he handed me over to Junior. We walked off to the sound of the good lieutenant quietly chuckling to himself.

Chapter 3

As we strolled through the auditorium, we were set upon by a mini horde of septuagenarians and octogenarians all talking at once. I could tell that Junior was feeling slightly overwhelmed; but he rose to the occasion with admirable panache, considering he was surrounded by a bunch of women old enough to be his grandmother—or even great-grandmother!

I dropped my coat and keys on a nearby bench and motioned Officer Jim to wait and said, "Ladies, please, I know this has been a rather strange day …."

"That's putting it mildly," Flor cracked, nudging Henrietta and grinning broadly.

"Oh, behave yourself, Flor!" Henri snapped in an effort to appear nonchalant.

"That's no fun! Come on. Tell us all the gruesome details."

Laughing, I nodded toward Junior. "You know I can't do that, Flor. I've been specifically ordered by the coppers to keep *schtum.* But I did want to check back with all of you to tell you that we'll have a make-up class at the end of this session. Now ladies, the police are going to want to speak with each of you about how we happened to … to … uh …."

"Trip over the body?" Not one to mince words, Henri finished for me.

"Uh … yes. So please behave yourselves and don't give the poor police officers a hard time." I replied, glancing back at young Officer O'Reilly, who was standing at attention, looking like he'd rather be anywhere else but there; like a soldier who is about to go into battle, without knowing when the enemy will attack.

"This is so excitin!" Charlotte Rae exclaimed again, her blonde tinted curls, bouncing up and down, big blue eyes alight and her Shirley Temple dimples on full display.

"Yeah, I'm just plotzing from all the excitement," Henri drawled in her inimitable transplanted New Yorker accent. "For this I moved to Connecticut? If I'd wanted this kind of excitement, I could have stayed in New York."

"Yes, but then we would never have met you and that would have been a great loss to us all." I responded, giving her a quick hug. Recalling that my young "police escort" was still waiting for me, I slowly inched toward the door.

"Listen girls, I've got to get going. I have to check in with the office secretaries and bring them up to date. They're probably dying of curiosity by now …. And I still need to call Tara and Lisa in Continuing Ed. to let them know. I don't even want to think about what poor Tara's going to say when she hears what's been going on! I'll see you all next week."

"God willing and we don't trip over another corpse," Henri commented dryly.

Laughing, I waved goodbye. Picking up my stuff, I signaled to Junior that I was finally ready. The poor kid hot footed it through the auditorium doors.

"Listen, Officer J … O' Reilly, I have to check in with the secretaries. Why don't you sit down for a minute? I'll try to be quick."

Throwing my coat and keys onto a nearby chair, I entered the inner sanctum—home to the two resident secretaries. The younger gal, Joanna Sparks, looked up at me and did a double take when she saw my "new look."

"Are you all right? What happened to your clothes?"

"They collected them for 'purposes of elimination', since I landed right on top of the poor guy—bags and all! Gonna unload them after the cops return the stuff." I shivered. "Doubt I could ever wear them again without remembering that poor dead man just lying there like a pile of discarded old clothes …. As you can see, I had to strip down and hand all my stuff over to the CSI guys. A real topper to this comedy of terrors, huh?"

"You poor thing!" exclaimed Joanna.

"Quite a fashion statement." Diane commented dryly.

"Gee, thanks, Di …."

"Any time," she grinned.

Diane, the older one and mistress of understatement, arched a shapely auburn eyebrow and said, "I understand you've had a rather interesting day."

"That's putting it mildly!" I snickered as I filled out my time card. This kind of 'interesting' I can live without."

"Aren't you a big mystery buff? The opportunity to follow a real live murder practically falls in your lap, and you're not the least bit curious?"

"More like I fell into it's … uh … his lap. Iewww!" I shivered, remembering. "Gives me the galloping heebie-jeebies just thinking about it. Of course, I'm curious, but I've already been warned off in no uncertain terms. You know the routine—'Mum's the word. Mind your own business.' etc and so forth."

"Mouth shut, yes. But you can still keep your ears open. There's a lot to learn by just sitting back and listening," Diane replied.

Joanna chimed in. "Yeah, you know how these seniors are. They know absolutely everything that's going on here and around town. Wanna know who's sick, who's just had a knee replacement or even who's dating who, they can tell you every time—in detail!"

"OK, OK, point taken." I said, throwing up my hands in mock surrender. "I'll keep my eyes and ears peeled, but the same goes for you two ladies. You are primely situated here, for scoping out the comings and goings of everyone."

"Not to mention the latest gossip," Joanna laughed.

"Thanks for the pep talk, girls. Well, I'd better get going. Would you ask Claudia to give me a call when she gets a chance? I need to know how she wants me to handle this situation."

"Will do," replied Diane. "Meanwhile, why don't you go home, take a nice warm shower and have a hot cup of something … or maybe something stronger," she winked.

"Good idea, I think I'll do just that. But first I've got to hit my long-suffering boss, Tara with the news. This is all she needs on top of getting ready for the next round of classes. Mind if I use your phone?"

"Be our guest. Why don't you use the one in the spare office?"

"Thanks! Much appreciated."

Finally getting to sit in a decent desk chair, I dialed the Continuing Ed. Office. Our wonderful secretary, Lisa answered on the second ring.

"Hi Lisa, is Tara around?"

"Hi Esme. How are you doing? Did your class go well today?"

I groaned. "Don't even ask! It's a very long story. Is Tara around?"

Concern in her voice, Lisa replied, "No, she's at a meeting. She'll be back in an hour or so. But what happened? Are you alright?"

"That depends on your interpretation of 'alright' … to make a long story short, I tripped over a dead body on my way up to class."

"Ay, Dios Mio! How are you?

"I'm fine," I sighed—except for a few bruises, my loss of dignity; not to mention the loss of my clothes and work bags as well. At least they let me keep my license and my car keys. Otherwise, I would have had to hitch a ride home with one of the cops. I'll tell you all about it after I've had a chance to recuperate. Meanwhile, just ask Tara to give me a call when she gets a chance. No hurry, I'm probably going to be crashing for the rest of the day—maybe longer."

"Don't worry about anything at this end, Esme. Just take care of yourself. I'll tell her you called. Let us know if there is anything we can do for you."

"Thanks! You are a true gem, Lisa! Have a good day." Hanging up, I headed back to the front of the office.

"Thanks for the use of the phone! Think I've hung around long enough. I know you ladies have your work cut out for you."

"For sure," groaned Joanna. "As if we don't have enough to do around here already."

"Speaking of which, I suppose I ought to collect Officer Junior over there and pick up my things."

"Actually, he's kinda cute," Joanna whispered. "You think he's single?"

"Are you kidding? He doesn't even look like he's old enough to shave yet. You want me to find out?"

"Oh no you don't!" both women cried out in unison.

"Yeah. You're like a bulldog, you don't let go," teased Diane.

"Are you kidding? Once you get started you won't stop until you know their whole life story!" Joanna groaned again.

"And then some," cracked Diane. "Leave the poor kid alone. He's still green under the collar. At least wait until he ferments a little. Speaking of which, looks like a couple of your ladies are making a beeline in his direction. Better get him out of here before they go to work on him!"

"OK. Leaving now …." At which point I left the office and retrieved my poor escort just in time to prevent my ladies from descending on him like a wake of vultures.

"Come on Officer Jim, excuse me, Officer O'Reilly. We'd better get you out of here before my ladies get hold of you. My car's just over there," I said, on entering the parking lot. As we headed for my midnight blue Mazda wagon, I couldn't resist the impulse to ask him just how old he was. "By the way, I hate to be nosy, but you look like you're young enough to be my kid. If you don't mind my asking—just how old are you?"

Blushing to the roots of his copper hair, he replied, "I don't mind. Older folks ask me all the time."

Ouch! Talk about payback—"older folks?"

"I'm twenty-four. I joined the academy right out of high school." he told me.

Double ouch, I grumbled to myself as I replied. "I was right, you are old enough to be my son. Actually, you're almost young enough to be my grandson … if I'd started earlier," I sighed.

"Don't worry, ma'am, you look pretty good for a grandmother."

Triple ouch! On hearing that, I knew it was time to get into my car before I had a minor heart attack. I thanked Officer Jimmy and climbed into the driver seat. Buckling up, I turned the key and gunned the engine. Fear in his eyes, Jimmy jumped out of the way, as I waved goodbye and took off at a more or less sedate pace. "Grandmother" indeed! This day was just getting better and better. Boy, did I need a drink and a long, long soak in the Jacuzzi!

Speed dialing my husband, Paul, "Hi Dear, heading home."

"Why so early?" he asked. "Doesn't your class run for an hour. Then lunch with the 'girls'?"

Wearily I explained. "It does, but today it didn't. Something happened."

I went on to regale him with an extremely abbreviated version of my misadventures, ending with a plea to turn on the Jacuzzi. I was planning on staying in there til I really turned into a dried up old prune.

When I got home, my little guy, Streak, was waiting at the door. The little salt and pepper version of Toto gave a shriek of joy and bounded into my arms, which by the way, isn't easy for a mini mutt! I gave him his usual cuddle, followed by his customary treat and headed for my bedroom.

Stripping down I climbed into the warm swirling waters of the Jacuzzi my hubby, Paul, gem that he is, had prepared for me.

Just as I was about to fall into blissful oblivion, he slipped in armed with a fragrant cup of my favorite tea and a much-needed muffin.

"How are you doing, dear? Thought you might need a little pick me up after your ordeal. By the way," he laughed, "I know you love your mysteries, but don't you think this is carrying it too far?"

"Uh … ya think? Reading them and watching them on the tube is one thing, but boy, I could have lived without the honor of literally tripping over one!"

"Well, just take it easy now and try to forget about everything for a little while. I'll leave you to your bath. Let me know if you need anything else."

Having said that he kissed me on the forehead, retrieved my now empty mug and headed toward the door. Turning, he said, "By the way dear, please don't get any ideas about trying to 'help' the police solve the case. I'm sure they are quite capable of doing it all by themselves."

I looked up at him, teasingly batting my eyes and replied innocently, "*Moi?* I wouldn't think of it! Don't forget to close the door on your way out."

"OK, but just remember what I said. This isn't a game, or even your idea of a puzzle."

"Yes dear. I'll remember dear. Now, please close the door and just let me veg!"

Chapter 4

I woke up in a cold sweat, having had a fitful night, tossing and turning. I'd been dreaming of little wizened zombie-like old men crawling out of the woodwork. Popping in and out of all sorts of nooks and crannies. Grabbing at me with their cold wet claws. Their equally cold dead eyes bored into me, until my skin crawled. I could almost feel their slimy wet clothing! I turned to Paul and he slid his arms around me in a protective embrace. Sleepily he looked down and stroking my sodden mahogany locks, he murmured, "Have a bad night?"

"The worst!" I replied. "Like I was living through one of those horrible *SyFy* horror flicks that you and our son are so fond of watching, when he visits."

"Wow, that is bad for you!" he replied. "Just remember, you've got the day off today, so try to relax. Why don't you take Streak out for a long walk later? Snap lots of pictures. That always helps you calm down, and he could definitely use the exercise."

"Speaking of pictures, the one recurring image which keeps running through my head is seeing that horrible dead body, the spittle dripping down his poor face! That's a vision I'll never be able to forget! I'll bet the guy was poisoned. His face had that bluish tinge, and he smelled of sweet almonds—you know, that sickly, cloying smell they talk about when someone's been slipped some cyanide? Hey! Remember what I told you about how you can get cyanide from peach and apple pits? I wonder if that's how they slipped to him. Ground up apple or peach pits in a smoothy. That would pack quite a punch wouldn't it?!"

Leaning on his elbow, Paul hit me with the full force of his piercing blue-gray eyes.

"There you go again. Didn't we just agree that you would let the cops handle this? I really don't think they'd appreciate any interference from an amateur—especially one who 'inhales' mystery novels! This is real life. You need to stay out of it and mind your own business. It's a dangerous game to play."

I stared back at him with my own big brown ones. "Don't I know it! This is definitely no game. But aren't you even the slightest bit interested in finding out what happened?" I asked after a short pause.

"No. I'll wait to read about it in the newspaper. It's not your business."

"It is my business!" I shouted. "I tripped over the poor guy!"

"You need to stay out of it! That's what the police are for."

Hearing our raised voices, poor Streak woke up and started barking hysterically. Paul snapped, "Now you've got the poor dog all worked up." Noticing the stricken look on my face, Paul calmed down. "I'm sorry, dear." Leaning over he gave me a quick kiss. "I realize you've had a rough time lately, but you have to know when to back off."

"Listen, I've gotta get ready for work. Why don't I let the little guy out of his crate so he can cuddle with his 'mommy'? Try to get some sleep. I'll even turn the phone ringer off so you're not disturbed."

After giving me another kiss, Paul rolled back over and climbed out of bed, padded over to Streak's crate and let him out. Streak made a flying leap onto the bed and then crawled under the covers, snuggling next to me. Heaving a big contented sigh, he went to sleep. Feeling the warmth of his plump little body, accompanied by his soft snuffling sounds, I began to relax. Melting into our cozy mattress, I soon fell into a deep sleep.

The next thing I knew, it was mid-afternoon. I had slept through the whole morning! Practically jumping out of bed, I threw on my warm, furry, fleece robe and shoved my feet into a pair of equally fuzzy purple slippers. I limped down the stairs, my own little fur ball following at my heels. We went through our somewhat belated morning ritual, where Streak bounded out of the house to do his thing and check for "messages" while I prepared his breakfast. Dry food complemented by a scoop of canned food, topped off with a slice of turkey and some pasta. Did I happen to mention that the little guy lived the life of a princeling? Talk about empty nest syndrome!

Next, I prepared my own breakfast, or should I say brunch, as I waited for "his highness" to return. Then I went over to my desk and checked the phone for messages. The light was blinking wildly, signaling that I had messages. Turning the ringer back on, I pressed the replay button and listened: "You have five messages," I heard the voicemail say.

First message, Tara Sinclair:

"Esme, sorry I missed your call. I got your message, or should I say 'messages'. That must have been one heck of a horrible experience! Your ladies are in quite a tizzy after your misadventure. The phone's been ringing off the hook, everyone asking how you're doing and if we've gotten any further information on the 'body in the basement' as it's now being called. They haven't been this hyped up since Hurricane Annie! Please give me a call when you're feeling better. By the way, that detective you spoke with yesterday, a Lieutenant Kai, also called. Said he tried to contact you at home, but it kept going straight to voicemail. Well, that's it for now. Try to get some rest. Call if you need me. And don't worry about your ladies. I'll have Lisa field all calls and tell them that you'll be in touch as soon as possible. Take care! I repeat, call me if you need me.

"By the way, also spoke with Claudia over at the Senior Center. She's got things covered on her end. The lieutenant's already connected with her as well."

Second Message, Leicester Police Department:

"Hello, Mrs. Fine. This is Lieutenant Ralph Kai. I have just a few more questions for you. Please call me when you can."

Third Message: Leicester Police department:

"Hello, Mrs. Fine. This is Lieutenant Kai, again. I really must speak with you to clear up a few questions. Please call me ASAP. You can contact me here at the department or on my cell phone. It is imperative that we talk!"

Fourth Message, Flor Ruiz:

"Hi, Kiddo. Just called to see how you're holding up after all the excitement. Had a visit from that big detective guy—Lieutenant Quay or something or other."

"It's Kai," I murmured to myself.

"Couldn't tell him much, since I arrived late—as usual. Missed all the fun! But the girls brought me up to snuff. I was able to give him a little background on who the guy who got himself topped might be. Call me and I'll fill you in, or better yet, let's meet for a cup of coffee. I'll leave you with a little teaser, luv .... Our victim wasn't that big mouthed jerk who's been so verbal about the new Center ... forgot his name ... starts with a 'J' or something … But …! It just might be that Little Hitler guy who got into it with him, you know, the one who's always making waves, or maybe it was that nice little guy … Harry something! Well that's all I got so far. Ta ta, for now. Call me!"

Pausing between messages, I wrote myself a note to return her call. Coffee and talk—my two favorite pastimes!

Fifth Message, Leicester Police Department:

"This is Lieutenant Kai again. Do I need to send an escort to pick you up? Call me!"

"OK, OK!" I shouted at the phone, "I got the message. You want me to call you." So I proceeded to do just that. He picked up on the second ring. Talk about being on top of things!

"Hello, this is Esme Fine, I understand you called."

"Yes. Several times. As I said in my message, we need to get some more information. Would you be able to speak with us today, if you're feeling up to it?"

"As a matter of fact, I can, Lieutenant. I'll be home all day still recuperating! Oops, almost forgot. I may be out for about an hour or so this afternoon. When do you want to stop by?"

"Now is as good a time as any, if that's convenient for you."

"Sure! Just give me about half an hour to straighten up. I'll make a pot of coffee. You guys do drink coffee don't you?"

Chuckling, he replied, "Yes ma'am we do. That's very thoughtful of you."

"No prob, I'm a Jewish mother. That's what we do."

The lieutenant chuckled again, in that deep rumbling way I'd heard before. "Alright, Mrs. Fine," he replied. "We'll be over shortly."

I let Streak back in, put away my dishes, quickly straightened up the house, then straightened myself out. Lastly, I brewed the coffee and set out a plate of cookies. Before I knew it the doorbell sounded and there on my front porch I saw the massive form of Lieutenant Kai accompanied by Officer Jimmy, as I'd affectionately come to think of him. I invited them in and led them through to the kitchen. As they settled at the table, I brought over the coffee and cookies, sat down and waited to be "grilled."

"OK, Lieutenant Kai. You mentioned that you have several more questions for me, so fire away."

"We just need a few more details and clarification, Mrs. Fine," he explained. Officer Jimmy was poised to take notes, pen in one hand, cookie in the other, I noticed smiling inwardly. Ahh …! He'd do a mother proud ….

"Have you given any further thought as to who our victim might be and what he might have been doing in that darkened hall?"

"Matter of fact I have, Lieutenant. There are at least two men I can think of who fit that description and as for what either one was doing there, that's easy. That stairway is a major traffic area during classes, since it leads directly up to the auditorium where most of the exercise classes are held, as well as to the Bingo room, the card room and of course—the cafeteria, where almost everyone hangs out at some time or other."

"Thanks for the clarification, Mrs Fine. Now, as you were saying, you think that you may have recognized the victim after all."

"Well, I can't say for sure, but either one would fit the bill. They are both your typical old Connecticut Yankees. One of the men's name is Adolf Betz. He's got sparse gray hair, which he wears in a greasy ponytail. Can't tell the eye color because he always wears tinted aviator glasses. He's a wiry little guy, not much taller than me—about five foot three or so; tries to make up for it by posturing and mouthing off to anyone and everyone. He's got a classic Napoleonic complex. Constantly trying to prove that he's tougher and smarter than everybody else. Definitely something of a troublemaker," I paused in my diatribe.

"Sounds like an unappetizing kind of guy," the lieutenant commented. Junior sat there, furiously writing with one hand while polishing off cookies with the other and nodding in agreement with what his superior was saying.

" 'Unappetizing'. The perfect description of the man. Used to show up at all the meetings and get into it with the presenters. It didn't matter who or what the meeting was about. Real little scrapper, too, our Mr. Betz. He just loves a good fight, physical as well as verbal, which is hard to believe from looking at him. As you can imagine, he has not ingratiated himself to many people. Very few of our members have anything good to say about that man."

I paused for another breath. "Even I found it hard to feel sorry for the guy. I'd have to say nobody would be surprised if he is indeed the 'body in the basement'. I'm told that's what it's now been dubbed—great title for a mystery story, don't you think?" I blurted out rather sardonically and then caught myself. Apologizing for my thoughtless outburst, shivering, I remembered the tortured face of that poor old man on the cold, hard stairs. "Oh, I'm so sorry, Lieutenant" I said, smacking myself on my mouth again. "No one deserves that kind of end, no matter how rude or obnoxious! To tell you the truth, I felt just a teeny bit sorry for him, despite all his pompous posturing and ranting. He must be one heck of a lonely and bitter man to act like that, always putting people's backs up."

"Thank you for that very in-depth description of Mr. Betz's character. Is there anything you can tell us about his choice of attire? It might help us to further ascertain if he is the man you found on the stairs."

"Actually, you could say that he kind of sticks out like a sore thumb."

"In what way? Specifics, please."

"He has a unique style of dress, for New England that is …. Adolf is one of two members who usually wear what I'd call, classic 'faux cowboy'—complete with black leather bolo, large, very expensive turquoise and silver belt buckle on a thick black leather belt, really grungy jeans, and ox-blood hammered leather boots. Walks with a rather strange gait, sort of pigeon-toed, as if that's the only way to keep his boots from falling off. Probably stuffs them with newspaper or something, too. He tops it all off with a ten gallon hat which is also at least one or two sizes too big for him, so he stuffs it with paper towels. And before you ask how I know, it's because I saw bits of towel sticking out when he pushed it back to scratch his head. Oh. I'm not sure if this is important yet, but he's always following this other 'wannabe' around. You know, the more I think about it, Adolf could not possibly be the poor man I ran into. His clothes were totally different."

"A very apt assessment, Mrs. Fine. Except for height and slight build, Mr. Betz' description does not tally with that of the victim. However, you mentioned another man who also fits the bill. What can you tell us about him?"

"Well, like many seniors of that age, the basics are the same. This gentleman, Harrold Browne, nickname Harry, also had sparse gray hair. But his was slightly frizzy, what there was of it. Looked like he tried rather unsuccessfully to trim it himself. He had brownish eyes. Was a little taller than me—again somewhere around five foot four. I think he was the taller of the two men. Like Adolf, he had a slight frame. Not wiry. Just painfully thin with a bit of a pot-belly. Looked like he didn't eat very regularly. He walked with a slight limp, as if he'd sustained an injury that had never healed properly. He struck me as an old soldier, who had seen it all—probably during the Vietnam Conflict, judging by his age. As a matter of fact, if it was Harry, I'd heard tell that he had earned a Purple Heart during one of the heavier skirmishes. That's how he got that injury. He was very modest about that. Once in a while he would mention it, but only by way of explaining why he was shipped back home."

"Can you remember how Mr. Browne dressed as well?"

"The few times I ran into him, Harry was usually wearing the same clothes—a rather tatty gray cardigan, very old but clean cargo pants, pockets overflowing with all kinds of odds and ends, from a pair of mini pliers to various coins of every size and origin. You could sometimes hear him coming with all that rattling. He always wore combat boots—even during the summer, also old, but well cared for. They were polished so well that you could almost see yourself in them. Looked like they were a remnant from his war days …." Suddenly, I gasped in mid-recitation.

"Mrs Fine, are you alright?" Lieutenant Kai inquired, leaning over with a look of concern on his ruddy face.

"Yes, I'm fine, Lieutenant." I answered, taking a deep breath. "It's just that I realized I've been talking about Harry in the past tense, and we don't even know for sure if it was him on the stairs. He's such a nice, harmless little guy. A real gentleman in his own way, unlike that Adolf, who's a nasty piece of work. Not that I wish him ill either. Judging from what I observed the few times our paths crossed, Harry seems to have had a hard, lonely life and deserves a break." I pulled myself together and looked the lieutenant in the eye. "Would you like me to continue?"

"Yes, please do, if you feel up to it. If not, we can always continue another day."

"No. Really, I'm fine now. Besides, I would like to get this over with, so that you can find out who the poor man is and why he was killed. What else would you like to know, Lieutenant?"

"Actually, let's backtrack for a moment," Kai replied in the middle of lifting a beefy, cookie lined paw.

"You mentioned that Harry—Mr. Browne, always had a pocketful of coins and other odds and ends on him. How did you know that?"

"Because, he was always jingling them and once or twice he actually dropped some. His pockets were always overflowing with junk. Now that I think of it, he was so proud of his 'collection', that he often showed one or two pieces to anyone who would take the time to listen to his far-fetched stories. That was his way of connecting with people. Generally speaking, he was rather shy. But when it came to his 'booty' he would light up like a Christmas tree, if you'll pardon the cliché. He just loved the attention when someone showed the slightest interest in hearing his stories or looking at his coins. Once or twice he even caught me off guard. Regaled me with some outrageous stories of his past escapades. I got the impression that he made them up as he went along, just to try to hold the listener's interest. Although, I must admit that some of his stories were quite fascinating to hear, even if most of them appeared to be figments of his imagination. His listeners really got caught up in them and were transported to foreign parts in their imagination as well. Oops, here I go again galloping off on another tangent. Why do you ask? Wasn't any of that stuff on the body when you looked?"

"Actually. No. There was nothing in his pockets when we checked. No wallet, no ID—not even a stray tissue. We did find it rather odd under the circumstances. So, what you're saying is, his pockets should have been chock-full of junk?"

"Yes, if it was poor Harry I tripped over. I wouldn't know about Adolf. I steered clear of that one."

"You, yourself did not check to see if he had any identification on him?"

"Are you kidding me? I've read and seen enough mystery shows to know that you never touch anything at the possible scene of a crime. Not to mention the fact that the very idea of going through someone's pockets, especially in that condition, is really repulsive. I'd be dousing my hands in disinfectant wipes for the rest of the day, if I had! I used to work in a psychiatric hospital where we'd have to drop everything whenever they called 'code red' and run to help. I'll never forget the time I was told to check the pockets of a client for drugs and sharp objects who was being 'bagged'. At least I had gloves on and found nothing dangerous. Sorry, I didn't mean to go off yet again. So, you were saying that you found absolutely nothing on him? That is strange."

"Yes," replied the lieutenant. "That's what we thought at the time. You've just confirmed our suspicions. Is there anything else you can remember about finding the body? Anything you may have noticed at the time, but forgotten to tell us after the shock of your discovery? It can be any little thing. Something that might have slipped your mind or seemed irrelevant at the time."

I paused to think about the question, before answering. "No. I don't think so … but if I do remember something later, I'll get right back to you. Like I said. It might be a good idea for you to talk to my ladies, though. I wouldn't be at all surprised if one of them spotted something I missed or saw or heard something that struck them as amiss … pardon the pun, but sometimes I can't help myself—especially when I'm nervous."

"No need to be nervous, Mrs. Fine. You've been very helpful. And in answer to your question, yes, we are planning on interviewing the members of your class again as well as anyone else who may have remembered something new which can help with our investigation. By the way, speaking of your ladies, I hope I don't need to remind you not to go off on a sleuthing expedition. Just let the police do their work. We're really pretty good at it, you know," he smiled. "Please bear in mind that this isn't a TV or mystery novel. Real murder can be a pretty nasty, dangerous business. We wouldn't want anything to happen to you or any of your ladies."

"Gee, you sound just like my husband. He said pretty much the same thing."

"No offense ma'am, but maybe you should listen to him. Sounds like a sensible person."

"OK, Lieutenant. I get the message loud and clear. NO AMATEUR SLEUTHING!"

"Good! Now I'll just finish this excellent cookie, then Officer O'Reilly and I will leave you in peace."

"Yeah, wonderful," chimed in Junior, mouth full of cookie.

Laughing, I replied, "Thank you, officers. Why don't you take some for the road? I've got plenty."

The lieutenant and his officer politely demurred, but only for a second—the "cookie siren" calling to them as I knew she would. I took a storage bag, filled it to the brim and handed it over as they headed toward the door. At the door, Lieutenant Kai shook my hand, almost crushing it in his vice-like grip. Boy did I pity the perp who ever tried to mess with him! Officer Jimmy thanked me profusely. I wondered if anyone ever fed that boy. They turned and let themselves out.

* * *

No sooner had I closed the door, then the phone started ringing. "Must be Henri," I thought to myself. Sometimes she has a sixth sense, and she always knows what's going on in the neighborhood. By the way, did I happen to mention that not only is Henri one of my most loyal students, she's also a good neighbor and an even better friend!

"Hi Hen, what's up?"

"What's up?" she echoed. "You tell me! I just saw that rather large cop and his minion leaving your place, so spill! Anything new to report on our case?"

Laughing, I replied, "First of all, Ms. H, it is not, I repeat—not 'our' case! Second of all, I told you, Lieutenant Kai has already warned me in no uncertain terms, not to get involved. He's got no time for amateurs, who might get in the way of the real investigation. That being said, the lieutenant did see fit to mention that there was nothing in any of the poor man's pockets, when they checked. He was wondering if any of us had checked for ID, when we found the body. I explained that we were a tad squeamish about looking. Figured we'd leave it to the police."

"So what else did the good detective say?"

"That was about it. I told you. He wasn't into sharing. All he did was ask me to go over my statement and wanted to know if I remembered anything else. He also reminded me, yet again, not to 'go off on a sleuthing expedition'. 'Let the police do their work'—his exact words."

Laughing, Henri replied, "Yeah, since when have you ever taken any-one's advice when you get it into your head to do something? So, what's the plan? Who do we talk to next?"

Throwing my hands in the air, I sighed, "OK, OK. I surrender! Boy are you an immovable force …."

"Got that right. So stop stalling and dish. I'm not getting any younger you know."

"Well, I think we should start in the cafeteria. Everyone there knows everyone else, so it stands to reason that the old man must have come across someone's radar, sometime. Check with your lunch buddies and see if they remember him. Meanwhile, I'll do my usual lunchtime meander. Then we can meet in the library and compare notes. Now I've really got to get moving or I'll never get anything done. I'm way behind schedule and this day is already practically shot. I'll meet you at the Center tomorrow right before the lunchtime rush. That'll give us some time to talk before we go into action."

"Sounds like a plan, Ez. See you tomorrow. I so can't wait to get started."

I could almost picture her rubbing her hands together in that gleefully wicked manner she has, when she's about to go into action. I said goodbye and hung up the phone. Shaking my head I mumbled to myself, "Boy am I in big trouble if the cops find out that my crew and I are about to go where no self-respecting little senior lady should go …."

Chapter 5

THE following day dawned sunny and bright. There was a distinct feel of spring in the air, even though we had a long way to go before the crocuses were ready to pop up their little heads and the forsythia started budding, heralding the arrival of that season of rebirth. Thinking of that reminded me of the other end of the cycle—death. Figures there'd be a murder in the depths of winter. Oh well, no time to get all philosophical. I had places to go and people to see—OK, one place to go—No. Two.

First stop, Continuing Ed. and my two favorite ladies. By the time I clicked the electric eye with my ID card, Tara was at the door, holding out a steaming cup of tea for me. Her trusty assistant and right-hand lady was right behind her with a plate full of my favorite peanut butter cookies. I'd had the presence of mind to call first making sure they were in. They fussed over me like a couple of anxious mother hens.

Pushing me onto one of the lovely pink peony print stuffed chairs, they took the other two and settled in to hear my bizarre tale.

"Unbelievable! You weren't kidding when you said it was surreal." Tara declared.

"Yes, you are very lucky that you did not run into the killer—if it was really murder."

"Don't I know it, Lisa! And I'm telling you, ladies, it was definitely murder! I mean, the poor guy's face was all swollen and a weird shade of grayish blue. Not only that, but there was this foam issuing from his mouth and the pungent smell of sweet almonds!"

"Cyanide." Lisa whispered. "I learned all about that during my training days in the Reserves."

"Stuff's bad news!" Tara concurred, shaking her head.

"A pretty painful way to go." I whimpered. "Finishing my tea and cookies, I stood up and prepared to take my leave.

"Thank you so much! I really needed to vent. Well, I'd better be going. Have to meet Henri and several of my ladies and acquaint them with the latest news—although I'd be willing to bet that they know more than I do. The senior gossip mill ...."

"For sure! Still the best form of communication," Tara Laughed as Lisa smiled her agreement.

Patting me on the shoulder, Tara walked me to the door. "Remember kiddo, anything you need, just call me. Even if all you want to do is vent some more."

"I'll remember."

"Take care—and be careful!"

I waved good-bye and headed back to my car. Next stop, the Senior Center ....

Lots of people to meet and greet. And this time I had an additional agenda. Finding out who would want to kill a nice, harmless old man like Harry. There I went again, taking it for granted that it was poor Harry's body I had tripped over. Suddenly it hit me—those silver flecks! That's what had been rolling around in the back of my mind. I'd better call Lieutenant Kai and let him know.

I arrived at the Center earlier than usual, just before the lunchtime crush. Henri, who usually arrives way before me, had not shown up yet, so I decided to make my usual rounds saying hi to the regulars and introducing myself to the "newbies." Time to check in with Arne (Arnoldine Frasier), our very own walking, talking social media person. She was just coming from the Senior Friendship Circle when I approached her. Arne knows absolutely everything about everyone. What she doesn't know is probably not worth knowing.

"Hey there, Arnoldine! What's new in the land of the Leicester Seniors?"

"Hiya Esme! As expected, the joint is really jumpin' with the news of your rather gruesome discovery. I hear you literally tripped over the corpse!"

"Groannn! Please don't remind me, the picture is indelibly etched on my brain for now and always! So what's everyone saying?"

"Oh, just the usual. They're taking bets as to who the guy is and how he died. Care to clue me in? I'd like to get the real story from you—not the 'Telephone' version that grows with every retelling."

"Sorry, Kiddo. I've been warned in no uncertain terms to keep it to myself—although there's not much more to tell. I'm in the dark the same as you. So what's the majority opinion as to the corpse's identity? Anybody been missing from the cafeteria or classes, bridge and/or bingo lately?"

"Funny you should ask. There are at least four old boys I know of personally, who haven't been around lately. Not a peep from any of them. As a matter of fact, I heard from the van driver, Ken, that one of them— Harry Browne—wasn't even home when he went to pick him up yesterday."

"Oh, yes? So who are the other three?"

"One is Herman Banks, but it turns out that he just went into the hospital for an unexpected procedure. He's still there, I believe."

"You mentioned Herman and Harry. Who are the other two?"

There's that vicious little runt, Adolf Betz—name suits him to a tee. Then there's that big guy, Norton Jones, you know, the obnoxious one, who's always spouting off about politics and 'what's wrong with our leaders today' ...."

"Funny that they've all gone MIA around the same time. I wonder if there's anything that ties them together?"

"I don't know, Ez .... That would be quite a coincidence. Don't you think you're stretching it a bit?"

"Possibly .... But like the police, I don't believe in coincidence. Maybe a couple here and there, but three men disappearing just when one of them is murdered?" Shaking my head. "I don't think so ...."

"Guess when you put it that way, I can see your point. So who should I start with first and what do you want to know?"

"Well let's try to eliminate the least likely one first. How about Jones? I think I remember him. Rather oily, large and flabby, full mustache. Favors western attire. Is he the one you're referring to?"

"That's him. Talk about an understatement!" Clapping me on the shoulder with a tiny, plump nutmeg colored hand, her beautiful coal-black eyes twinkling with humor, she elaborated. "If you ask me, the guy looks like the Pillsbury Dough Boy before he went on a diet. He's like a walking talking cartoon character. Has a great big old mustache that makes him look like a giant 'Yosemite Sam'. Full blubbery lips, not sexy just gross. A big mouth in more ways than one—wider than the great outdoors! Now there's a candidate for victim of the month. I can easily imagine someone being tempted to knock him off. But of course, people are rarely murdered just for being obnoxious—or are they?"

"Yes, but he's too tall. The man I … gag … tripped over, was not much bigger than me, from what little I could see …, but you never know. There still might be a connection between him and one of the others. Isn't he the guy who had words with Adolf Betz?"

"Are you kidding? They had more than words and not just once. They almost came to blows at one of the community meetings and Jeannie Gardner had to step in and separate them. It was a real freak show—that pugnacious little runt, Betz, up against that big flabby slob. Unbelievable!"

I reached out and patted her arm, cooing softly. "OK. OK, Arne. Don't get so worked up. It's not great for the blood pressure."

"You're right, Ez … but when I think about those two, it makes my blood boil—especially that Adolf Betz!" Arnoldine spat out disdainfully.

"I agree, but that won't help us figure out whose body that was lying in the stairwell. Can you tell me anything else about Betz? Something you might have seen or heard in passing?"

"When it comes to knowing anything about that one, I'd be willing to bet that what you see is what you get, and I want no part of it. Know what I mean?"

"Unfortunately, I do." Wistfully adding, "But I sometimes wonder what could have happened to make him that way."

"Well, all I can say is I have no desire whatsoever to know any more. He's a real piece of work! In his case I'd say he was just born bent. You run into that sometimes."

"Understood. That just leaves Harry Browne. I'm really worried that his is the body I saw, and this is one time I very much hope I'm wrong!" I sighed heavily.

"Hmm. Harry Browne. Yes, I know him. Everyone knows sweet, funny, quirky Harry Browne of the overflowing pockets and over the top tales. He kind of keeps himself to himself—except when it comes to showing off his precious coins. He's as quiet and self-effacing as Adolf is a big mouthed bully."

"Yes, I noticed the same thing. That's what I told the police when they interviewed me a second time. He was always jangling those coins in his pockets. And I remember those wonderful tall tales of his. You ever been privy to one of them?"

Arne grinned. "Of course! Who hasn't?"

"That's just the problem! If the victim turns out to be Harry, there'll be no dearth of suspects having cause to do the poor guy in—assuming his stories are true. Who knows? One of those coins might be very priceless. Stranger things have been known to occur ...."

"So, to recap. Harry and Adolf both hang out in the cafeteria almost every day and you haven't seen either of them lately and the driver said Harry wasn't in when he went on his rounds. Right?"

"Right. As I told you, I haven't seen hide nor hair of either one for a few days. Then again, whenever I see that little fascist coming, I usually take off running in the opposite direction!" she continued somewhat vehemently.

"Thanks for giving me the skinny on what's been going on since my unfortunate encounter with a corpse. Keep your eyes and ears open for anything else that might be relevant to the murder."

"UH OH! I feel a raging case of sleuth gone wild coming on. So what do you want me to do now boss?" she asked, tipping an imaginary hat.

"I want you to contact Lieutenant Kai or his young sidekick, if you stumble across anything that strikes you as relevant or just plain unusual."

"Got it! Will do, *Mon Capitan*," she replied, making a mock salute.

"And don't forget to keep us in the loop ... " came a rather strident voice from behind. Henri had crept up so quietly that I nearly jumped out of my own shoes.

"Henri, you almost gave me a minor heart attack! How about warning a person, before you sneak up on her—especially one who has already had more than her share of shocks."

"Sorry, kiddo," Henri replied in mock penitence. "Been recruiting again?" Henri turned her attention to Arne. "How are you doing Arne? Has our fearless leader been enlisting you and your special talent for getting people to talk?"

Arne laughed. "Of course. What else is new?"

"Now girls, this is not a game. Real people can get hurt when they interfere in stuff that has nothing to do with them. Remember, one poor man has already been murdered. We don't even know for sure who he is yet. I'd really hate for anything to happen to my peeps. All I want you to do is stay abreast of what people are saying and then pass the info along to the big guy."

"OK, point taken. But remember, between us girls, we have more access to the inner workings of this place than the cops. You know the gossip mill grinds busily away. As soon as we officially know who the poor guy is, we can swing into action."

"Not to mention who did what to whom and why," Arne added.

"I agree! Which is why I said to keep listening .... Speaking of which, thanks again, Arne. You are an absolute fount of information as usual! Continue your cafeteria schmoozing and pass along any good gossip you might hear. But don't forget to inform the police right away!"

"You got it!" Arne gave another mock salute.

"As for you, Henri, it goes without saying that I'm depending on you as always."

"Now you're talking!" Henri declared. "So what's next on the agenda?"

"What's next is ... much as you'd like to keep all of this info to ourselves, I'm going to have to call Lieutenant Kai and bring him up to date. Before they can proceed any further, the police have to put a name to the victim. They still need to come up with motive and opportunity, and it's pretty hard to do either when dealing with a nameless corpse."

"I guess so," conceded a very disappointed Henri.

"That's right! But we can still do a bit of snooping to find out who the poor old guy is, can't we?" Arne asked.

"Of course we can," replied Henri in her usual 'the decision is made' voice. No swaying that gal when she's made up her mind.

"Uh. No. I really don't think that would be a very good idea. I'm sure the police will be giving us the official word any time now. As I already mentioned, they can't really launch a full investigation until then."

"Oh, alright." Henri replied sulkily. "But you will let us know as soon as you hear from that big cop—yes?"

"Yes." I replied, laughing. "Anyone ever tell you that you are absolutely incorrigible!"

Henri grinned. "Yeah, all the time. But I'm lovable too, aren't I?"

"Weell ...."

"Arne ... don't say a word." I laughed again, giving them a collective hug.

"Listen girls, I really need to get moving, especially if I want to bring the lieutenant up to date. Take care and try not to get into any trouble!" Waving goodbye, I grabbed my bags and ran for the door before anyone else could stop me. Seniors are sometimes like that—no boundaries ....

Still smiling over the antics of my ladies, I headed for my car. As I turned to leave, I literally collided with Chuck Shackleton.

"Whoa there, little lady!" he laughed, reaching out a hand to steady me, a hint of a wink in his twinkling hazel eyes. "Where's the fire?"

"Hiya, Chuck," I winked back, straightening myself out. "You're just the person I was hoping to run into, although not literally."

Chuck, a tall, rangy sort of man in his late sixties, is the former captain of the Leicester Fire Department and our resident fire expert. Hence, the reference to fires. With his down-to-earth attitude and jovial personality, he is also one of my favorite people.

"So what can I do you for? Got any 'fires' need putting out?" he asked, chuckling at his own joke.

"Actually, you could say that—in a way. You know how I always worry about my peeps when I haven't seen or heard from them in a while. I was wondering if you had run into that guy who always dresses like an old-fashioned cowboy, Adolf Betz? I think that's his name."

"Since when has the 'Faux Cowboy' been one of your 'peeps'?"

"Come on Chuck, you know me! I can't help but get into conversations with everyone."

Laughing, Chuck replied, "That's why we all like you. But really, what possible interest can you have in our resident 'bad boy'?"

"Weell ... it's like this ... I'm sure you've already heard about my run in with a corpse. Just about everyone has by now. The police want to know if I recognized him, but I'm still not sure. I've pretty much narrowed it down to two men: Adolf Betz and Harry Browne. The problem is, that except for the way they dress, they both look alike. Anyway, I'm very much afraid it could be Harry, judging by the clothes .... But ... it could just as easily be Betz, in a departure from his usual gear."

"Okay, I'm with you so far. What is it you'd like to know?"

"I guess I'd like to hear any thoughts you might have on the matter. You see, Arne—you know, Arnoldine Frasier?"

"Yes our local town crier."

"Yes, that's her. She said that Betz and Jones were going at it big time at one of the community meetings. Almost came to blows … Jeannie Gardner had to step in and separate them.

"That sounds like Betz. Always looking for a fight. When he's not doing that, you'll find him looking to cash in on someone else's deal!"

"But she also told me that it was the last time she'd seen either of them around."

"Well, you can set your mind at ease as far as those two are concerned. I know for a fact that Betz heard Jones tell everyone he was heading out West to check on some business 'opportunities'. Knowing Betz, I'd be willing to bet, pardon the pun, that Betz figured Jones was on to something and decided to follow suit. Played it real cagey as usual, but what else is new?"

"Oh, thanks for bringing me up to speed. By the way, what about Harry Browne? He's also a regular. Seen him lately? Know if he's alright?"

"Funny you should mention Harry. I've been wondering what happened to him, myself. Nice little guy—totally different from that big blowhard, Jones and that slimy little Hitler, Betz … I keep waiting for him to execute a '*sieg heil*'. That guy really gets up my nose!"

"Anyway," Chuck continued, "as you know, Harry's real quiet. Doesn't share much—except when it comes to those wild stories of his. Then he doesn't stop! To hear him talk, you'd think he must have been some kind of adventurer back in the day. Got a kick out of his stories. Everyone did! Couldn't stand the constant clinking of those coins, though. Always rattling them around … drove me nuts! He seems like a real sad guy, you know?" Chuck shook his head. "Probably just lonely and looking for some attention. That's the main reason I always try to stop and talk to everyone, or at least say hello. Just like you. They often have so much to offer, but no one to share it with."

"I know. That's just what I told Lieutenant Kai. Speaking of whom, do you mind if I sic Lieutenant Kai on you? He'll definitely be interested in what you've just told me."

"Not at all, little lady. I'll be happy to talk to the lieutenant. I wish I could have been more help."

"Are ya kidding me? You've been a great help. What you shared with me will be of use to the good lieutenant as well. Thanks, Chuck!"

"By the way, if you want to find out more about Harry Browne, you might check with Thom, you know, Thom Davis He's a good buddy of

Harry's. Kinda took the poor little guy under his wing. I know he loves to listen to those stories of his. Practically memorized several. Could probably write a book."

"Yes, they are extremely entertaining and not a little creative. Which is your favorite?"

"I particularly got a kick out of the coin stories. Harry was always taking out a coin or two and going off on a whole dissertation on how he got 'em," Chuck continued. "I remember the day he showed us one of his most valuable coins. It was one we hadn't seen before. Solid gold. Looked real old, too. Come to think of it, Norton, the blowhard, was there. His eyes got as round as saucers and he started licking his chops, like he'd just discovered El Dorado. Now that I think about it, Norton decided to take a nice long trip out West, just around that time. I believe he mentioned Arizona. Funny coincidence that …."

"Yes. Isn't it?" The wheels starting to whirl about madly in my brain.

"Well, I'd better be heading out." I said, smiling and getting ready to take off at a trot. "See you later, big guy." I have a habit of calling all men "big guy" and the ladies, "kiddo." My memory is like a sieve when it comes to names.

Grinning, Chuck saluted and headed off to his usual hangout in the card room. I moved toward the door, my brain still reeling a mile a minute from what I'd just heard. I guessed it was time for another round of coffee and talk with Lieutenant Kai and his minion, Junior, as I now thought of him.

Chapter 6

Having arrived home, as I unlocked the door and let myself in, I heard the phone ringing, announcing that I had a call from the local police station. Dropping my things I lunged for the phone, grabbing it just before it went into voicemail. Sure enough, it was Lieutenant Kai, himself.

"Hi, Lieutenant. You must have read my mind. I had a very interesting conversation with one of the gentlemen at the Senior Center today. His name's Chuck Shackleton, and he may be able to shed some more light on the identity of the poor man I found on the stairs."

"Hello Mrs. Fine. That's very interesting. I'm looking forward to what you and he have to say. However, the reason I called is to inform you that we now have positive identification of the person you ... uh ... tripped over and I thought you'd want to know. The victim is your acquaintance, Harrold Browne. If you have some time today, I'd like to come over and ask you a few more questions."

"Of course, Lieutenant! I kind of figured it was him. The more I thought about it, the more certain I was. There was just something so familiar about the body, even in that grotesquely twisted state. Then it dawned on me. It was his eyes, the silver flecks. I didn't know Harry very well. Just to say 'Hi, how are you?' ... that sort of thing whenever I saw him; but I liked him very much. I just can't understand who would want to hurt such a sweet, harmless little man. He never had a mean word for anybody." Pulling myself together I asked the lieutenant when he would like to stop by.

"Now, if it's convenient for you. Won't take long. Just need some additional background information, and then you can bring us up to date on what you've heard."

"Sure, but can you give me about fifteen minutes or so? I just got in this minute and haven't eaten lunch yet. And I still have to let my dog out for his daily walkabout."

"That'll be fine. We'll be there in about half an hour. That should give you time to settle down and do what you need to do."

"Yes. Plenty of time. By the way, will Officer Jim … Officer O'Reilly, be with you? I know how much he loves my cookies. Looks like he could use a few extra pounds."

Once again, Kai's booming laugh burst out over the wire, almost splitting my ear drums. "Yes, but there's really no need for you to concern yourself about our comfort."

"Please, Lieutenant Kai, as I've already told you, I'm a Jewish mother. That's what we do. Besides, I have a son who's not all that much older than Officer O'Reilly. I know first hand about the horrible eating habits of young men their age and believe me, it won't kill me to offer you both a little refreshment."

"Alright, Mrs. Fine, point taken.", laughed the lieutenant, a little more quietly this time. "We'll see you shortly."

I grabbed a quick lunch, let Streak out, and proceeded to brew yet another pot of coffee and a green tea for me. No sooner had I placed the cups, dishes and another batch of cookies on the table than the bell rang. I opened the door and there stood the detective, cradling little Streak in his massive arms. The little guy was licking him like he was some great big, succulent piece of meat (which he probably was to a dog). Behind the detective, young Jimmy stood deferentially, hat in hand, notepad in pocket. Inviting them in, I headed back to the kitchen. Lieutenant Kai gently deposited Streak onto his fuzzy little doggy sofa—I believe I already explained that my dog is a little princeling. He turned around several times and fell into a rapturous, snoring sleep, to the great amusement of both detectives. Inviting them to sit down, I brought the pot over to the table and filled their cups.

Chuckling, the lieutenant said, "Now that the little fella's settled in, maybe we can get down to business. As I explained when I called, we have irrefutable proof that the victim was your acquaintance, Harry Browne. I won't go into details. The reason we are here is, you had mentioned that, although you didn't have much contact with him, you knew of others who had. Do you happen to remember any of those others in addition to

Mr. Shackelton?" he asked, consulting his notes. "We would really like to talk with them in order to get a clearer picture of what kind of person Mr. Browne was and who might have had reason to want him dead."

"I understand, Lieutenant, but as I stated earlier, I speak to so many people during my 'travels' that I don't always remember who said what or who sat with whom."

"We realize that, Mrs. Fine. Just tell us what you can. For instance, you had mentioned that Mr Browne was always telling stories about his adventures and carried around all sorts of stuff in his pockets, showing them off. Can you remember anyone in particular, who may have exhibited more than a passing interest in these show-and-tells? Anyone go out of his or her way to seek him out?"

"Funny you should ask, Lieutenant. Chuck Shackleton is the man you need talk to. He actually noticed just such an exchange." I proceeded to sum up what Chuck had told me.

"Oh, I almost forgot. You might want to talk with Thom Davis as well. Chuck told me that Thom was the closest thing to a best friend that Harry had."

"Thanks for the update. Opens up several new lines of inquiry. By the way, I'll need the name and address of Mr. Shackleton and Mr. Davis, if you have them."

"Of course, Lieutenant. I've got their info right here."

"We'll have to locate Norton Jones and Adolf Betz as well. Both of their names have come up several times as persons of interest. Quite a coincidence, eh, O'Reilly? And what do I always say about coincidences?"

Jimmy snapped to attention at once, almost choking on the cookie he was polishing off.

"You don't believe in coincidences," the young policeman exclaimed, spewing forth a mouthful of crumbs.

"Right!"

"Neither do I!"

Turning his attention back to the matter at hand, he continued. "Did Mr. Shackleton happen to mention where out West, Jones and Betz were headed? It's a big country out there."

"No, he didn't. Chuck said he was headed out West somewhere. Wait a minute! I do remember. He said something about Arizona. Spoke of mines in connection with both of them. I just don't remember the specifics."

"No worries. It often happens, especially in stressful situations. It'll probably come back to you when you least expect it. Just give me a call if you remember anything else. And again, I can't emphasize enough the importance of reporting anything at all, even if it seems unimportant to you."

"I'll remember. I've already spoken to my ladies and told them to contact you if they hear or see anything that might ring a bell. Just take some of what they tell you with a grain of salt. They have quite active imaginations and sadly, this is the most exciting thing that's happened to them in years—in some cases, ever!"

"We'll bear that in mind. I hope you've reminded them that this is not a game."

"Yes I have, Lieutenant. Umpteen times! That doesn't mean they're going to listen. They are adults, you know, and I certainly can't tell them what to do or not to do."

"That goes without saying, but you don't need to encourage them either," he replied rather more sternly than before.

"Understood," I answered meekly, mentally crossing my fingers behind me.

"Well, we've kept you long enough, and you've given us a lot to think about." The detective stood up. Towering over me, he continued, "We'll be in touch if we have any more questions. Thanks again for this delightful repast," Kai said as he and Officer Jim prepared to leave. Shaking hands, I saw them out.

Closing the door behind them, I leaned back, sighing deeply and tried to process all that I had learned today. Then I laughed, wondering what the neighbors must be thinking by now. Was this going to become a habit? Shaking my head, I poured myself another cup of tea. Next, a quick nap in the hopes of calming my teeming brain.

* * *

I woke up an hour later, my thoughts tumbling about all over the place. Unable to sleep, I decided to put them on paper, as is my wont, when I'm feeling stymied. I grabbed one of the many pads lying around the house and sat down to make a list of what I knew and what I suspected from everything I'd seen and heard in the past couple of days.

Question number one: Why would anyone want to pull the plug on such a harmless, unimposing little man as Harry? It's not like he was rich or had anything worth stealing. Or had he? What if someone had heard some of his tall tales and decided they were true? What if they actually were true, and he had been carrying around something of real value in those baggy, capacious pockets of his? If so, what on earth could it be—a semi priceless old coin? Or one connected to hidden treasure? Was it a valuable piece of antique jewelry? What exactly was it that had driven a man—or woman, for that matter, to kill? Mentally dragging myself off that line of thought, I continued with my list.

Question number two: How was he killed? Assuming Harry was poisoned; which I was quite sure he was—cyanide—judging from the bluish tinge and foam oozing out of his mouth, topped off by the very strong smell of bitter almonds on his breath. It had to be some form of the stuff, one which was slower acting (note to myself: check on other forms of cyanide). This narrowed things down considerably. But how and when could the cyanide have been administered to him without anyone getting caught?

Cyanide is a very popular poison in the mystery novel universe and, of course, it was the go-to capsule during several wars. If someone was captured, or caught spying, all he, or she had to do was bite down and it would be all over. Speaking of which, I remembered reading somewhere that in fatal doses of potassium and sodium cyanide, symptoms might not occur for ten to twenty minutes and in some cases death might take up to half an hour. How that poor man must have suffered if that was the case! I could hardly bear the thought of that poor man in excruciating pain, dying all alone on that cold, dank staircase! I managed with great difficulty to pull myself out of my funk and get back to focusing on the matter at hand. This whole thing was just an exercise in futility, since the good lieutenant was not exactly into sharing.

Maybe I could wheedle the info out of him. No. That wouldn't work, since I had already commented on the state of the body. Knowing what a careful cop he was, I was sure he'd already checked on that stuff. Oh well! I guess I'd just have to wait, like everyone else, until the information was made public. At least I could help by finding out more about Harry. Who might have had a motive to do away with him? I still had my trusty ladies scoping out the situation. I'd have to check back with them next time I was at the Center.

As all this was running through my mind, the phone rang. It was Henri calling to see how things were going—talk about ESP! Making a mad dash for the phone, I picked it up, breathlessly answering, "Hiya Hen! I was just thinking about you."

"Hi yourself. You sound like you've just finished a road race. Stop and catch your breath. I think I can wait a few seconds."

So I did.

"That's better. Have you heard any more from that rather imposing copper and his young sidekick?"

"Come on, Hen. You know darn well they were just here a little while ago. You live right next door. You probably also saw me go upstairs and figured I was going to crash when I closed the blinds, which is why you waited to call me til now."

"Oh, alright, 'Sherlock'. You caught me red-handed. So … what did the big fella want this time?"

"The usual."

"And that would be …?"

"Not much," I replied, maddeningly taking my time. "They have officially identified the body. And before you say anything, yes, it's poor Harry Browne."

Suddenly sobered, Hen cried out, "OMG! Listen kiddo, I'll be right over. Leave the door unlocked and you just sit down and have another cuppa. Mama Hen is on the way."

Before I could even thank her, she'd hung up the phone. Taking her sage advice, I did as I was told—poured myself a large one and took down a mug for her. Just as I sat down, I heard the door gently open and light footsteps briskly padding toward the kitchen.

"It's alright, Ez," Henri said. Wrapping her arm around my shoulder and giving it a squeeze, she softly cooed, "I'm here now, dear. So tell Mama H what's going on. But first, how are you holding up? You're looking a little paler than usual and your pulse is beating a mile a minute!" she said gently lifting my wrist and checking her watch.

Suddenly the floodgates opened and I began to sob uncontrollably, more like blubbered. "Who would want to kill that nice old guy? He wouldn't even step on an ant. What kind of sicko kills someone like him and in such a cruel way, too?"

"So it's definitely Harry, is it?"

"No doubt about it," I sniffled loudly. "I wasn't privy to the specifics, but I'm guessing they were able to identify him from his dental and/or military records. You remember, he walked with a marked limp and his shoes were always spit shined to within an inch of their life. And we'd already heard that he was in Nam."

"Of course! That's typical of military training. I guess we were all afraid it was him."

"I think I knew from the start, but I just didn't want to believe it. I always said there was something very familiar about him, even in that state. It was those eyes … rheumy—like that old man in The Telltale Heart, but I could still see those silver flecks."

"Do they think he was poisoned?"

"They aren't saying, but I'd be willing to bet that's what it was, judging from what I saw."

"And I'd give odds that you'd be right. Having been a nurse for all these years, I can usually spot the signs a mile away."

"Shame on me. I almost forgot with all the craziness of the past few days … seems more like a year," I repeated almost to myself. "You're always regaling me with all those delightfully gruesome hospital stories which, by the way, I could probably live without. After hearing them I plan on staying far away from hospitals if mortally possible," I laughed.

"After what you've been through, kiddo, I'm surprised you even remember your name."

I laughed. "Well, I can always depend on you to remind me, while lightening up a difficult situation at the same time. Thanks for being you."

"You're welcome … and here's a tissue. Your face is a mess."

"I know." I snuffled into the tissue.

"By the way Hen, I ran into Chuck Shackleton, you know, the big guy who used to be a running back and a firefighter? Now, the only running he does is bridge. Might call him the MVP of card games."

"OK! I get the picture. Chuck, the Bridge player. I've seen him around occasionally. Devoted to the game. Smart guy and very observant. What about him? Did he have any worthwhile info to impart? I assume he heard about the old guy croaking on the stairs. Did he know Harry?"

"As a matter of fact my nosy friend, he recognized poor Harry from my description. He also knows that very annoying man, Norton Jones, and his nemesis, Adolf Betz. Rumor has it that both of them are now being considered persons of interest, having conveniently disappeared in the wilds of the Southwest. Chuck had several conversations with them. He even saw the two of them talking once or twice. That in itself is very strange, since they're always at each other's throats. Chuck also remembered Harry showing off his little treasures to himself and those two while reminiscing about the good old days. He used to think that it was all talk until he checked out a particularly fascinating specimen one day. When Chuck took a closer look, it dawned on him that Harry might actually have acquired something of real value. Chuck described the piece to me. It was a gold coin and very old. However, what really made me sit up and take notice, was the fact that Norton and Adolf had the same reaction. According to Chuck, and I quote: 'His eyes got as round as saucers and he started licking his chops'. Of course this is all conjecture on both our parts. There is currently no proof since the coins conveniently have disappeared. However, don't you think it's awfully curious that Norton took off for parts unknown right after Harry was murdered and the coins went missing? And shortly after that, Adolf Betz followed closely at his heels? A bit too convenient if you ask me."

"Aha! So that's why you called the big guy, huh? I gather that he was impressed?"

"Well, I wouldn't exactly describe him as impressed, but he certainly seemed interested in the information and was planning on making inquiries even as we speak."

"You see, we are helping with the investigation!" barked Henri. "People talk to us quicker than they would to the cops. You know that. You read it all the time in mysteries."

"Yes, but might I remind you that this is real life and not a book. People can get hurt when they stick their noses where they don't belong, as the lieutenant has reminded me again and again. How about we give the poor guy a break and let him get on with the investigation minus our interference?" I said.

"Sure," Henri replied, an alarming twinkle in her eye, which always warned me that she wasn't going to back off. No way, no how. Henri is an absolute terror once she takes the bit in her mouth. I just had to make sure she didn't get into any trouble. Boy, was I in for one heck of a wild ride!

Chapter 7

Monday morning. I woke up with a dreadful headache, my brain all fuzzy from nerves and lack of sleep. This was becoming one very bad habit! Dragging myself out of bed, I headed to the bathroom to begin my daily ablutions. Taking one look at the image in the mirror, I groaned at the rather sleep-deprived apparition peering back at me. Tufts of fine mahogany brown hair stuck out all over my head like some demented version of Alfalfa of *Little Rascals* fame. Newly developed wrinkles in a formerly smooth face. Haunted, wild, dark eyes. Sighing, I shook my head and muttered, "It's going to take more than makeup to do anything with this mess!"

If this was an example of what it's like to be a senior citizen, I'm not sure I wanted any part of it! But then, as my very wise mother had often said, many years ago, "What's the alternative, dear?"

"Yes, what is the alternative?" I repeated as I stoically proceeded to put my stressed, sleep ravaged face to rights. I washed my face, slathering on the moisturizer. After a few well aimed touches of shadow and liner, I studied the results. Sighing again, I fluffed up my hair and drenched it in hairspray.

"OK, not as bad as I thought, but not so great either—thank God for Estée Lauder and Clinique!" Chuckling to myself, I headed for my spacious walk-in closet. I grabbed my dance leggings and one of my many tunic tops—this one, hot pink with lace trim of the same color. Noticing that the tunic was looser than usual, I remembered I hadn't eaten much since this whole nightmare had begun. At least one good thing had come out of it. What I had tried to do with diet and exercise for the last few months made nary a dent, but tripping over a poor old dead guy had done the trick. Talk about irony!

Grabbing my coat, dance tote and smoothy. I made a beeline for my car. This time I arrived at work well in advance of my ladies. Running up the stairs, I couldn't help thinking of the last time I had done this. Shaking my head to dispel the gruesome image, I put on my best smile and headed toward the auditorium. "Showtime!" I whispered to myself as I headed through the double doors.

Who should I see when I entered the room, but Rosemary. Often the first to arrive, she approached me with that big, bright smile of hers, beautiful hazel eyes twinkling with humor. Holding a Starbucks bag, Rosemary shoved her offering into my now eager grasp and handed me a nice large mocha latte. Does that woman know me or what? Groaning with anticipation and delight, I threw caution to the wind and dug in; my only excuse being that I was under a lot of stress.

The girls, as I like to refer them, slowly shuffled in, with Flor Ruiz bringing up the rear. Have I mentioned that my ladies take their ever loving time showing up? Flor might be habitually late, but she's also my most devoted student. Flor has been with me for at least thirty years. She's followed me as I made the usual rounds of the Senior Centers. She's also one of my biggest fans and promoters. While I was polishing off the last of the buttery croissant I had ravaged and licking the crumbs from my lips, the girls converged upon me and smothered me in hugs and kisses asking how I was doing after my ordeal. I gently detached myself from the circle of love and thanked them all for their concern reminding them that it was time to dance. Did I also mention that my ladies sometimes behaved more like excited high school girls than dignified older women? I was always telling them that they were worse than my high school kids when it came to settling down and paying attention. This morning I also added that all questions would be answered during our weekly lunch.

As long as I can remember—and believe me, it's a long time!—I have been going out for lunch or dessert with my students after class. As a matter of fact, I've often been told that's why they love my class so much. We've been together so long that we're more than teacher and students— we're close friends, who would do almost anything for one another. This was about to be proven when they jumped on the "let's solve a mystery" bandwagon! Groaning inwardly, I pasted a happy "let's dance smile" on my face and proceeded to put them through their paces—with a little tougher workout than usual. I grinned again; this time for real, thinking, "Boy, isn't it great to be on the other side of the stage!"

Class went smoothly. We did our warmup exercises, rib, hip and tummy isolations, vibrated, shimmied, twirled our veils and generally cut loose. Of course, we finished with our regular relaxation and cool down exercises, followed by their favorite inspirational song: "Somewhere Over The Rainbow." After that workout, we were ready to dig into lunch. Flor and I were the last to leave—as usual! First, I had to put away my music, return my boom box to its little shelf, then wash up. Leaving my dance things on, I added a scarf and changed into boots. I grabbed my jacket and hat and ran out the door. Seems I'm always running somewhere.

As we entered our little Main Street Café, I was set upon by Henri and my other regulars yet again. The Café is located at the top of Main, right across the street from the Robert W. Remington Town Hall. The Center was named in honor of one of our greatest Town Managers, Mr. Robert W. Remington, or Mr. Bob as he was affectionately known.

His father, Jonathan W. Remington, was one of the first Jews to settle here in Leicester and had literally been responsible for putting the town of Leicester on the map in 1897. Up until then it had been a sleepy little hamlet with a small Main Street and a tiny Green, surrounded by white and Wedgwood Blue clapboard colonials, salt boxes and Victorians with their gingerbread details. We even have some beautiful Edwardian homes.

Heir to the Remington Silk Mill fortune, Mr. Bob followed in his Father's footsteps. He made a point of encouraging the development and growth of cottage industry and supported the arts, saying that they would attract the gentler, more discriminating tourist crowds. He was also responsible for coming up with the town slogan. Gradually, Leicester became a thriving artisan center attracting art and crafts lovers as well as antique hunters from all over New England.

A number of up and coming interstate railroads were expanding their territories and Mr. Bob managed to convince the NBRR Company to make a stop at the northern edge of town on its way to and from New York and Boston. As a result, Leicester became a popular stopover for travelers, many swearing that they would one day retire to this beautiful city village.

But, I digress. Back to the mystery of the old man on the stairs. I brought the ladies up to date on what I had learned—which was very little and what I had told Lieutenant Kai. With ghoulish glee, several of them loudly voiced opinions as to how poor Harry might have met his end. Henri put her two cents in here and there as did Arne. Once again, Marina was the voice of reason. "Calm down girls and let Esme continue," she told them.

Rosemary, the practical one, added, "Yes. Please continue. Then let us know what you'd like us to do."

"Well, I'm not sure what we can or should do for that matter," I replied.

"I suppose it wouldn't hurt to ask around about poor little Harrold Browne," Rosemary suggested. "You know. See if anyone had more than a passing acquaintance … you know, more than 'Hi how are you?' and 'How's the food?'."

"Come to think of it, there is someone else who was friendly with Harry." added Marina. "That sweet old gentleman, who sits in the last row of the lunchroom. Always smiles and says hello to everyone who enters. He's about five foot nine or ten—kind of plump and uses a walker. Always wears tees with signage and a plaid flannel shirt over that."

"Do you mean Thom Davis, Mar?"

"Yes! That's the man. He's known for taking the newbies and shy guys under his wing. Shows them the lay of the land. Knows who's who and what's going on when and where. I'm sure I've seen them eating together and having some very animated discussions. As a matter of fact, I even saw Harry showing Thom one of those special coins he was always going on about. Maybe one of us could talk with him?"

"Great idea, Marina. Which one of you ladies knows Thom and has a rapport with him?"

"That'd be me." Henri declared. "I usually sit at his table during lunch."

"Hey, don't forget me!" Arnoldine called out. "We're lunch mates, remember?"

"How could I ever forget!" Henri muttered under her breath. She continued out loud. "Yes, we both sit right next to the guy, and he's definitely sweet on our Arne. You should see how he stares at her. Poor guy actually blushes when she returns his look."

It was Arne's turn to blush. "TMI, Hen," Arne retorted, as a lovely shade of maroon spread across her warm dark features. "Now you're making me blush! But Henri's right. Thom's always asking me if I'd like to join him for Movie or Dance Night at the Center. He probably would open up to me."

"Great! Then I expect you to turn on your significant charm and get

Thom to talk about Harry. He may just know or have heard something that could help us get to the bottom of things."

"Will do, *Mon Capitan!*"

"Now that's taken care of," I grinned. "Any other ideas who we might connect with?"

"I just remembered something else," said Marina. "Harry used to confide in Jeannie Gardner, the Social Worker. She might have seen or heard something during her conversations with him. Of course, she couldn't discuss anything confidential, but she should know more about him than anyone else. She and I do lunch every so often. Why don't I ask her if she can help? I know she was quite fond of Harry. He always entertained her with his tales of the good old days and derring-do—would you believe, that's actually how he described them."

"Sounds like a plan, Marina. Are you going to be meeting with her any time this week?"

"Yes, I am. Want me to ask her to give you a call, when she gets a chance?"

"That would be great! I might even call her myself, or drop in at her office and say hello."

That taken care of, I turned my attention back to Rosemary.

"On another note. Rosemary, as Recording Secretary of the Advisory Board, you're always attending various meetings. Is there anything in particular you remember about the obstreperous Mr. Norton Jones or Adolf Betz? Did you ever notice either of them talking to, or more likely at Harry? Did Harry ever attend any of the meetings?"

Rosemary tapped her cheek thoughtfully. "Hmm ... I believe they both attended several meetings about potential building sites for a new Senior Center. Those two are a couple of know-it-alls—think they have all the answers to everything."

"Where have we heard that before?" Henri interjected wryly."

"That's the truth!" Arne added.

"Alright ladies, let's let Rosemary finish."

"Thanks, Esme! I spoke with Harry several times as well—and yes, before you ask, he did show some of his coins to Norton and whoever else expressed interest. Most of the people feigned interest, just to be kind. However, Norton was a totally different story. His eyes positively lit up on seeing one particular coin. He asked to take a closer look. I actually saw the coin, myself. As you all know, I'm interested in antique and vintage collectibles. The coin was gold, maybe an inch and a half in diameter. I didn't get a close look at it, but from what I could tell, it was very worn and had a picture of a woman in Victorian garb on one side and what appeared to be some sort of coat of arms on the other."

Chuckling, I commented, "Boy, for someone who didn't get a good look, you certainly observed quite a bit!"

"Well, you know how it is. Like you, I notice all things bright and golden."

"OK! Now we have two more avenues to explore.

one Harry's background.

two Messrs. Jones and Betz.

Anything else ladies, before we call it quits for the day?"

Jayne Hathaway, one of our newbies, a rather quiet, shy septuagenarian, meekly raised her hand. She had recently joined our little belly dancing cadre, after becoming widowed. Now she was one of our most ardent participants!

"As some of you may have heard, I used to work in the town library. Now I just volunteer a few days a week, when I'm not hanging out with you ladies, that is," Jayne giggled nervously. "If you get more information on the coin that caught everyone's interest, I can research it online and in some of our older books. Just a sketch will suffice."

The ladies all called out at once.

"What a wonderful idea."

"Great idea."

"You go, girl!"

I added my two cents. "Sounds like a plan. Marina, Rosemary, do you think one or both of you can sketch out or get hold of any pix of that coin?"

"I don't see why not," Marina replied.

"And I'm not too bad at the sketching part," Rosemary added. "I'll give it a try."

"Great! Well, I think we've gotten a lot accomplished today, but just remember, as Lieutenant Kai has told us ad infinitum.

"More like 'ad nauseam', " Henri cracked, not so *sotto voce* ....

Directing my gaze toward Henri and then back at my ladies, I continued. "Look girls, this is not a game. There are dangerous people out there. So, if you do find out anything of importance, make sure you inform him first. Now, if there are no further comments I really need to get back to work.

Got a couple of classes to prepare for. See you all later!" With that, I hugged everyone, grabbed my coat and hat and scooted towards the stairs. As I passed through the cafeteria, I saw Arne making a beeline for her usual table sidling up to Thom. Dear Arne. I could always count on her.

* * *

Wasting no time, Arnoldine went right into her act. Sitting down next to him, she pulled her chair as close as she could get. "Guess by now you've heard about your buddy Harry. Terrible isn't it?"

"I know, I've been thinking about it ever since I heard. You know, he's one of the people on the top of my list." Taking a crumpled, folded piece of paper from his flannel pocket, he held it up for her to see. "I've been keeping a list of people for years. You know, people who are friendly, kind to each other and always helpful. He's right near the top. See?" Shyly looking at her, his cherubic face turning a soft shade of pink, he whispered. "You're on the very top, you know."

Arnoldine gazed into his clouded hazel eyes with her deep dark ones. The poor man almost turned to jelly. Patting his arthritis-riddled claw-like hand, she smiled, theatrically striking her heart with her own warm, dark one. "I'm honored and touched."

Henri sat on the other side of Arne, watching her performance. "Oh my Gawd," she groaned, mentally shoving two fingers in her mouth. "That woman should win an Emmy for Corniest performance! Ouch!" She grunted, receiving a well aimed elbow in her scrawny side by the woman in question. Meanwhile, Arne was going full throttle in her interrogation.

"I don't suppose you have any idea why anyone would want to hurt him," Arne continued, inching ever closer to her 'innocent prey'. "After all, you were one of Harry's only true friends. I remember that you took him under your wing when he first came here. When everyone else made fun of him behind his back you always defended him. That's true friendship!"

"I suppose so," Thom mumbled thoughtfully.

"Most of all, you believed in him, when very few others did. You knew that his stories were true and not tall tales." Then she changed tack and got right to the point.

"So what do you know that no one else does?"

"That a girl! Right down to business," Henri muttered under her breath. "Boy! Is she a player or what …?" This received another dig in her side.

"What'd you do that for?"

"Shhsh!" Arne hissed under her breath.

Thom closed his eyes in thought, then opening them wide, he answered. "You know, he showed me a number of his the coins, just like he did with everyone else. But this time it was different. That mean Adolf Betz and nosy Norton were right behind us, and they both got a good look. You should have seen Norton's eyes light up … like a Christmas tree! And Adolf almost choked on the coffee he was drinking."

Arne tried to hide her excitement. "What did the coin look like?"

"Just looked like a dark yellow coin, with a picture of a pretty lady in an old-fashioned outfit. I don't know why everyone's carrying on so much. It's just a dirty old coin as far as I can tell—not anywhere as interesting as that map he has hanging on the wall in his apartment. I used to go there for a game of dominoes and sometimes gin rummy."

This time Henri, who had been sitting, avidly taking in every word, almost choked on her own coffee. "Well I'll be damned …," she muttered to herself, so engrossed in her own thoughts was she, that she almost missed the most important part of the conversation.

Arne practically jumped out of her chair. "Map! What map?"

"Looked like a very old map … like the ones they used to have back in the eighteen hundreds. It was framed and hanging on the wall along with some other old maps and pictures. He collected them, you know."

"No. I didn't know." By this time Arne was almost on top of poor Thom … although according to Henri, he was loving every minute!

"Well, this map was different from the others. It was hand-printed and included some roughly drawn pictures of desert terrain, caves and such. One night he took it down and showed it to me. Even winked at me … kind of conspiratorially like. He told me that it was a sort of treasure map. Somewhere in the Southwest. So I asked him why he'd never used it.

"Shook his head sadly and said, 'Why would I? I have no relatives to share it with. I live alone. I'm already comfortably settled. So why bother? In a way it's more fun to make up stories in my mind about what it would be like to be rich.' But that was Harry for you. Perfectly happy with his memories and the adventures he'd had in the past. Just wanted to be quiet.

To sit back and share his stories with friends and acquaintances." Sighing, Thom sat back and sipped his tea.

Touched, Arne reached out and patted his hand again. "Must've been hard remembering all the good times you shared with Harry."

"Yes, it was, but it helped to share with you. By the way, they're showing one of our favorite movies this Friday, *The Treasure of Sierra Madre*. How about going with me? We can stop across the street at Sophia Kenny's for a quick dinner and then come here."

"Talk about coincidence …," Arne thought. Aloud she said, "Sounds good. How 'bout I meet you there and we head back here together? Popcorn's on me."

"Great! Movie's at seven, five thirty for dinner OK with you?

"Sure. Well, I'd better be moving along. Gotta get ready for class tomorrow." Standing up, she turned to Henri. "You coming, Hen? We got lots to do before class."

Henri took the hint. "I hear you loud and clear, Arne." She pushed her chair back and followed Arne toward the exit as they both turned and waved to Thom.

"Boy did you get a ton of info, Arne!"

Arne snickered. "That's OK. I'm used to your potty mouth by now, but you'd better try to tone it down once in a while. You know how PC some of the girls can be."

"Yeah, I know you're right. But it's all my crazy college psych professor's fault! He used to make us practice cursing. Said it was great mechanism for venting and dealing with stress in a 'healthy' manner. Before he started in on that psycho-babble, the strongest language that ever passed through these pearly whites was 'fiddlesticks' or 'Oh shoot'. I'm telling you, it's positively addictive!"

"Well, at least it's not drugs or booze. Ready to report to Esme?"

"You bet! She'll be absolutely gobsmacked, as she's so fond of saying."

The two friends linked arms and shimmied out the door.

Chapter 8

WHEN I arrived home, my two "boys" were waiting for me as usual—both wanting their dinners. Streak sniffed me all over to make sure it was really me. Convinced that it was, he proceeded to stand on his little back legs and lick whatever part of me he could reach. I bent down, gave him a good cuddle, while he bestowed sloppy, wet kisses on my face. Paul came next, wipe in hand. After swiping said face, he added his own not so sloppy one.

"How was your day?" he asked, helping me off with my coat. "Any more misadventures?"

"Heaven forfend!" I retorted. "Nope, the most excitement I had was listening to the girls and helping them plan our next move."

"What next move? I thought you were going to leave it to the police."

"I know, I know! But you of all people must realize that seniors are usually a little wary of sharing information with the powers that be. That includes the cops. My ladies hear things—stuff that people would never tell the police. Besides, as you've heard me say umpteen times, I'm kind of like a bartender. People like to talk to me. They share all sorts of stuff that they'd never have the heart to tell the police."

"That's not the point, Esme," Paul said grabbing me by the shoulders as if to shake some sense into me. He repeated it again, for emphasis. "That's not the point and you know it. You and your ladies are playing at a very dangerous game. What if the bad guys find out what you're up to? Worse yet, what if one of you actually stumbles onto something that can lead to the murderer's identity? Have you even given serious thought to that? Whoever it is has already killed once and has nothing to lose and everything to gain by shutting you up."

"You're scaring me, Paul!" I cried, easing myself out from under his grip and backing away.

"That was my intention. You should be scared—very scared! Who says you won't be next if you keep up with this harebrained scheme of yours?"

"It is not 'harebrained'!" I retorted. "I know what I'm doing. I've been keeping Lieutenant Kai apprised of everything all along, and I told my ladies to do the same thing."

"How do I know you're not keeping anything from me? And while we're at it, what happens if Lieutenant Kai is unavailable when you call? What would you do then?"

"I'd leave him a message and keep trying. Besides, I've always got my big brave hubby to protect me, if I ever need help." I said, sidling up to him and stroking him on his shiny bald pate.

"Esme …," he said, gently pushing me away, "That isn't going to work this time. I'm concerned for your safety and you'd better be, too …."

Just then the phone rang. It was Jayne, probably calling to report on her research. Cutting the hubby off mid-rant, I made a grab for the phone. "Hold on. I was just going over something with Paul."

"Oh," she stammered, "I can call back."

"No. Your timing is perfect. Only take me a sec …." Covering the mouthpiece with my hand, I whispered, "Alright dear, calm down. I promise to be careful and try to keep my big mouth shut; but right now I need to take this call. It's one of my new ladies and she's still quite inhibited."

"Maybe, you should take some lessons from her," Paul muttered as he walked away.

"OK! Message received loud and clear! Go back to your book and relax while I take this call. Then I've got to get out of these clothes and jump in the shower." I blew him a kiss and continued.

"Sorry for the hold up, Jayne. How are you doing? Don't tell me you've already found something? We just finished our meeting a short while ago."

"I hope I didn't interrupt anything, Esme." she said timidly.

"Not at all, kiddo! So what's up?"

"Well, it turns out that I had to run some errands near the library anyway, so I thought I'd get a head start on my research."

"Great! Have you come up with anything helpful, yet?"

"Yes, I think so," she replied. "You know that coin that one of the girls drew a picture of? I found one just like it in an old history book. Comes from a batch that was stolen during transport to Australia. It's all here in newspaper reports of the time. You see, once again the coins were involved in yet another robbery. This one on a stagecoach in California. The papers really had a field day! It had everything: murder, mayhem, heroes and scoundrels."

"You have got to be kidding me!" I exclaimed. "Tell me all about it and try not to leave out a thing!"

"All right. I'll try, but there's oh so much to tell." Jayne went on to give me a detailed explanation from the original theft of the coins through the arrest and execution of the criminals involved.

"OMG!" I said. "Talk about truth being stranger than fiction. This is beginning to sound like one of those old time westerns with a little film noir thrown in for good measure. That's quite a story, Jayne, and it jibes with some of the tall stories Harry shared with a number of people at the Senior Center. Were you able to check out the book or make copies of the relevant pages?"

"I sure was. I've got the book right in front of me and I made extra copies for the ladies. I was also able to print out relevant passages of the news stories. There were even a number of penny dreadfuls written about it. Couldn't get hold of any of them, since they're extremely rare, and I doubt very much that any collectors would be willing to share. However, I did get the names and plot descriptions of a couple."

"Boy have you been busy ... and all in a matter of hours. You are absolutely amazing! I'd like you to share this whole story with the girls—from soup to nuts."

"I ... I guess so," she stammered. "If you think it will help."

"Are ya kidding me? They'll be absolutely knocked out by it! Thank you so much for all your hard work! Listen, I have to go now, but there's just one more thing I need you to do."

"Uh, Oh. What is it this time?"

I laughed. "Don't worry, this part is easy and very important! Unfortunately, I just got reamed out by my overly protective husband, who said that we should stay out of it and pass along any info to the police. So I need you to do just that. Pass everything on to Lieutenant Kai or his young assistant, Jimmy O'Reilly. Can you do that for me?"

"Everything? The book, the picture and the articles?"

"Yes. Everything!"

"Alright. I'll drop it all off to the Lieutenant." Suddenly I heard her giggle. The tension broken. "This is getting positively exciting!" She said goodbye and hung up, still giggling.

It was good to watch Jayne finally coming out of her shell and starting to be happy again. She had been married to her high school sweetheart for over fifty years and had never dated any other men before or even after being widowed.

A frisson of fear suddenly hit me as I zoned in on the lecture my husband had just given me. I sure hoped I wasn't putting my ladies or myself at risk as he feared. Boy, was I glad I had told Jayne to pass the stuff on to Lieutenant Kai. I wondered how he'd react to the info … then that imaginary little imp of trouble landed on my shoulder, whispering in my ear: "Call the Lieutenant. Invite him and Junior over for more cookies and Java. See what he has to say." And that's exactly what I did.

* * *

I finally got to strip down and jump in the shower. Putting on my comfy slob around clothes, I stopped in my hubby's office and made nice, nice.

"Listen dear, I know you're worried about me, but I promise not to do anything too stupid …."

" 'Do' being the operative word, Esme. You shouldn't be doing anything. I told you just leave it to the police!"

"I am leaving it to them. Just providing them with info they might not have been privy to. I'm heading downstairs to call Lieutenant Kai and pass along everything the girls and I have already learned. Okay?"

"Okay." With that he leaned over and planted a kiss on my nose. Meaning all was forgiven. Temporarily ….

I went down to the kitchen for a quick snack of tea and whole wheat toast slathered with goat cheese and fig and orange preserves. Next, I picked up the phone and dialed my favorite detective, munching away while waiting for him to pick up. The phone was answered by Junior, who stated that the Lieutenant was in the middle of another call.

"Would you like to hold while I see if he's available?" He inquired. "Or would you prefer to have Lieutenant Kai call you back?"

"I'll wait." I replied as he placed me on hold. "I'll bet that's Jayne," I muttered to myself, as I continued crunching. Five minutes later, just as I'd finished the last of my toast and tea, Lieutenant Kai's voice came on the line.

"Hello, Mrs. Fine. To what do I owe the pleasure of this call? I just got off the phone with one of your students—a Mrs Jayne Hathaway. Thank you for telling her to contact me. So. Any more information you'd care to share?"

"Actually, that's what I called about. The info Jayne passed along to you. I just wanted to make sure she'd gotten hold of you. It seemed like some important stuff."

"Thank you for your concern. She did. Was there anything else you needed to talk to me about?"

I paused. "No ... no, that was all ... just wondering ... do you think it will help you with your investigation?"

I could almost picture him grinning as he replied. "Mrs. Fine, is this your idea of a fishing expedition? Because if it is, you know I can't share any information with you. I hope you're not planning a little amateur sleuthing of your own. Remember what I told you earlier."

"How could I forget. You keep drumming it into my poor little head, like one of my old high school teachers: Don't get involved. Leave it to the experts ... on and on til I have every word indelibly etched in my brain!" This time, I distinctly heard a slight snicker escape his lips. The man was insufferable—but he was right.

"Well, if that's all, you'll excuse me if I say goodbye. I've got an investigation to run."

"Umm ... umm ... " I stuttered. "I guess that's all for now ... just one more question. You are checking on the coin connection aren't you?"

"Goodbye, Mrs. Fine!" He hung up. Yeah. Sure ... like I was actually going to back off now. Guess it was time to continue our own search into the coin connection and the whereabouts of Norton and Adolf. Wouldn't be at all surprised if those two turned out to be in cahoots!

Chapter 9

A week later the girls and I all got together as usual for lunch. This time we had a specific agenda, so we ordered takeout and met in one of the empty card rooms at the Center. The air was positively buzzing with excitement and anticipation. Everyone seemed to have something to share.

Jayne went first. Taking out the book she'd found at the library, she handed out copies of Rosemary's drawing and the one in the book. There was a general intake of breath as the ladies compared the two coins. They were identical! Suddenly everyone went absolutely quiet—which for my ladies was a first. As the importance of the information finally sank in they all started talking at once.

"Ladies, let's try to exercise a little self-control here and allow Jayne discuss her findings. There'll be plenty of time for questions and comments later. Remember we've got the whole room to ourselves until they close the building at four and it's only just turned two. Go on Jayne tell us what you've found out about this coin."

"Well," Jayne began, "Marina's guess was correct. The coin is from the early 1800s and as you can see there is definitely a picture of a woman. Not just any woman, it's a representation of the young Queen Victoria, herself. It was minted shortly after she ascended the throne at age eighteen. See, right here. You can just barely read the date on the side—1838," Jayne pointed to the right side of the face. "Here on the other side is her royal crest. Below it the denomination. However, this is where it gets really fascinating. Although the coins were minted they were never put into circulation!"

As one, a group gasp escaped the women, piercing the silence.

Jayne continued. "As you probably know, Victoria was a very mercurial woman. One never knew what would set her off. Apparently, that's what happened here. The newly minted queen took one look at the image etched onto the coins and declared that it did not do her justice. She had them shipped out to Australia, where very few people would notice whose visage was on them. Those who did, couldn't care less, since most of the population there was still made up of criminals and other undesirables; people who had been shipped over years before."

"So how on earth did that lil' ol' coin end up in po' lil' ol' Harry's pocket?" Charlotte Rae drawled.

"Good question …." Clearly enjoying her time in the limelight, Jayne paused once again.

"The coins disappeared on the way to New South Wales, Australia. Not enough to raise anyone's suspicion, but quite enough to set someone up for life or, in this case—several someones. It was thought that one of the sailors must have helped himself to them or, maybe even one of the guards charged with the responsibility of delivering the shipment to the storehouse. More about that later. The coins were never found and to this day, no one knows for sure who stole them or how they were spirited away. A number of theories have floated around through the years. However, the predominant theory is that it was something of an inside job. One of the officials in charge of the delivery is thought to have had a partner on the ship and another in the storage facility, where the coins were to be kept before being put into circulation. You see, they did not have an official branch of the mint until 1855, when the British Royal Mint was opened."

"Wow! And you got all that from this book!" Arne exclaimed.

"Not quite all. I got the last bit of info off the internet. Saved a great deal of time and research, but I have noted the relevant parts from the article and made copies for all of you to check out."

"Hmmm …, maybe Ah should take some courses on surfin' the web," murmured Charlotte Rae.

"Maybe we all should take a couple of refresher courses. A lot has changed since we were first introduced to personal computers back in the prehistoric times," Henri smirked.

"Actually, computer technology is changing every day. What was once brand new, is usually obsolete within a couple of years—sometimes even faster." Jayne explained. Taking out two more stapled sheets, she handed them to Marina, who passed them out.

"Looks like we just hit pay dirt thanks to Jayne's research and Rosemary's drawing," Marina commented.

Jayne blushed with pleasure. Visibly drawing herself up with dignity to her full five foot two inches, she thanked Marina and Rosemary and continued with the final part of her research.

"Thanks for the kudos. By the way, we found out a little more about what actually happened to the missing coins."

"You didn't!" exclaimed Melisande. Up until then she'd been too mesmerized by the recitation to say anything.

"Actually, I did."

"So tell us already! Ah just can't stand the suspense!" Charlotte Rae declared, her accent getting thicker as it did when she was excited.

"That's what I was about to do if you'll bear with me a little longer."

"Shut up and give the poor woman a chance to continue!" Henri snapped, exasperated. At that point I felt it was time to reel my ladies back in.

"Girls, please simmer down and listen to the rest of Jayne's findings. I told you, there will be time for questions and comments when she's done.

"Go ahead Jayne, the floor is all yours."

Blushing yet again, Jayne continued. "Thanks, Esme. The next part is even more exciting than the first. It seems that whoever stole the coins managed to slip onto a ship headed for the United States—San Francisco, to be exact. Would you believe I found an item in one of the old newspapers mentioning it? Guess an ocean trip between Australia and San Francisco was not a usual undertaking during the mid-eighteenth century."

"Wait a minute, Jayne," squawked Henri. "How in the Big H did a whole shipment of freshly minted gold coins manage to disappear in the first place? Didn't they usually have specially trained men guarding the stuff in the first place?"

"You'd think so, wouldn't you? That very question left me quite stymied as well. So, I dug a little further and found out that three British navel men were hand chosen and tasked with the special detail of guarding the shipment. It was locked in a trunk in the First Mate's cabin, but the Captain would have held onto the key. The First Mate was a very old and trusted navy man himself. However, he was getting on in years and this was supposed to be his last trip."

"Let me guess," Mel—always the amateur detective—asked. "The guy was overworked and underpaid and decided he wanted to retire in style …."

"Yes," Jayne replied. "But he needed help, so he recruited the guards with the promise of splitting the money four ways."

"Boy, this is getting more confusin' by the minute," Charlotte murmured.

"You're not kidding!" Flor added. "I still don't get it. How did they manage to pull it off?"

I groaned inwardly. This is getting more obfuscated by the minute. At the rate we're going, we'll still be here when the building closes. What on earth have I let myself in for? Maybe Paul was right. I should have let it go and left it to the police handle.

I was so wrapped up in my own thoughts that I almost missed what Jayne said next.

"I'll try to clarify any confusion. You see, the First Mate had connections and because he was a well respected long serving member of the crew, no one would have suspected him, least of all the Captain, who apparently had been mentored by him. Given the information at hand, it was thought that the first mate and the three guards came up with a plan enabling them to snatch the coins, then take off before anyone became the wiser."

"The plan being?", Henri asked archly.

"Actually it would have been beautifully simple. Somehow, the first mate must have managed to make a copy of the key to the trunk in which the gold was stored. The four conspirators must have switched the gold for something of equal weight. What happened next, again, no one really knows for sure. But we can make an educated guess based on what few facts were available at the time. The First Mate left the ship, then disappeared before the chest was opened. When they discovered the switch, the authorities conducted a thorough search, but he had slipped through the cracks. It was presumed that he must have taken off to somewhere in the outback, far from the reach of the law, where no one really knew what had happened in New South Wales. During my research, I read somewhere that an old seafaring man had purchased a small farm. Bought a couple of horses, a tractor, actually a portable barn engine, and settled down to raise wheat."

Thrown for a loop, Henri practically shouted." Hold it Jayne! Back up a little. How did you find that little tidbit?"

Rosemary and Melisande grinned. "The cloud of course!"

"Yes, another fascinating item I found during my research. As a matter of fact, that's how I managed to locate the former First Mate. You see, the barn engine, which resembled a mini locomotive, had just gone into production. A great deal of interest was stirred up as a result and there were a number of articles and ads mentioning it."

"Hence the discovery of the possible location of our man," 'Detective' Mel supplied.

"Exactly. As for the other three, they probably jumped ship as soon as it anchored in port. No one reported seeing them leave. It was rumored at the time that they had disguised themselves and signed on with a freighter bound for San Francisco. Several men fitting their description were later mentioned regarding the robbery of a stagecoach heading northeast. News of the robbery was splashed all over the front pages of newspapers between here and the Pacific Southwest!"

"Stagecoach robbery!" whooped Arne, rubbing her plump little hands together, intrigued. "Now we're getting somewhere! What stagecoach robbery? Was anybody killed? Did those sailors have anything to do with the murders?" Mel exclaimed, her curly locks bouncing up and down in her excitement.

Overwhelmed by the barrage of questions shot at her, Jayne held up her hands. "Please, girls. One question at a time."

"Yeah. Back off will you and give the poor gal a break already?" Henri snapped.

"Go ahead, Jayne. What's the deal with the stagecoach robbery?"

Taking a deep breath, Jayne continued. "Well, it was like this. As I explained earlier, the three sailors jumped ship as soon as it pulled into port. They figured they'd be home free once the cargo ship set sail. Unfortunately they hadn't bargained on what happened next."

"Ah can't wait to hear what happened next!" Charlotte Rae exclaimed, unable to curb her excitement.

"Zip it, woman!" Henri barked. "Jayne was about to tell us."

"Oops ... " Charlotte Rae gushed apologetically. "Sorry. Ah just get so excited .... Please continue, Ms. Jayne."

"That's alright, Charlotte Rae. As I was about to explain, some of you may know, that back in the day, stagecoaches were plagued by vicious gangs constantly attacking them. Wells Fargo didn't exist yet, so the coach companies had to take their chances or hire professionals to guard them ...."

That's where the expression 'riding shotgun' came from. A coachman and a bodyguard would have ridden up front to fend off bandits—especially when they were carrying a delivery of cash and during the extended trips between coasts. Speculation was that the original coin thieves believed to be the three sailors had ended up on a stagecoach in the southwest. That's when they ran out of luck. On the way, the coach was set upon by a ruthless gang of outlaws. Two of the sailors were killed trying to hold onto their swag."

"Big mistake!" Flor muttered.

"Now I'm confused," Arnoldine, scratched her head. "What happened to the gold coins? I'm guessing that the gang got away with most of it."

Jayne answered. "Yes. They did. As I said, the robbery turned out to be a sensational story. It had something for everyone. Bathos. Pathos. Murder. Mayhem. Everything readers craved and what publishers thrived on. The publishers took full advantage of the lurid details, blowing them way out of proportion. All the papers large and small rushed to jump on the bandwagon and beat out their competitors, so there was a great deal written on it. Went on for months until the severe earthquake at San Jose, Santa Clara and Monterey sometime in 1839 finally replaced it as front page news. To add to this three-ring circus, the writers of Penny Dreadfuls turned up in hordes, cranking out a whole series of stories based on the robbery."

Taking a swig of water, Jayne continued. "According to eye-witness accounts, one of the boxes that the coins were stashed in broke open as the thieves were dragging them off the coach. That's when, according to another passenger—'all hell broke loose!' Two of the sailors were not about to give up without a fight. But they were outnumbered by men and lethal weapons. All they had to defend themselves were a couple of knives and their fists. Both were shot. One died instantly. The other was hastily patched up by the coachman, with the help of one of the passengers, after the robbers took off.

"The robbers scrambled to scoop up as many of the coins as possible. A number of the passengers, including the third and youngest sailor, took advantage of the chaos to grab some coins for themselves."

"Wait a minute," roared Henri, more incensed than usual. "What were the driver and the guard doing during all the pandemonium?"

"What indeed?" Marina murmured.

"Another excellent question. The guard managed to get off several shots before he himself was hit in his shooting arm. The driver, literally had his hands full trying to calm his hysterical horses, who were out of control."

Once again, soft-hearted Charlotte Rae's hand shot to her mouth. "Oh those po' lil' ol' horses! I hope they weren't hurt."

Henri snickered: "Leave it to you to worry about horses when people have been shot."

"There's not much more to tell regarding the actual robbery. Suffice it to say, the bandits shoved their haul in their saddlebags, jumped on their horses and took off 'hell for leather' as the other sailor lay bleeding to death on the side of the road."

Charlotte Rae's hand shot to her mouth again. "How absolutely horrible! Ah sure hope they finally caught those wicked, wicked scoundrels and hung 'em from the highest tree!"

"How very bloodthirsty of you, Charlotte Rae." Rosemary replied laconically.

Flor chimed in irately. "Charlotte Rae's right! Those SOBs deserved to be made an example of!"

"OK ladies," I said, "time's a flying, how about letting Jayne get on with the story?"

This met with a chorus of mumbled apologies, as Jayne continued.

"If it makes you feel any better," Jayne said, "all the robbers were eventually caught and hanged. However, the injured sailor died and was buried somewhere along the way."

"What happened to the booty?" trumpeted Flor.

"The coins were never recovered."

"Since the rest of the passengers and the driver were relatively unscathed, it was agreed that the coach should continue on its journey, making a stop along the way in the next town to take care of any injuries and report the robbery and murder to the local sheriff."

"So how did the coins end up in Harry's pockets and the rest somewhere out west?" Rosemary asked.

At that point, I happened to look at my watch and noticed that it was almost closing time for the Senior Center, and it appeared that Jayne had a great deal more information to relay. Time for me to step in. "That's a very good question, Ro." I caught Jayne's eye, she nodded slightly.

"I'm sure Jayne will be able to provide the answer. This has been a fascinating, totally engrossing, session for us all, but it's almost four o'clock and we need to be heading out shortly. Obviously, Jayne has a lot more information to impart, but she's probably running out of steam by now, as are the rest of us. I'm sure we're all ready for a short snack break, so why don't we adjourn across the street to Sophia Kenny's and continue our meeting there?"

"Sounds good to me." Marina commented, as she got up and stretched. The others followed suit. Chattering excitedly among themselves, they all agreed. One by one they grabbed their things and headed towards the double doors. I called out to them to grab the table in the back, as Marina, Jayne and I gathered our paperwork, coats and hats and prepared to follow suit.

* * *

We reconvened at our favorite little mom-and-pop place. It was a cozy family restaurant, located in a refurbished cottage. It had a lovely little reception room at the back—sunny all year round and toasty warm during the cold New England winters. We often hung out there because of our ever-increasing numbers. For over twenty-five years, it had been run by a lovely Korean couple who had recently retired and passed the store into the very capable hands of their son, Kenny. Kenny proved to be every bit as gracious as his parents. My ladies and I practically lived there, often going for lunch or just a cup of coffee and one of their marvelous muffins after class. Sophia, an old friend and program backer, greeted us warmly as we entered. Although she and her husband had officially retired, she could often be found back in the kitchen, helping her son, Kenny—especially on busier days. Luckily for us, this was one of them.

"Good afternoon Miss Esme. It is so nice to see you again."

"And you," I replied, giving her a swift hug. "I really miss you! But Kenny has been taking good care of us. Have all my ladies arrived?"

"Yes, they have just seated themselves and await your arrival. They have already ordered their drinks."

"Well, then we'd better not keep them waiting any longer."

"Would you like me to bring you your usual green tea?"

"That would be great!" I turned to Marina and Jayne. "How about you two? Coffee or tea? It's on me in appreciation for all your hard work."

"Espresso for me, thanks," replied Marina.

"Just hot chocolate for me," said Jayne. "And a large cup of water, no ice. I'm parched!"

Marina and I looked at each other and back at Jayne. "I'm not surprised after the marathon session you just conducted."

Marina grinned. "Not to mention all the research work you've had to do. Quite impressive! All the information you've come up with so quickly."

"I hope I didn't go too overboard," she replied, biting her lower lip.

"Are you kidding? You gave an absolutely wonderful presentation! I've never seen the likes of Flor, Charlotte Rae and even Mel so mesmerized—they barely moved!"

"Not to mention Henri," Marina added wryly. "She hardly opened her mouth."

"Thanks for the kudos. I guess it's time to present Part 2 of this very long and winding saga," she sighed.

Laughing, we each placed an arm through hers and led her toward the back room.

Rosemary was the first to notice our entrance and patted the seat next to her.

"Here she is, the heroine of the moment!" She exclaimed.

Everyone at the table grabbed their mugs and saluted Jayne. As soon as we seated ourselves, Henri, being Henri, jumped right in.

"It's about time you three arrived. We're waiting for the second installment of this mystery story."

Jayne laughed self-consciously. "Just give me a minute to gather my thoughts and take a quick drink of water. OK, what was I up to?"

Our Miss Marple struck again. Before anyone else even had a chance to comment, she brought everyone up to date.

"You were up to the part where the stagecoach was robbed, two of the original thieves dead and the third one scrambling for the gold pieces along with the rest of the passengers."

Having re-hydrated, Jayne continued her narration. "According to legend, after they stole the money, the robbers buried it somewhere in the high desert in an old abandoned silver mine. They made a map showing the location, but were caught before they could collect it. However …," she paused, "and this is where it gets really interesting. One of the robbers managed to pass the map on to his wife before he was caught and hanged.

Unfortunately, she was so devastated by the loss of her husband, she hid the map where she hoped no one would find it, and she wouldn't have to look at it ever again. As far as his wife was concerned it was blood money and she wanted nothing to do with it."

"Oh mah goodness …," sighed Charlotte Rae, vigorously fanning herself with her copy of the handouts. "Ah just don't know if I can stand the suspense. What happened to all those lovely gold coins, after those dirty ol' bandits buried them in the mine?"

"And I want to know where Harry comes into all of this." Rosemary added.

"I'm getting to that. It's the most relevant part with regard to Harry and his coins.

"Years later, as fate would have it, the great-great-great-grandson of the stagecoach robber, a nice boy named Joe Bommarito, was drafted into the army and sent to Vietnam. He was critically injured during an ambush and was rushed to the 95th Evacuation Hospital in Da Nang, where he met Harry. They became fast friends and apparently Joe told Harry the story of the robbery, the map and stash of gold coins he'd inherited from his own grandfather on his eighteenth birthday. Ironically, he was drafted just after he turned eighteen and never had a chance to collect the rest of the coins. Sadly, he died of his wounds several weeks before he was due to be demobbed along with Harry. Since he had no close family left, the young man, Joe, wrote a will leaving the map and the key to a safe deposit box in a bank in Sedona, to Harry."

"Oh my Gawd!" exclaimed Henri, her New York accent slipping out in her discomposure. "Sounds like a plot straight out of Alfred Hitchcock."

"Sure does," Rosemary added, "but remember what they say: 'Truth is often stranger than fiction.'"

"Think we could backtrack here?" asked Melisande. "A couple of loose ends need tightening up. For one thing, how come none of the other predecessors of this kid Joe never went looking?"

"I should have known you'd spot that, Mel." Jayne smiled. "Another set of weird circumstances. Turns out the map was never discovered, but the story was passed down from father to son, until Joe's grandfather accidentally found the map when he was repairing the fireplace in his home. The same one the robber and his family had lived in all those years ago. Apparently it was one solid little piece of real estate, and very few renovations were made through the years, other than installing modern bathrooms and updating the kitchen."

"And you know this how?" Henri asked skeptically?

"Oh, well, I don't know for sure, but I managed to locate several of the original newspaper articles about the robbery. They mentioned the town it occurred in and hinted at where the robbers lived. I just put two and two together, made a couple of calls to real estate agents in Sedona and hit pay dirt. It's not that big a town, and would you believe that they have limited the number of people who can move there?

"On a more sobering note, the more I read about those coins, the more I realize that robber's wife was right. There's blood on them. It's almost as if they were cursed. Just about everyone who ever came in contact with them met with a violent death. First the sailors, then the robbers. Even that poor young man, Joe, and finally our Harry! Who knows how many other deaths those cursed coins might have been responsible for?"

We all looked at each other and shuddered as Jayne's remark hit home. I wondered how many other lives might be destroyed or lost before those coins were finally found and hopefully returned to their original destination.

Marina finally broke the shocked silence. "So that's how Harry happened to come into possession of a small fortune in gold coins. Absolutely Amazing!"

"It sure is," I added, shaking my head. "Unbelievable!"

"That was my reaction, when I tripped over the information."

"Please don't say 'tripped'," I groaned. "Brings back a very disturbing scene!"

"Oh, I'm so sorry, Esme! How thoughtless of me. For a moment there I'd almost forgotten about your own ordeal."

I patted her arm. "Oh don't mind me, Jayne. It's still just a little fresh in my mind. Why don't you bring your narration full circle and tell the girls what you found out about the rest of the stash that the bandits took off with?"

"Boy, this just gets better and better," Mel said.

"Yeah, they should turn this into a movie," Flor added. "I'd sure pay to see it!"

"Oh, don't be such a ghoul, Flor. Although, I have to admit I'd probably check it out myself," Henri snickered.

Once again, I was forced to take control, before our meeting turned into a free for all.

"Girls, ya think we can focus and get back to the matter at hand? Jayne is beginning to run out of steam again."

"That's alright, Esme. I understand how they feel. It's pretty much how I reacted on first reading about all this. Fortunately we've just about come to the end of the story—at least as far as the coins and my research are concerned."

At this point I stood up and thanked Jayne for all her hard work. "Ladies, I think we should give Jayne a big hand for her major contribution to our investigation."

Blushing furiously, Jayne returned to her seat as the ladies, following my lead, stood up and cheered.

"Well ladies, thanks to this wealth of information, Jayne has opened up a number of avenues to pursue. Anyone else got something to add or bring us up to date on? Marina, have you had a chance to talk with Jeannie yet?"

"As a matter of fact, I have. This is somewhat anticlimactic after Jayne's revelations. However, it's still important with regard to Harry's backstory, if you'll pardon the literary allusion. We had quite a long chat about Harry. Everyone knew that he was a kind, but very lonely old gentleman. Jeannie concurred that he was always ready to talk to anyone who would listen. She had several meetings with him, during which he shared some of his background as well as his stories. Like the rest of us, at first she took most of his tales with a grain of salt, but gradually a number of them began to ring true, even if they did sound rather far-fetched. For one thing, Harry described people and places in great detail—as if he had really experienced them personally. Several of the places were out west. One of them was Sedona. During another of their sessions, he even showed her several of the coins. After looking them over, she was convinced they were the real thing. Jeannie suggested that he keep them in a safe place, like a bank. She also warned him that it was not a good idea to flaunt them around so freely, since they could easily be stolen and pocketed by almost anyone."

"What did he say to that?" asked Rosemary—ever the pragmatist.

"He said pretty much what you'd expect him to say. Told her not to worry, that he'd had them for a long time and saw no reason why he shouldn't continue with the way things were. He also told her, somewhat cryptically, that he only had a small collection at home. The others were in a very safe place. I guess that turned out to be pretty true, assuming they're still buried where the cowboys left them."

"Did she mention any specific stories he told her—especially concerning the coins?" I asked.

"Yes. Gave her quite an earful as I understand. As a matter of fact, when I told Jeannie why I wanted to know, she actually offered to repeat some of the stories, as long as there was nothing confidential in them that would interfere with her client's privacy rights. She even suggested that you contact her and make an appointment to discuss anything that might help us find out what happened to poor Harry. She also informed me that she would schedule an appointment with Lieutenant Kai as well."

"That's great!" I replied. "It's too late to try to contact Jeannie tonight. She'll be long gone by now. I'll call her first thing in the morning.

"Boy, we sure are moving along at a good pace, ladies! Anyone else have something you want to add?" I waited. Seeing no takers, I suggested that we call it a day.

"You all have my phone number and email address. Contact me if you come up with anything else of interest or if you just want to chat, either online or in person. Better yet, contact the lieutenant first. Then call me. Thanks for all your support and ideas! See you in a few."

As the group disbanded I hastily grabbed my things and prepared to take off at a gallop. Unfortunately, I was headed off at the pass by a passel of geriatric fillies, all wanting a piece of me. I held up my hand for quiet. "Ladies, please give yourselves and me a break. I know you're all psyched and champing at the bit, but it's been a very long, albeit stimulating, day. Speaking for myself, I need to head home and chew on all the information we've just received. I suggest you do the same. Go home. Grab a nice cup of tea or something stronger and just veg out. Let's all take a page from Scarlet O'Hara and 'think about it tomorrow' …."

And then I left.

Chapter 10

I was out like a light having finally collapsed from exhaustion. Dreaming again about hordes of little old men—but this time they were being chased by a bunch of little old ladies, dressed in Harem pants and wearing noisy jingling hip belts, I was awakened by a shrill ringing sound in my ears. Groggily rolling over, my brain clicked in and I grabbed the phone. I wondered who on earth would call me so early. Checking the Caller ID, I answered. Henrietta of course.

"Henrietta Hirshfeld, what are you doing calling at this unearthly hour?" I croaked.

"What early? Take a look at your clock, kiddo. It's after 10 AM. You should be making tracks by now. Remember, you said you'd call Jeannie this morning."

I sat up quickly, practically knocking over the bedside lamp as I checked my clock.

"OMG! It's a good thing you called Henri, I must have set my alarm for PM instead of AM."

Henri laughed. "That's what you get for running around like a madwoman. So what's the plan? When do we meet with Jeannie?"

"What 'we'? There is no 'we', when it comes to Jeannie. I need to catch her in her office before she gets too involved with clients. Of course, it would be a good idea if I call her first, in case she's too busy."

Henri's voice held a touch of frost as she replied, "Well excuse me! I thought we were a team. I didn't mean to encroach on your territory …."

"Oh Henri, I didn't mean to offend you. It's just been a rough couple of weeks with barely any sleep and last night I finally crashed thoroughly and well."

Defrosting a little, Henri replied, "I understand, kiddo. It's been quite a roller coaster for all of us—but especially for you, tripping over poor Harry like that."

"Please don't remind me!" I groaned. "Had another one of my nightmares about little old men, but this time they were being chased by what appeared to be our belly dancing ladies."

Henrietta practically choked trying to control her laughter.

"Oh my, you have had quite a night! Belly dancing battle-axes, huh?"

"More like a swarm of Valkyries." I giggled despite myself. "Can't you just picture little Mel or Charlotte Rae in a helmet with horns or Arnoldine in a leather bustier, wearing long blonde braids?"

Henri guffawed. "Puhlease, you'll give me day mares just picturing it! Seriously though, I'm sorry I woke you. But you did say that you'd be contacting Jeannie first thing this morning, so I thought it was safe to call you."

"And a darn good thing you did too! I might have slept through half the day, I'd better get going. I also have to bring the good lieutenant up to speed again today. Thanks for checking in. I'll let you know if I hear anything useful from Jeannie. You know that Lieutenant Kai is not about to share any of that personal stuff with us any more than Jeannie."

"Yeah, I know, Ez. Sure isn't easy for us amateurs. Besides, anything that personal might not even be on the web. Although, these days you can find out where someone lives, what they wear, even what they had for breakfast."

I could hear the quaver in her voice as she said this.

"It's downright scary! If you even sneeze the wrong way, someone will post it online."

"That's for sure!"

"I don't know … maybe we should leave it to the experts and 'sit this one out' as my hubby would say and Lieutenant Kai would reiterate."

Changing her tune, Henri snapped "Give me a break! How often have you ignored your hubby's advice?"

"Well …."

Before I could answer, Henri continued her rant. When that woman gets started there's no stopping her until she runs out of steam. Showing no signs of winding down at that moment, I let her rave on, while I listened with half an ear.

"Furthermore," Henri continued. "Since when have you ever given up without a fight? Aren't you the one who agreed that we ladies could give the cops a run for their money? Remember. Our friends and acquaintances would rather confide in us than a bunch of strangers—especially of the police variety. Now get your scrawny little rear end out of bed and go do your thing."

Laughing, I replied, "Yes mom. Getting out of bed now. Gotta get ready to roll … and Hen, great pep talk! Guess I needed it …."

"Anytime. Mama Henri's always here for you."

"I know that. And it's much appreciated. Talk to you soon."

"I'll be waiting with bated breath."

I hung up the phone. Throwing off the covers, I almost dislodged poor Streak, who had managed to insinuate his little self under them. I jumped out of bed, pulled on my favorite raggedy old robe and ratty slippers. Padding over to my little home office, I sat down and dialed Jeannie's number. She picked up after the first couple of rings.

"Hi Esme. I was wondering when you'd call. Marina told me the rather gruesome details about how you found poor Harry. She said you had several questions about him. Thought I might be able to answer.

"Yes, that's about the size of it."

"I'll be happy to oblige, if it will help to clear up why he was killed."

"Thanks, Jeannie. I realize how busy you always are. I really appreciate your willingness to make time to talk with me. When would you be able to meet?"

"How about getting together today for lunch across the street. I could use a break. One PM good for you? It should be relatively quiet by then, so we can talk freely."

"Perfect! One PM it is. I imagine you've had your hands full, since the murder."

"That's a bit of an understatement! Things have definitely been more chaotic than usual. Everyone's just plain devastated about poor Harry's passing and then there are those who are afraid that the killer will strike again."

"I know. Got the same reaction from my ladies. When they weren't busy sleuthing that is …."

I could hear her laughing over the phone.

"Well, I'd better get back to work if I want to escape in time for lunch."

"Okay. Thanks again. See you in a few."

We said our goodbyes. Hanging up, I raced into Paul's home office to tell him my plans. Barely listening—thank goodness, he nodded his acknowledgment and turned back to his computer. I quickly threw off my robe and changed into a comfortable pair of blue jeans and my favorite navy blue sweater. I brushed my teeth, ran a brush through my hair and finished with my eyebrow pencil—my one vanity. I never go anywhere without it, since someone once mistook me for my friend's mother. Running back to Paul's room, I gave him a quick peck on the head and stooped down to pat Streak, who was lying in his usual morning spot, with his head on Paul's foot. Having a couple of hours to spare, I headed downstairs, grabbed a quick breakfast and then headed back up to my own compact office to conduct a little research of my own with the help of the "Great Google."

Clicking on my browser I typed in "Harrold Browne." Soon I was neck deep in "Harrold Brownes," so I added his approximate age and what little I knew about his address. Miraculously, the information popped up right before my eyes:

"Harrold Browne, born in Newark, New Jersey, September 12th, 1945."

He would have just turned 75. I sighed and continued reading.

> Enlisted in the Marines in 1967 … Served two tours in Vietnam, from 1968 to August 1970 until he was severely injured by a booby trap during the summer campaign in Quang Nam.

So engrossed was I in my research that I didn't even hear Streak enter the room until I felt a small, warm, wet tongue on my ankle. Reaching down I picked him up, gave him a good cuddle and placed him on my lap, where he instantly fell asleep. Stroking his silky little ears, I whispered, "Maybe I can find some additional info on what happened to Harry after he was injured and how he ended up here in Leicester. It's worth a try. What do you think puppy?" The little guy snored his reply. I took that as a sign to read on. Clicking several more sites I finally found what I was looking for. There it was in black and white—right in our own town newspaper; a list of casualties during the month of August 1970: Lance Corporal Harrold J. Browne. The next time I found mention of Harry was in an article on recovering vets, dated several years later. Bingo! He had been sent to the rehab center at the veterans' hospital one town over from ours.

I was on a roll!

The next mention, dated 1975, was an announcement of the marriage of LCpl. Harrold Browne to Gerda Grant. The article went on to list attendees: the ring bearer, Gerda's son Richard Grant and the flower girl, daughter, Shelby Grant—accompanied by a picture no less! The picture showed a serious looking young boy of about five and an adorable little Shirley Temple type toddler, looking like she was about to star in her own show.

Boy had I hit pay dirt!

I was jerked back to the present by the incessant ringing of my phone. Running to grab it before it went to voicemail, I managed to pick up on the last ring. Henri....

"Hi Hen. What's up?"

"Hi yourself, Ez. I thought you weren't gonna answer. Almost hung up .... Just called to see if you managed to touch base with Jeannie."

"I did. We're meeting for lunch at one this afternoon. Across the street from the Center. I'm glad you called. You won't believe what I just found online! I exclaimed."

"Actually, I would. It's amazing what you can find surfing the web these days. So what'd you trip over this time?"

I groaned.

"Oops, wrong choice of words. Sorry Ez."

"That's okay. I've got to get used to hearing that word again .... By the way, why don't you stop over for some coffee? I've got a slew of stuff to show you."

"Don't you have to get ready for your lunch date."

"I do. But there's still time and thought you'd want to hear what I found out regarding Harry's time in Nam and how he ended up here in Connecticut."

"Wow, now I am intrigued! Be there in a tick!" Henri slammed the phone down practically bursting my eardrum. Before I knew it she was at the door.

"What did you do, run all the way?" Henri sat down as I placed a nice hot coffee and blueberry corn muffin in front of her.

"Well, sounded like you've got a lot to report and not much time to do it. Lunch date ... Jeannie? Remember?"

"I know! But this is important and you're my sounding board."

"Gee thanks ... I think." Henri consulted her Fitbit. "Okay, fire away. You've got about twenty minutes before you have to head out. Clock is ticking ... " she mumbled through a mouthful of muffin. "So, what's got you so revved that it can't wait 'til after your meeting?"

Helping myself to a muffin, I poured some tea into my favorite mystery book mug, and sat down opposite her.

"It's about Harry's former wife—that's what!"

"Well, what do you know? I'd heard a rumor that Harry had married a nurse or someone he'd met while recuperating in a veteran's hospital, but I thought it was just that—a rumor."

"Turns out it's true. Gerda Grant. They were married back in '75. I just found the announcement in an old copy of our newspaper. And get this—the article also listed her two kids."

"Two kids, huh? Must have been a divorcee or maybe even a widow?"

"Good question. I was wondering the same thing. Just about to dig further when you called. Care to join me in a little research?"

"Are ya kidding? You couldn't keep me away! Wait a minute ...." Glancing at her Fitbit, again, Henri let loose with a shrill whistle fit to burst the eardrums.

"Uhh, Oh ... Ez, do you know what time it is?"

"Nooo .... Why, what's the matter?"

"I hate to tell you, kiddo, but it's after 12:30. Don't you think you ought to get off your little tush and head on over to the restaurant?"

"Oh, No! Damn good thing you stopped by. I was so caught up in my research that I completely lost track of the time. If you hadn't called when you did, poor Jeannie would be cooling her heels while I was somewhere off in the cloud. I'd better get moving. I honestly don't know what I would do without you, Hen!"

Planting a quick kiss on her cheek, I rushed to the closet and pulled out my coat. Slipping into it and shoving a hat on my unruly curls, I grabbed my gloves, cell phone and tote bag. Dashing over to the stairs, I yelled up to Paul, "Hey, dear, throw down my notebook, will you?"

"Where is it?"

"In my office. On the Desk."

Paul picked up said notebook, brought it over to where I stood below and handed it down to me between the stair posts. I turned and made a dash for the door.

Henri came up behind me. "Slow down, Ez. You'll give yourself a heart attack at the rate you're going. You've still got a little time. It only takes about ten minutes to get there—even the way you drive."

"You're right as usual. Gotta calm down."

"Good! All set now, kiddo?"

Checking to make sure I had remembered everything, I gave Henri a big hug and exhaled deeply. "Think so. I'll catch you up on what Jeannie has to say later."

"Sounds like a plan …."

I called goodbye to the hubby and patted Streak, who had followed me downstairs. Ushering my friend out the door, I followed closely behind. Once in the car, garage door going up, I pulled myself together and turned the key.

I made it to the Senior Center just in time to park, grab my things and head across the street to Sophia Kenny's.

My mouth watered just thinking of what I was going to order.

Chapter 11

I had just entered the restaurant and sat down at our favorite table in the farthest corner of the little eatery, when the waitress, Heather Grey, approached.

"Hi Esme, How're you doing? Can't stay away, huh?" Heather grinned. Green tea as usual?"

"Of course, thanks. And coffee for Jeannie. I see her coming now," I said, looking out the large picture window, as Jeannie crossed the street, copious bag in hand. Idly, I wondered which of us had the most stuff crammed into our bags.

"Great! Be right back."

"Perfect timing!" I said as Jeannie came over to the table. "I just ordered our drinks. Coffee for you right?" I grinned as Jeannie set her things down and settled into the opposite seat.

"Great. Thanks!"

Our efficient young waitress returned armed with menus and our drinks.

"Hi Jeannie. Nice to see you."

"You too, Heather."

"Ladies, I'll be back in a tick to take your orders," Heather said and bustled off to greet another customer.

"That young woman is amazing! I predict that she'll be running her own place before long."

"Definitely! I wish more young people were as motivated as she is these days," Jeannie sighed. We both picked up our menus and went about the business of choosing our meals. Today, I ordered the Portabella Caprese Ciabatta Special with all my favorite foods wrapped into one divine ciabatta, my mouth watering yet again. Jeannie had her usual soup and salad—today's choice, Vegetarian Mushroom Lentil, another one of my faves. Having given our orders to Heather, we settled in for a long talk—hopefully, Jeannie doing most of the talking; me listening, with a few well aimed questions.

"So, Esme, I understand you're into sleuthing mode now. How goes the investigation? Have you and your ladies come up with any good stuff yet?"

Laughing I replied, "Guess the grapevine's in full swing, huh? Yes, the girls and I have actually run across some rather interesting information, but you're not here to grill me, remember? It's the other way around. I'm here to pick your brain." I smiled. "As I explained on the phone, I'm very interested in the stories Harry shared with you, and anything else he may have said in passing that might have struck a chord after the fact." I paused, holding up my hands. "And before you say it—No, I'm not looking to invade poor Harry's privacy, nor compromise your ethics."

Jeannie smiled her encouragement.

"I just want to hear … No. Make that, *need* to hear about some of those tall tales of his, which now appear to have been not so 'tall' after all. Unfortunately, at least one person believed them enough to commit murder. Obviously, that's something we all want to find out."

"I understand. You know I'm just as interested in helping to expose the party responsible for such a ghastly crime. I can't even imagine how much Harry must have suffered in those last few moments!"

"That's exactly how I feel. Remember, I'm the one who found him like that. It was absolutely horrible! I still have nightmares almost every night … sometimes even during the day, if I close my eyes for a minute. I just can't wipe the picture from my mind. I feel this driving need to discover who was responsible, as much for my own peace of mind as for Harry's sake."

"Of course, Esme, but I don't know that I can tell you much more than you've already heard from his friends and acquaintances, such as they were."

"Why don't you let me be the judge of that? For instance, anything you know regarding Harry's coin stories. They appear to feature prominently in his life, and I am absolutely convinced that they contributed to his death!"

"First of all, I should explain that I never met with Harry as a client. However, I did talk with him occasionally in the cafeteria, while waiting for clients to finish their lunch. Sometimes, he shared bits here and there about his earlier life."

"There! You see, I knew you'd be able to help. Please go on."

"Well, on one of those occasions, Harry spoke about how lonely, he'd been until he joined our Senior Center. He began to open up and share with me his background. Apparently, he had no family to speak of. He had no sibs and his parents had passed on before he enlisted in the Marines ... sounded like that might have been the deciding factor in his joining up."

I nodded. "Sadly, from the little I've heard about Harry, I'd say you were right. So, what else did he have to say?"

"He met and married a young Eurasian girl, named Lien Nguyen (pronounced, Lee-yin. Nue-En). Her first name means Lotus Flower.

"That is so pretty," I murmured dreamily .... "Wait ... What ...? Did I hear you correctly? You're telling me Harry'd been married once before? Are you kidding me?"

"Yes, that's what I said. Why on earth would I kid about something like that, Esme? Harry did say that they met while he and several others were reconnoitering her village and the surrounding terrain. She was only seventeen. He even told me he gave her a gold locket as a wedding gift, with both their pictures in it. Unfortunately, he was badly wounded during one of the skirmishes at Quang Nam during the Summer of '70—just a couple of months after he and Lien were married. His injuries were so severe that he was sent to a hospital in Nam. Then, demobbed and eventually sent back to a VA hospital right here in Connecticut for more surgeries."

I gasped! "What happened to Lien?"

"Tragically, Harry and Lien lost touch after he was injured—and to add insult to injury, Lien's papers got lost in the chaos that followed and she was left behind."

"Talk about Murphy's law! Sounds like the worst kind of soap opera! What happened to the poor girl? Did he tell you?"

Jeannie exhaled deeply. "It gets worse. While he was in the hospital ... sorry, I forget the name, he received word that his wife was dead. There had been an attack on her village. They identified her by the tiny wedding picture in the locket she was wearing when they found her."

"OMG! That's absolutely horrible—poor, hapless Harry!"

"I know. It's a miracle the locket wasn't stolen or destroyed during the conflagration, or he would never have even gotten closure. Which leads me to the next part of the story. The part you've expressed great interest in hearing about."

"The coins?"

Jeannie grinned. "Yes. The coins. Harry told me that while in the hospital in Nam he'd heard about a cache of rare coins from a young man in the bed next to his. The young man—"

"Who we now know is Joe Bommarito." I cut in bringing her up to date on the latest info I had received from Jayne.

"Harry did mention that it was a very nice Italian boy: 'too young to have his life cut short in a war no one could win' … those were his exact words. Joe told him all about the map his grandfather had given him, along with a gold coin on a colorful braided lanyard, which the boy—and he was still a boy—only nineteen years old …." Shaking her head wearily, she continued. "The young man wore it around his neck for good luck."

"Talk about 'ironic' … " I murmured. "What happened next?"

"He told Harry that his granddad had also gifted him with a number of the same issue. The rest were locked away in a safe deposit box at a savings bank in Sedona."

"That jibes with what we've heard from Jayne Hathaway, during her research."

Taking several bites of salad, Jeannie commented dryly.

"I'm guessing that you've also heard about the will."

It was my turn to grin. "You'd be guessing correctly. Having no other family besides his grandfather, the poor kid actually wrote a will naming Harry as his heir. He left written instructions as to the name and address of the grandfather's solicitors. By then, grandpa had died, leaving Joe all alone in the world."

Jeannie's face clouded over. "I'm beginning to wonder if those coins are cursed."

"You know, Jayne said the same thing. Death and destruction seems to follow them everywhere—right down through the generations."

"By the way, before I forget, Harry even showed me the key to the box. Like Joe, he took to wearing it all the time, hanging from a brown leather cord."

"Hold it!" I jumped in. "There was no key around Harry's neck when I found him. Did you happen to mention this to Lieutenant Kai?"

"No. Why would I? He didn't ask and I didn't think to comment on it."

"Whoa! I think that's something we all missed. No one ever said anything about a key. Must've kept it tucked inside his shirt. You'd better tell Lieutenant Kai about that right away! I'll bet the murderer took it, although I don't know how or when," I paused in reflection. Thinking out loud I continued. "It had to have happened before I tripped over the body. I never left until the police showed up. He was already pretty cold to the touch when I checked for a pulse." I shook my head, nauseated at the thought that someone could cold-heartedly steal something from a dead man—or worse … I shivered inwardly. The guy could have been dying when it was stolen. "What kind of sick SOB is capable of such desecration!" I cried.

"The murdering kind," Jeannie murmured. Reaching out, she gently patted my hand. "A very sick one as you so aptly pointed out. Try not to get yourself all worked up. There's not much we can do about that travesty now, and it certainly won't help catch him or her; but we can put our heads together to try to unmask the butcher responsible. How about continuing in that vein?"

With great effort I managed to regain my composure. "You're right. I'm okay now. Thanks." Deep breath. "So where were we? Anything else?"

"Just the usual. Except … " finger tapping her lips. "Though, now that I think about it, he also mentioned running into his stepdaughter after all these years." Jeannie paused. "I believe her name was Shelby. He didn't give a last name."

Practically jumping out of my seat, I blurted out: "Grant. Shelby Grant. Mother: Gerda Grant—before she became Mrs. Harrold Browne," I remarked snarkily.

"Really, Esmeralda," Jeannie declared, a pained expression marring her delicate features.

I apologized sheepishly. "I know. I know. Sorry. I just get so aggravated. Please continue. I'll try not to interrupt again. You were saying …?"

Somewhat mollified, Jeannie replied, "Look, Esme, to make things simpler, why don't you just clue me in as to what you already know and/or suspect? That way we won't waste any more time going round in circles."

I clued her in ….

Brow furrowed, Jeannie summarized.

"Alright. We know that Harry had a rather rough, very lonely life. All he ever wanted was a family of his own and that did not come to fruition. His young wife was dead. Four years of being shunted from one VA hospital to another until he finally ends up here in Connecticut."

I took up the narrative. "Enter Gerda Grant, a savvy divorcee with two little kids—a ready-made family. Just what Harry's been craving."

"It's a classic scenario as you well know, Esme. We see it all the time."

"Right. Mrs. Grant knows a live one when she sees one and makes a beeline for the poor guy. From your talks with Harry I'm sure you've figured out the rest by now, Jeannie."

"The implication being: like mother like daughter; but what can this possibly have to do with Harry's murder and who is responsible?"

"Elementary my dear Ms. Gardner. It could have everything to do with it. Suspects. A passel of 'em! And don't forget those missing coins either."

"I can't understand how you can be so cynical Esme. It's just not like the usual upbeat, glass is half full gal we've all come to love and respect."

"Yeah, well I've never tripped over a corpse before either. Somehow that can affect a gal's attitude."

"Listen, Esme, I realize that must have been a horrible experience for you, to put it mildly."

"That's for sure!"

"But you're becoming absolutely obsessed with this whole murder investigation."

"Ya think?"

"Look, my friend, I can tell when a person is stressed to the max—ready to snap ... and Esme, that's you. You need to take a break. Back off and let the experts do the heavy work."

"Everything you say is true, but I just can't seem to stop myself. I have this overweening need do something—anything! I can't sit by and leave it to someone else—not even the police ...." Worn out by my sudden outburst I finally wound down.

Shocked, Jeannie quickly shifted to counselor mode.

Reaching out to me again, she murmured, "I am so sorry, Esme. I didn't realize what a disastrous impact finding Harry in that manner has had on you. Of course, I'll do anything I can to help you find the answers you need. But please, please leave the dangerous stuff to the police! You have to trust them."

"Thanks, Jeannie," I whispered hoarsely. "Sorry about my little outburst. Listen, can you just tell me how Harry came to reconnect with Shelby in the first place? It might be important. So ... Harry had just crossed paths with Shelby, but you never met her?"

"Correct. All he said was her name is Shelby, and he'd married her mother when she was still a toddler." Jeannie sighed. "I hate to admit it, but I was only listening with half an ear when Harry launched into one of his monologues."

"I understand. I'm often guilty of that myself—especially when it comes to my more loquacious friends. But maybe he said something that might have stuck in the back of your mind. Something you didn't realize at the time."

"Maybe ... I'm not sure." Jeannie closed her eyes trying to picture past discussions. Suddenly, eyes fluttering open, Jeannie burst out. "Wait a minute! I do remember something."

"What? What is it?"

Catching my sense of urgency, Jeannie replied breathlessly. "The last time I spoke with Harry he said that he'd told Shelby he was changing his will to leave the majority of his estate to her. He knew of no other living relatives besides her brother, Richard, and he hadn't heard from him in years. He also mentioned that he gave Shelby a ruby the size of a small acorn; he'd picked it while in Nam. Called it a welcome home gift and added that there were more where that came from. They were safely locked away in his bank deposit box along with a stash of old gold coins. Shelby would receive the lot on his death."

On hearing this tidbit, I almost slid off the edge of my chair.

"OMG! Talk about motive! I don't suppose you informed Lieutenant Kai of any of this."

"Nooo ... I didn't realize it might be relevant. Do you think I should call and let him know?"

"Definitely! If for no other reason than the fact that Shelby was one of the very few people who actually visited Harry—probably the last from what you said. She also showed inordinate interest in his little 'treasures'."

Jeannie gasped again as realization of what she had just told me dawned on her. "Oh no!" She murmured. "You're right. I'd better call the Lieutenant right away!"

The game was afoot! Rubbing my hands together, I added, "Now all we have to do is find out if Harry actually followed through with his promise."

"No, Esme. That's Lieutenant Kai's job."

"I guess you're right. Besides, no lawyers worth their salt would ever pass that info along unless it was already public record."

Jeannie finished the last of her soup and checked her watch.

"I hope I've been of some help, Esme, but now I have to get back to work."

"You've been an absolute fount of info, Jeannie. Thanks to you there are a number of avenues to explore. Don't forget to call the lieutenant as soon you get back to the office."

"I promise." Jeannie paused, hazel eyes boring into my brown ones. "Uh ... Esme ... I don't like that look in your eyes."

"What? I don't know what you're talking about." I gazed innocently back at her. Jeannie didn't blink.

"Esme ... I recognize that look. You've got something planned in that cagey mind of yours. Remember this is murder we're talking about—cold blooded murder! It's one thing to want to find answers, but quite another to go looking for trouble in pursuit of them. Leave the detecting to the detectives. That big policeman seems to know his job—not to mention looking very intimidating."

"But that's just it, Jeannie. He looks too intimidating. Towers over everyone. Not only that, but you and I both know that seniors are more apt to share what they know with one of their own, than a policeman—especially one built like a sumo wrestler!"

"Oh ... I don't know ...," Jeannie smiled wryly. "I think several of your ladies can more than hold their own when interviewed by him."

Remembering my ladies' excitement when they first met Kai and his young partner, I had to admit that my friend had a point. That's why she's so good at her job.

"I know. I've heard it all before. Still ...."

Gathering her things, Jeannie got up. "Please Esme, you're not dealing with a recalcitrant senior here. We're talking about someone who's already killed once. What makes you think he or she will stop there if threatened?"

I sighed heavily. "My husband said the same thing. So did the lieutenant himself—numerous times."

"Then I suggest you take their advice. Listen, I've really got to run. See you later." Slipping into her coat she was out the door before I could answer. Needless to say, I ignored her very sage advice and proceeded to come up with a crazy plan to unmask the murderer.

I should have listened ....

Chapter 12

As I had expected, there was an obit in the *Senior Newsletter* and the *Leicester Town Crier*. It listed the passing of Harrold Browne. What it didn't list was cause of death. However, it did include a notice that the funeral service would be held at 11 AM on Wednesday in the auditorium of the Leicester Senior Center, since he was not affiliated with any religious institution. It would also allow his many friends and acquaintances to attend. Refreshments were to be donated by the local Army and Navy Club, of which Harry was a decorated member. The article went on to provide the usual information about surviving family members; one of whom was his stepdaughter, Shelby Grant Browne, who lived right in the neighboring town of Winston, Connecticut. Furthermore, in addition to working as an herbalist in a nearby health store, she just happened to be a Paralegal Intake Specialist at the High Mount Nursing Facility on Mountain Road in Leicester. As such, she would have access to information regarding which resident was prescribed certain kinds of prescription drugs—very convenient.

Here it was—just the opportunity to put my plan into action. I could safely attend with everyone else. I'd choose an opportune time to introduce myself and extend my condolences. Then I'd casually—as if it just dawned on me—comment that I'd love to hear more about Harry in his younger days. Would she be interested in getting together sometime for coffee—or in my case, tea? If she took me up on my offer, I'd suggest Flo's Coffee Hut.

I called Henri. Sure enough, she picked up on the first ring as if she'd been waiting by the phone. Does that woman know me or what?

The day of the funeral dawned sunny and clear with a distinct nip in the air. I dressed in my usual go-to-funeral clothes. It seemed like they were seeing more action by the week. Every other day, one heard about another death. That was one of the more depressing drawbacks of working with older populations. Just when you got to know and care about your students, one of them was gone.

I pulled on my black tencel slacks, followed by a black mock turtleneck and finished off the outfit off with a nice conservative gray plaid blazer and black nubuck pumps. I added the usual accessories, consisting of a pair of small silver hoop earrings and my ever present Chai (Life) necklace for good luck. I quickly grabbed one of my favorite Greek yogurts. I phoned Henri, as I shoveled it in, to let her know I was on my way. Yelling goodbye to Paul, I gave Streak one last cuddle as I headed out the door. Henri was already waiting for me at the end of her driveway.

As soon as she set foot in the car Henry took me to task.

"So, Esme. Time for that little catch up conversation we were supposed to have after your lunch meeting with Jeannie. Did she hit you with any good stuff?"

"She sure did! Good thing you're sitting down 'cause you are absolutely going to freak out when you hear what she had to say!"

"Enough already! Cut to the chase … we only have ten minutes before we arrive at the center."

"Okay! Turns out that, although Harry wasn't one of her clients, he shared a great deal with her. Would you believe that our quiet, mild-mannered Harry was actually married not once, but twice? He met and married a young Vietnamese woman during his second tour of Nam."

"OMG! You've got to be kidding!"

"I most certainly am not! Harry, himself, told Jeannie."

"Well, what do you know? He had some sort of a life after all—before Gerda and company entered the picture. Tell me more."

"Her name was Lien … means Lotus Flower … isn't that a beautiful name?" Once again I was in danger of going off into dreamland again until my dear friend smacked me in the arm and brought me crashing down to earth.

"Earth to Esme. Clock's ticking …."

"Tragically, from there on everything went downhill for him. Apparently, he was injured shortly after they married and she wasn't allowed to

this can't be just a weird coincidence. There's no way there can be another woman about the same age and who has those eyes."

"Are you nuts? How could that be the former wife—and with a daughter in tow?"

"I don't know, but it's them. Somehow, she must have survived and made it to the states."

Skeptically, Henri replied. "I don't know Ez. That's a pretty big leap, even for you …."

"I am telling you as sure as I'm sitting here—that's Harry's first wife and that's her daughter. I'd swear it! I don't know how she managed to survive and even reunite with her daughter … not to mention how they ended up here, but I'm sure going to find out!"

"Oh NOOO!" Henri groaned. "I don't like where this is heading. Please don't tell me we're going after those two now! What about our number one suspect?" Henri replied snarkily.

"Yes, what about our suspect?" Flor chimed in.

"Wait … what suspect?" she asked, somewhat perplexed. Before I could even answer, our resident Southern belle added her two cents.

"Am ah missin' somethin' here? What wife? What suspect? Is someone gonna enlighten me, before ah positively die from curiosity?"

I sighed, shaking my head.

Henri patted my shoulder. "Take a deep breath kiddo before you address this bunch. If you don't say something soon, we're in for a minor rebellion."

Smiling despite myself I switched my attention to the three waiting avidly awaiting an answer.

"Look, girls. It's a very long story. Suffice it to say, those women sitting up front are all related to Harry in one way or other."

They let loose with a collective gasp, with Flor having the last say.

"You've got some big explaining to do, Esme!" She protested.

"I know, and I promise to explain everything in due time, but right now we really ought to concentrate on the service, don't you think? After all that's what we're here for. To pay our last respects to Harry and give him the send-off he deserves."

"Oh, alright … " grumbled Flor, "but it better be good!"

"Ah guess ah can wait," sulked Charlotte Rae.

Arnoldine concurred, doing her best to hide her frustration.

"And I'm still waiting to hear what you're going to do about that one!" Henri muttered, inclining her head to the striking auburn haired middle-aged woman, in a black pencil skirt. Shelby Grant Browne. Her skirt was both short and tight, leaving little to the imagination and paired with black suede thigh high boots. She sat stiff backed in the front row, a solitary figure surrounded by members of the military who were preparing to give her the flag that had adorned the casket.

"Hold it! There's something really weird going on up there!" Arne exclaimed. "Look!" We all turned as one; just in time to see the two women I had noticed, standing up and moving rapidly to the center of the room where the soldiers were getting ready to present the now folded flag to Shelby Grant Browne.

The older woman, who I had already figured was Lien, rushed up to the soldiers crying out.

"Stop! That flag belongs to my daughter and me. Harrold Browne was my husband. The father of my daughter. I have my marriage certificate. It will prove that I am telling the truth."

Suddenly the packed hall went completely silent as all eyes turned to the soldiers and the three women glaring wordlessly at each other. The soldier who had been preparing to pass the flag on to Shelby, saluted all three women, then executing a clean turn toward Lien and her daughter, he saluted again. Bowing smartly, he handed the precious item over to the grief stricken mother and daughter. Turning, he strode over to take his place as one of the pallbearers. Stepping in front, he signaled to the others to wheel the casket to the back of the hall and through the lobby. Henri and I leaned over and watched the procession as they headed out the door and loaded the casket into the waiting hearse.

The mourners followed, Lien and her daughter furtively exchanging hostile glances with Shelby. The building positively vibrated with unreleased tension! At last the door closed on the scene as the driver of the hearse positioned it in front of the already long line of cars in the procession to the town cemetery. With its imminent departure, the hall slowly came back to life. Everyone talking at once. Some dashing for their cars. Heads shaking, openly speculating on the drama that had just taken place. Wild theories were interspersed with even wilder hints at some sort of conspiracy.

The five of us heaved a breath of relief. Charlotte Rae was the first to speak.

"Ma goodness that was quite a scene! Even more excitin' than when my daddy finally broke down and gave his permission for ma nuptials to my Yankee boy."

Arnoldine just shook her head in bewilderment and kept repeating as if by way of a mantra: "Well I'll be darned. What on earth just happened?"

I could almost detect the slightest sign of a smile vying with the present look of solemnity Henri had plastered on her face as she listened to the others.

"What about us?" Flor, Charlotte Rae and Arne echoed in unison.

"Yes," Flor continued. "You left us completely in the dark. What's this about two wives and two daughters?"

"Yeah!" Arne said. "We didn't know that Harry even had one, let alone two!"

I sighed, a deep one, this time. Cradling my poor throbbing head between my hands I answered. "It's a very, very, long story and this is not the time or place to share it. Suffice it to say, that at this stage, I don't know much more than you. However, I promise to bring you all up to speed ASAP, with whatever information I do have. But right now we've got more important things to take care of."

"Such as?" Henri asked archly.

"Well for one thing, it appears that we'll have to abort our original plan to extend our condolences. But first things first. It looks like all the mourners have started for the cemetery. We'd better follow suit and join the procession before they leave without us."

"OK. Then what?" an impatient Henri asked.

"Then we head back here to the cafeteria and hope we have a chance to connect with each of them if possible. I'm dying to know how Harry's wife and daughter made it out alive—let alone to the States. Talk about a minor miracle!"

Being equally curious, the others agreed that would be the best plan of action at this time. Furthermore, we decided to get together back at the Senior Center and offer our condolences to the now expanded little group of mourners if possible. Off we went to fetch our respective vehicles and join the others in line.

Henri and I headed to my car, picking up a Funeral Procession flag along the way. As we climbed into the car, Henri, who as I've already explained, is not the most patient woman around, jumped on me as soon as the door closed.

"So. Am I to understand, there has been a change of plans regarding the stalking of Shelby Grant Browne, who you still consider our main suspect?"

"You understand correctly. Shelby's not going anywhere, and we have more important matters to take care of."

Henri snorted. "The stalking of the other characters in this very bizarre melodrama, I take it?"

"Well, I wouldn't put it that way exactly," I replied slightly offended, although I knew that she was right. "But, yes. We really need to find out what happened to that poor woman and her daughter after they were left behind. How did they dodge death? How did they find each other again? Most importantly—how on earth did they escape and what took them so long to find Harry?"

"Don't forget. Who helped them to get here? I can't wait to hear that one …," Henri replied dryly.

"Well, that's exactly what we are going to do my friend. First we have to find out where they are currently living. Then we pay our respects."

"And how do you think you're going to come up with all of that info in the immediate future? Remember, we only have Lien's married name to go on. How do we know she didn't marry someone else and change it? After all, she would have been very young when she married Harry and had that baby."

Seventeen to be exact."

"My, you have been a busy little beaver," Henri cut in, her voice dripping sarcasm. " 'Great Google', I assume?".

Ignoring her pointed remarks, I continued. "Yes, it is truly amazing the wealth of information you can obtain on The Cloud … or is it the Mist? Remember, that's how we discovered all that info about Harry's military days—not to mention what we learned about the next Mrs Browne. But I thought I already told you about that on the drive over."

"No. You did not." Henri grunted, hands firmly attached to hips.

"Oh, that's right. I didn't get the chance to finish bringing you up to date. It's just that the shock of seeing those two women in the flesh, knocked everything else out of my mind. Sorry …," I replied sheepishly.

Once again, my dear old friend couldn't maintain her indignation, the hint of a smile creeping onto her lips. "OK. I give up. I'm almost afraid to ask. What's the plan?"

"I told you. We find out where they live and pay them a visit. Simple as that."

"My dear Esme. Having known you for eons, I have come to realize that nothing is 'simple as that'. So clue me in. Exactly what is rattling around in that tangled maze you call a brain?"

"Just this. We make contact with them during the luncheon and ask if we may pay them a visit in a few days to see how they're holding up. That's all."

Henri groaned. "Well at least they're not suspects in that perverse mind of yours. They're not are they?" she added, a worried look on her face.

"No, my friend. If I'm any judge of character at all, I'd say most definitely NOT."

Henri breathed a breath of relief. "Well that's one less thing to worry about with you. But what makes you so sure?"

"Several things. First of all, did you see their faces? Dripping with tears, real tears, not manufactured ones. And when Lien spoke up, there was unfeigned anguish in her voice. Lastly, as far as I can tell, neither of them had anything to gain. They probably weren't listed in Harry's will since he thought Lien was dead, and he never even knew of the existence of a daughter. No. It couldn't be them. Besides, for all we know, they might not even have been in town when he was murdered."

"And that's one of the many things you want to find out." Henri finished for me.

"Exactly! Now, can we give it a break at least until we return to the Center?"

"Oh, alright. But as soon as we sit down to lunch I want to hear everything—absolutely everything. Not the abridged version!"

I smiled in spite of myself. Henri has always had that effect on me. "Yes, Mom."

The tension broken, we both laughed. Just in time to disembark at the cemetery, which was already overflowing with people wanting to give Harry a big sendoff.

The service was very touching. Because Harry was a Purple Heart recipient it ended with the equivalent of a well-deserved Twenty-one Gun

Salute. Then we all piled back into our cars for the informal procession back to the Senior Center, where a generous luncheon had been laid out.

Chapter 13

SINCE we were early arrivals, we had our pick of tables to choose from. The arrangement of the seating in the Center cafeteria is much the same as many public institutions—a series of long rectangular tables set up in two sets of five rows each, with an aisle between them and one on either side. Sometimes for special occasions they're arranged in one large rectangle around the room.

Claudia had gone all out to prepare a special meal in memory of our resident fallen hero. The secretaries were on hand as well to help out wherever needed. Henri and I took some seats toward the middle of the cafeteria, so we could watch people coming and going from both the back door of the room and the main one leading into the auditorium. The seats for the service had already been cleared away by Ace, our wonderful Jack-of-all-trades and Felix, our go-to security guard, who was always around when you needed him.

Henri and I sat quietly talking, each keeping an eye on both doors. Catching sight of us, Arne and Charlotte Rae bustled over to our table and made themselves comfortable, eyes bulging with anticipation. They were followed shortly by several more of my little dance group: Mel, Marina, Rosemary, and Flor strolling in late as usual. Everyone crowded into the vacant seats on both sides of the table.

Mel, being slightly hard of hearing, broke the ice. "Well, isn't this cozy? We have almost enough to hold our dance class. Anyone care to shimmy?" The ladies started to giggle nervously. Receiving an arch look from Henri, they caught themselves mid-laughter and quieted down. All heads turned to Henri and me as Mel continued in a stage whisper. "Sorry. Just nerves. Never did like funerals—especially those of murdered persons."

"And how many of those have you actually been to?" Henri sniped.

Ignoring Henri's crack, Mel continued. "So what's the latest on our case? Anything new to report?"

I turned to Mel, speaking into her good ear. "Not much more than what you've already witnessed."

"Remember, Ms. Esme, you did tell us that you'd bring us up to speed on the latest developments," said Charlotte Rae. "Didn't she, Arnoldine?"

"She sure did!" Turning back to me, Arne continued. "I was there when you said so, less than an hour ago."

"Ladies, how about we give it a break for a bit. This really is not, I repeat—not the time or place to pursue our inquiries. The wrong person might hear."

"Or worse still," Henri cut in. "The murderer might hear. Then we'd all be in danger."

Excited, Charlotte Rae drawled, "Ah can see the headlines now: 'Senior Belly Dance Students Land in Local Hospital. Victims of Attempted Mass Poisoning.'"

I nearly choked on that one. "OK ladies, now we're really getting out of control. This is a serious matter. Dead serious! No pun intended. The murderer could very well be here. Having gotten away with it so far, who's to stop him or her from doing it again to protect their own identity?"

Ever the voice of reason, Marina added, "Esme's right, girls. It's not a good idea to tempt fate. Speaking of which, check out who's coming our way now." All followed her glance as they saw Claudia heading toward them.

"Yeah. Can it girls," Henri muttered. "We certainly don't want her to know what we've been up to. She'd put the kibosh on our whole enterprise, before we even started."

"We really don't want to involve anyone else in this," I added, putting in my own two cents. "Especially the administration! Claudia would be obliged to report it to Lieutenant Kai, if she found out."

"Yeah, the poop would really hit the fan!" Flor squawked.

"And that very large policeman might even place us all under house arrest. Ma poor daddy'd be rollin' in his grave if he knew what his lil' ol' daughter's been up to!"

"That's right," Rosemary laughed, patting her friend on the back. "We wouldn't want your dear departed daddy rolling in his grave, would we, girls?"

That broke the tension once and for all as my ladies burst into another nervous giggle fest.

"Shh!" Marina whispered. "Here come the mourners now. We need to calm down and show them some respect." Henri and I exchanged glances and followed suit as the three ladies slowly passed through the hall and entered the cafeteria. I couldn't help but notice the guarded, antagonistic looks radiating from the three of them.

"I wonder what's going on with those women? If looks could kill, one or more of them would be dead." Arne whispered.

"Uhh … rather poor choice of words don't you think?" Henri chided.

Arne's hands shot to her mouth. "OMG, you're right! I can't believe I just said that. They've all lost someone they cared about. And in such a violent way. No wonder they look like that."

Henri muttered under her breath, loud enough for only me to hear. "That might be true for at least one of them. The other not so much."

"Quiet!" I snapped *sotto voce.* "Do you want people to hear us. Remember, we've got practically the whole class here right now. Do you really want to take a chance that one of them will hear you? Let's just eat and clue everyone else in later. I'm sure most of our ladies have already figured out quite a bit on their own, but we really don't need to advertise for anyone else's benefit. How about meeting at my house while Paul's out? I'll catch you up then. And NO. To reiterate. I have no intention of calling on Ms. Shelby Grant Browne in the near future … at least not until we find out more about her."

"Yeah. Where have I heard that before?"

"Thanks for that sterling vote of confidence, Hen! Ya know, you've had your moments as well." I cracked. "How 'bout we get back to the matter at hand and see where it takes us?"

"Ha! Now who's being the feisty one?" Henri snickered. "Well, I'm glad you've decided to shelve your original plan for a little while longer. Definitely had to be one of your dumber ideas, and that's saying something!"

"Thanks again, Hen. I can always count on you to bring me crashing down to earth."

"You're welcome!" She smirked.

"Besides," I continued huffily, "I've already explained that we have more immediate concerns to address."

"I know." Henri answered wearily. "We have to reach out to Harry's first wife and daughter. Pay our condolences, although I'm not sure what that will achieve."

"Well, don't you want to speak with them? Hear how they managed to escape that hell-hole, Nam, and find their way here?"

"Of course I do, but I feel like such a ghoul encroaching on their misery during this awful time."

"Listen. Have you ever thought that maybe they'd appreciate a sympathetic ear to tell their troubles to—in this case four?"

"When you put it that way, I guess I can understand. But let's face it. We'll be snooping as much as empathizing—and you know it!"

Henri was right. I colored furiously. Feeling like I'd just been smacked in the face, I chose my words carefully. "You're absolutely right, Hen. I have been behaving rather egocentrically and not thinking of other people's feelings."

"Wha'? Am I hearing correctly? Little Esme admitting she's wrong, for a change? Are you sure you're feeling OK? Got a fever or something," she mimed checking out my forehead.

"OK! I get the picture. Message received loud and clear. But you of all people, should be able to understand how I feel."

"Say no more kiddo. I do understand, but others might not. Aren't you the one always reminding us about boundaries? All I'm asking is that you take that into consideration, before you go off half-cocked."

"Thanks, Henri You are a very wise woman, in your own gruff way."

"From you, I take that as a supreme compliment." Henri grinned, squeezing my shoulder and getting back to the business of eating. Good old Henri. Wouldn't trade her for the world. Addressing the food on my dish I proceeded to chow down.

"Now this is what I call a great spread!" Henri sighed, happily full of good old-fashioned New England cooking. "Figure we needed a little break from the tension. What better way to do that than by filling our faces," she grinned. "OK, ready to continue. At least you can't get into too much trouble visiting our newcomers. Somehow, I can't see those two women masterminding a murder either—especially not Harry's. They seemed totally bereft. Besides, what earthly reason could they possibly have anyway, if poor Harry didn't even know his wife was alive?"

"Very true." I replied. "No. As I said, they don't strike me as cold-blooded murderesses. They've been through so much already."

"Glad we're on the same page for a change. So, when do we head over there—wherever 'there' is?"

"Henri, you are a living doll." I said embracing her in a sideways hug."

"Yeah, just call me Barbie."

I almost spewed out the tea I was drinking. "Henri, you are absolutely incorrigible!"

"Yeah, but that's why you love me," she grinned.

"Probably …. I'll let you know later. Right now I just want to finish this lovely lunch in peace."

An hour later things were beginning to wind down. Dessert had been brought around on the old reliable metal trolleys. Decaf tea and coffee cups were refilled one last time. The strain of the day had given way to full bellies and quiet conversations. Looking at my ladies, I couldn't help but smile at how close a family unit they'd become. Now it was time to make my exit—but not before I assured them of further revelations to come.

Leaning forward, I quietly addressed the group. All eyes turned to me expectantly. "Well ladies, I'm glad to see most of our class has turned out to give Harry a lovely send off. I know you're all waiting to hear the latest on our unofficial investigation into the events leading up to Harry's death. First let me remind you that anything you hear or find out for yourselves should be reported immediately to the detectives handling the case. Do not—I repeat—do not try your hands at sleuthing. Remember, there's a murderer out there. One who would stop at nothing to keep from being identified."

Marina smiled indulgently. "I trust that goes for you as well, Esme."

"Of course it does." I replied. "Henri and I intend to pay a condolence call to each of Harry's relations. That's all. If you would like to be support-ive, I suggest you do the same—but call first. We don't want to overwhelm them."

"What about that kerfuffle we witnessed?" Charlotte Rae declared. "Aren't y'all gonna clue us in like you promised?"

"Yeah, Esme." Flor barked. "We'd like to know what brought about that little show between those ladies."

I raised my hands for silence. "I understand you're all hyped up about that incident. I promise to fill you in as soon as I've done more research. Right now, I'm as much in the dark as you. So let's plan on meeting after class for our usual lunch in Sophia's little room in the back, so we can have some privacy."

"Sounds like a plan," Rosemary said. The others agreed.

"Great! And now I'd better take off if I want to find the rest of that info for you." That said, I grabbed my stuff, blew kisses to them and headed toward the lobby, Henri practically lock stepping in time with me.

* * *

Once in the lobby, I turned to Henri. Dragging her into the library room off the lobby, I shut the door.

Henri freaked out. "What are you up to now and why the hell did you drag me in here?!"

"Quiet, I don't want anyone to hear …."

"Hear what?" She hissed.

"Listen, I didn't want to add to an already difficult situation, but I meant what I said about introducing ourselves to Lien and her daughter and officially paying our respects."

"Your point?"

I rolled my eyes. "My point is that we need to catch them before they head out."

She replied snarkily. "And how are you going to do that without any of the girls noticing?"

"We're going to wait in here until we see Lien and her daughter leaving. Then we'll just casually run into them and offer our condolences …."

Henri shook her head. "You know, Esme, I'm really beginning to worry about you. You've become utterly obsessed with this whole thing. Don't you think you're getting a little carried away? And what makes you think we can pull this off without anyone noticing?"

"I've thought about that. The way I figure it is, if we accidentally catch up, nobody will think anything of it."

"Do you hear yourself, Ez? Remember who we're dealing with here.

Those ladies of yours are sharp as the proverbial tack … and what's more—they are all onto you!"

"OK, OK. I know, but this is the only chance we'll have to meet Lien and her daughter. It's not as if we know where they live and can make a phone call …."

Henri threw her hands up in the air. "I give up! This is probably one of the lamest ideas you've come up with yet, and I must be a total idiot even to listen to you, but like they say—in for a penny, in for a pound. At least I can be here in case you dig yourself in too deep."

"Thanks, Hen. I knew I could rely on you!" Giving Henri a big hug, I pushed her into one of the overstuffed leather chairs nearest the door and peeked out.

Groaning, she slumped into the depths of the chair. "I just know that I'm going to live to regret this …."

"Shhh! Here they come now. And they're alone for a change. Now's our chance!" I dragged her out of the chair and hurried out of the room, just in time to come face to face with the grieving mother and daughter.

"Excuse me ladies, my name is Esmeralda Fine and this is my good friend Henrietta Hirshfeld. We just wanted to convey our condolences for your loss."

Lien replied in a soft bell-like voice. "Thank you. That is very kind of you. Did you know my husband very well?"

"Actually. No. I only knew him to say 'Hi' and 'How are you?'. He was always friendly and a real gentleman."

"Yes, that sounds like my Harry. May I introduce you to my daughter, Linh? Sadly, she never had a chance to meet her father. We became separated before she was born." Lien took out a wrinkled, handkerchief wet from tears as her daughter stepped forward to shake hand. "My poor Harry never even knew he was a father."

"I am pleased to meet you. Everyone has been so kind and told me stories about my father. I almost feel that I knew him. And I am so happy to meet you both as well!"

Sucking in my breath, as Henri looked on I prepared to tell them my macabre connection to Harry.

"I should explain that I am the person who found him."

Both women gasped!

"That must have been terrible for you, finding my father like that."

"It was! And because of it, I somehow feel a psychic connection to him and to you. Henri and I were wondering if we might pay you a visit when things quiet down for you. You see, we're Jewish and in our religion, as in yours as well, we pay a Shiva call and bring a meal to the grieving family. I believe you have a similar custom."

"We do," Lien replied.

"Would you mind if we did the same for you? We'd really like to get to know you and hear how you happened to come to the states."

"That would be lovely. It would do us much good to be able to share our story with you." Lien replied, taking out a small notepad and pen. "Let me give you our address and phone number."

Gracing me with a telling look, Henri, who had been silent the whole time—unusual for her—finally found her voice.

"You have our deepest sympathy. I'm very sorry that we could not have met under happier circumstances. We look forward to visiting with you. But I'm sure you're worn out by now and we don't want to hold you up."

Linh put a protective arm around her mother. "Thank you. It has been quite a trying day for both of us. Everyone has been so very kind. I speak for my mother and myself when I say that you will be very welcome any time you decide to visit."

Reaching out, Henri and I shook hands with the mother and daughter. "Thank you, Linh. Henri and I will be in touch very soon."

Grabbing our coats and bags from the library, we headed out close behind ....

By the time I got home, I was exhausted! The funeral had taken a lot out of me. Add to that the subsequent drama brought about as the result of the latest revelation that both Lien and her daughter were alive and well and living in Connecticut.

Chapter 14

THURSDAY afternoon. We had just finished shimmying, tummy rippling, et al. and were now sitting down to a well-earned meal at Sophia's. We had the place to ourselves, since the lunchtime rush had already abated. I was just bringing the group up to date on all Henri and I had gleaned from Google and my talk with Jeannie.

I addressed my students-cum-amateur-detectives. "Well ladies, that's all I can tell you for now."

As expected there were the usual murmurs and surprised exclamations followed by questions being hurled at me from all directions. I fielded them with the deftness of a baseball player. Having heard all the info earlier and strongly expressed her opinion, Henri kept uncharacteristically still— glaring at me from time to time. The others couldn't wait to hear what parts they would play in our little investigation.

Practical Marina was the first to inquire, "What do the police have to say regarding the case?"

The police, in the form of Lieutenant Kai and his minion have warned us off in no uncertain terms. 'Mind your own business. Let the experts handle the case.' "

"As usual." our frustrated Miss Marple announced.

"Thanks for the clarification, Mel." I replied facetiously. Taking up where I'd left off, "Lieutenant Kai further stated that we should inform him if anything relevant to the case turned up, and not—I repeat—not try to handle it ourselves."

At this point Henri cut in. "Which of course, Esme has no intention of complying with."

I managed to maintain some degree of aplomb. "I have no intention of putting myself in harm's way if that's what you mean. As I've already told Henri, all I want to do is pay my respects to the parties involved."

"And maybe along the way they'll let something slip—correct?"

"Maybe …," I stammered, realizing how lame I actually sounded. Everyone's eyes shifted from one to the other of us, as if watching a tennis game. Henri delivered the final volley.

"And maybe, one of your suspects just might catch on and make you the next victim."

Everyone gasped as the thrust hit home, followed by shocked silence.

Marina wisely observed that it was time to offer more practical solutions. She was seconded by Jeannie, who had just walked through the door and sat down at the table.

"Hello everyone. Sorry I'm late. Just finished with a client. I have to agree with Marina. Obviously we all bring a lot to the table in our own ways. However, we need to trust that the police have things under control. We must let Lieutenant Kai do his job, without throwing obstacles in his way. If you happen to notice or hear something that doesn't quite sit right with you, tell the lieutenant or his young assistant." Then she bestowed the full force of her arresting gaze on me. "And as for you, my dear impulsive friend, try not to jump in feet first—something that will get you into trouble."

I sighed inwardly. Aloud, I told everyone what they wanted to hear.

"I guess you're right. Maybe it is time to accept a more passive role and let the lieutenant and his staff get on with it." The whole time I spoke, Henri steadily eyeballed me, knowing full well that I wouldn't … No—couldn't back down. My mind accepted that my friends were right, but if I were being truly honest with myself, I had to admit I was incapable of letting go—like a dog with a bone. I was that dog and consequences be damned.

Chapter 15

Two days later, I was on my way to personally extend my condolences to Lien and her daughter, Linh, accompanied by a very skeptical Henrietta Hirshfeld, ever echoing her own mantra: "I still think this is a crazy idea."

"What crazy? How many times have we attended Shiva at a house in mourning? It's what we do as Jews and as fellow human beings. You were all there for me when my sister passed away. I was there when you lost your brother. It's what we do."

"Don't you dare compare that to what we're doing now! It's not the same at all and you know it! These women are strangers to us and we to them. For all intents and purposes we are invading their privacy. Have you even thought about how they might feel? They've already been through so much, and here we are, about to rip open old wounds they may want to remain closed."

"I've thought of almost nothing else since I recognized them at the funeral. I felt it. I knew they were Harry's family. You know I get these feelings sometime—runs in my family."

"There you go again with that ESP crap. I've heard all about it ad nauseam." She exclaimed. "I'm not saying that I don't believe you. I just don't think this is the time to trot that out."

"Henri, you're a dear friend. You've made your point and I don't want to argue with you, especially now. But you also know me well enough to realize that I can't back down when we're so close to finding out the truth about what happened to Harry, as well as how his beautiful family was ripped apart. Those poor women have been trying to reunite with him for years and what happens when they finally find him? He's dead. Murdered by some cold-blooded person. For what … money, jewels? What's worth taking a person's life over?!"

"Alright already. I give up!" an exasperated Henri declared, arms flying into the air.

By this time we had reached their house, located in the southeast portion of the state. It was a small, well cared for dove-gray cottage with white trim. The house sat on the far corner of a cul-de-sac, surrounded by acres of fields which had once been rich farmland. I pulled in next to a pristine white wooden mailbox and did a quick double take. Poking Henri in the shoulder, I pointed to the box: L. Sterling, 18 Lotus Lane.

"What the …?" Henri burst out. "What's the deal there?"

"I wonder if she remarried?"

Snickering, Henri replied "Well, if we get out of this car and knock on the door, we'll soon find out." Suiting word to action, she unbuckled her seat belt and pushed open the door.

"Are you just gonna sit there zoning out or are you coming, girl?" Rudely jerked back to reality, I nodded. Unhooking my belt, I threw open the car door and stepped out onto the pavement. "Yes I'm coming. You sure have changed your tune. What happened to, 'I still think it's a crazy idea.'?" I mimicked.

"OK," She nodded grudgingly. "Maybe it wasn't such a crazy idea after all. Now would you please get a move on and hit the bell?"

Laughing despite myself, I replied as we headed for the door. "And you call me impulsive? OK, I'm moving, but we're going to knock, not lean on the bell." I reached out for the dragon shaped knob and gently knocked.

Henri could barely contain her excitement. "Boy I can't wait to hear what she and her daughter have to say. This case gets curiouser and curiouser by the minute."

We heard the muffled sound of sandals on the tile from within. The door was opened by Lien herself, dressed in traditional Vietnamese mourning attire consisting of a long white gauze tunic over softly flowing white pants of the same fabric and loosely tied at the waist. Her long black hair, sprinkled with silvery gray, was kept in place by a wide white band tied at the back of her head. She was followed by her daughter, Linh, similarly dressed, with the addition of a sheer white muslin veil, covering her warm brown hair. It was kept in place by a wide band, identical to her mother's. Both ladies bowed their heads slightly in welcome. There were candles of all sizes spread around the house and sticks of incense in long narrow vases everywhere. The scent of cedar and cinnamon filled the air.

Lien warmly took both our hands in her tiny ones as she bid us enter. "Good afternoon ladies. We are most touched and honored to have you visit our humble abode. As you can imagine, we are much alone here and do not have many visitors."

"We are honored to be invited." Henri and I nodded our heads in return.

Having done my homework, I knew that it was the custom to bring gifts of flowers, food, candies and other delicacies to a house in mourning, similar to our own tradition when paying a Shiva call. So I had gone out of my way to purchase an exotic bouquet of winter flowers: pristine white Snowdrops, Yellow Jasmine, white Winter Honeysuckle and pale pink Camellias. The effect was striking. The fragrance, absolutely intoxicating! I had also baked my special apple kugel, by way of offering one of our own traditional dishes. We had practiced our presentation beforehand, so as not to commit any *faux pas* by accident. Henri would offer the flowers to Lien. I'd give the casserole to her daughter, Linh. Henri stepped forward and presented Lien with the flowers. I was just about to give Linh the kugel, when she looked up at me with those beautiful silver flecked brown eyes—Harry's eyes. Suddenly I reeled very slightly from the shock. Linh quickly reached out to steady me.

"Are you all right? You have suddenly gone quite pale." A look of concern in those eyes, she asked, "May I get you a glass of water?"

"No. I am fine. It was just looking into your eyes, that threw me momentarily. They are the spitting image of your father's eyes."

"Yes, my mother has often commented on how much I resemble my father. As you know, I never met him. But my mother has kept him alive for me in spirit." She smiled at her mother. "They had a very short time together, but he left her with a lifetime of beautiful memories which she has passed on to me." Staring out into space, Linh continued, as if in a trance. "So much so, I feel I have always known him."

Lien draped her arm around her daughter's shoulder, breaking the spell. Linh looked down at the dish she still held, declaring, "Oh my goodness, where are my manners? Here I am holding this delightfully scented dish while you are still standing here in the cold. Please, please let me take your coats while mother shows you into our parlor. You can warm yourselves by the fire. Meanwhile, I will bring this into the kitchen and prepare a little tea."

"We hope you will join us for tea." her mother added, bowing again.

That said, Lien turned and led Henri and me through to the back of the house. We entered a warm, brightly lit room, surrounded on all sides by paintings, wood block prints and magnificent art scrolls adorning the walls. The walls themselves were covered with a pale shade of natural beige grass cloth, almost like that of sun bleached parchment. There was a large bay window to the right, facing one of the loveliest miniature oriental gardens I've ever seen. It had a variety of statuary, from religious figurines to stone dragons, cranes and pagodas of every size. One of the pagodas was a bird bath, currently being used by a pair of sparrows bathing in the afternoon sun. To the left was a smaller window which looked out on a lovely patio filled with winter flowers and miniature trees in beautifully painted and carved planters. The overall effect was that of a private little paradise.

The room itself bordered on minimalist—something my husband Paul would have loved. The only furniture consisted of a warm pale beige plush overstuffed sofa perfectly centered in front of a simple red brick fireplace framed in natural teak trim and a colorful mosaic at the base of it. An overstuffed chair of the same fabric as the sofa sat to the left of the fireplace. To the right of it was a worn, obviously well-loved, baby soft, nutmeg brown leather recliner. This was *feng shui* at its best and most restful.

"Please sit down." Lien said. "The sofa is quite comfortable. Wonderful for having a—how do you say it—a nice long schmooze?" She giggled.

That broke the ice. Laughing as well, we settled comfortably into the depths of what proved to be down filled cushions. I sighed happily. Boy, Lien sure wasn't kidding! I could easily fall asleep right then and there. I had to remind myself that we weren't here just for a visit. We were on a mission! And it looked like Lien and her daughter were on one as well. You know what they say: "great minds think alike."

Just as I was in danger of completely surrendering to Morpheus, Linh quietly re-entered the room pushing an ornately carved acacia cart loaded down with exotic goodies. It contained a heat-resistant, clear glass teapot with a lotus flower floating inside and a few green tea leaves for good measure. I'd read that lotus tea is one of the healthiest teas around. Good for lowering blood pressure, insomnia and stress … boy did I need to buy some! Laid out on a fine bone china platter was an array of delicious desserts: Ban

Dau Xanh (mung bean pastry), Che Troi Nuroc (sticky rice balls in ginger syrup), Che Chuoi (Banana with sago pearls in coconut milk) and my all-time fave, Banh Tieu (Vietnamese version of a doughnut) coated in sesame seeds. Just the sight of them made my mouth water, like Pavlov's dogs. Linh passed the tray around and poured us each a glass of tea, then poured one for herself. Next she scooped a large spoonful of my kugel onto delicate bone china plates with an intricate lotus design and passed them out along with sets of beautiful bamboo chopsticks ... hmm, never tried eating kugel with chopsticks—talk about East meets West. Not one to pass up a new experience I took up my chopsticks and had a go.

Henri and I dug in as if we hadn't eaten for days. Slowly the lotus tea took effect as all the tension of the past few days melted away. I let the peaceful atmosphere flow over me. Glancing at my friend, I noticed it was having an equally cathartic effect on her. Beside us, Lien and Linh had taken up their chopsticks and were gingerly working their way through the kugel, murmuring their appreciation.

Satiated, the four of us replaced our dishes onto the cart, but lingered over the heavenly brew. It was time for that long talk. Unexpectedly Linh took the lead.

"I will straighten up here, she announced, gathering everything but the tea and returning the lot to the tea cart. I know that my mother has much to ask you about my dear father, so I shall leave you to it. I too, would like to hear more about him. With that she wheeled the cart out of the room.

Smiling sweetly, Lien faced us and repeated, "Now it is time for our schmooze, yes?"

Grinning, I answered. "Yes. This would be a great time, if that's what you'd really like to do."

"It is. I have been waiting a very long time to hear how my Harry has fared, but before we continue, I am sure you are wondering about the name on the mailbox."

"Well, it had crossed our minds." Henri chimed in unusually subtly for her.

"I am sure you have already heard, my husband was severely wounded, shortly after we married. I was separated from him before I could even tell him that I was with child. They would not even let me see him. I was in anguish. Harry had already filled out the papers for me to rejoin him in your country, but somehow the papers were destroyed or misplaced during one of the many skirmishes between the VC and the Americans. I still had my certificate of marriage, but it was not enough and Harry had already been transferred to a hospital here in New England. I went to stay with my elder sister Li Nguyen until my daughter was born. She had been sharing an apartment with our widowed aunt, Van Li, who also had a daughter my age, named Bich. Bich and I bore a very slight likeness to each other, which my selfish cousin used to her advantage. She had seen my pendant with our wedding picture and wanted it for her own. One night shortly after my daughter was born she crept into our room and stole it. I was heartbroken! Aside from my beautiful daughter, it was the one thing I had to remember my Harry. I did not know at the time that she had taken it. I just thought that it had been lost during childbirth."

"That is so sad! What happened next?"

"Unfortunately, my cousin was caught in the crossfire of a fight between the North and South Vietnamese. She was severely burned and died of her wounds. My poor Aunt Van Li, fearing the effect it would have on her little sister, identified the body by the pendant—not knowing that her daughter, Bich, had stolen it, and it was her own daughter who was lying there, burnt beyond recognition."

At this point, Henri, who had been listening intently, broke in. "I don't understand," she said shaking her head. "How is it that your aunt did not find out her mistake when she returned home?"

"That is the problem with war. When my aunt returned home, it was to find an empty house. While she was away, identifying what she thought were my remains, I returned from visiting another village. To add to the confusion, my mother, daughter and I had been forced to flee from the invading army. She never saw her sister again. Eventually, my mother received the pendant with a note of condolence for her loss. By then I had already fled with my daughter to the safety of the American side. My mother refused to leave, and I could not persuade her to come with us. I still remember her last words as we said goodbye. I will translate for you:

> My darling girl, I am too old to change and cannot bear to leave
> my country, as torn as it is now. My wish is for you to leave
> this place and seek your own destiny in a safer place. Go. Find
> your man and be as one again. Remember me with kindness.
> Know that I will always love and be with you, if only in spirit.

Then she kissed us both and turned back toward our war torn village. I walked on carrying my precious baby girl and never looked back."

By the time Lien had finished I was practically in tears. Henri reached into her capacious bag and pulled out a pack of tissues, shoving them at me, while stoically holding back her own tears.

Poor Lien was so taken by my reaction, that she leaned toward me, pressing my hand in hers.

"Please do not distress yourself, Miss Esme. My fortunes did improve. You see, I ended up working as a cook and nanny for an American family living in Vietnam. They had twins, close to the same age as my Linh. They took us under their wing and saw to it that we were not harmed in any way. Their children became Linh's closest playmates and their mother even taught us English. While there, I met a widowed Medic, named Gerald Sterling, who developed a fondness for me and my daughter. He was a much older gentleman—about fifty-seven years old. He had lost his wife a number of years earlier and had no children of his own. He knew I had a husband somewhere in New England—that much I had been able to find out from the military. When it was time for him to return to the states, Gerald asked if I would allow him to adopt me and my child, saying that he regarded me as the daughter he would have loved to have. Like me, he had no family of his own. We would become that family. He even offered to put out 'feelers', as you say, and try to locate my Harry. It was like a dream come true! I would go to the United States and just maybe, reunite with my beloved Harry. Three months later, all the papers signed, my guardian angel, Gerald, bundled us into a car, headed for the airport and home—our home."

"OK, now I need one of those tissues," Henri declared gruffly. "Your story is like a modern fairy tale with a twist. You'd make a million if you ever sold it to the movies."

"I have all I could ever want or need right now, right here. The only thing missing is my husband. I would have given millions to have had one more day with him, but sadly that was not to be."

By this time, Linh had finished up in the kitchen and returned to the parlor. Giving her mother a hug, she sat back in her own chair to listen to our discussion.

"Mother is right. We have everything we need. We have our health, a comfortable home and most of all—each other. Sadly, I too am grieved to have never met my father. But I was not totally without a father figure, was I mother? Papa Gerald served in the role and did a most excellent job of it. We had him in our lives for over thirty years. He was the only father, although more like the grand-papa, I ever knew."

"And a devoted father to me." added Lien. "I could not have asked for a better one. It is because of him that we are now independent and answer to no one. Unfortunately, he passed on before he could locate my Harry. He did leave us with enough information so that we were finally able to find him—although too late. I should very much like to discover the identity of the cold-hearted killer who tore Harry from me yet again!"

Here was the perfect opening, handed to me on a silver platter!

"And that is exactly what we would like to do. As I explained when we first met, I did not know Harry well. However …," I paused trying to find the next words. "However, I was the one who found him and it has haunted me ever since. I dream about poor Harry almost every night. I need to find his murderer and help lay him to rest once and for all!"

Total silence. My hostesses sat very still, processing what I had just revealed. Linh was the first to recover her composure. "Oh my poor Miss Esme. No wonder you reacted so strongly when you looked into my eyes! I believe we have much to discuss and learn from each other."

Linh sure wasn't kidding.

Chapter 16

"So where do we go from here?" Henri asked no one in particular, as three pairs of eyes turned in her direction. "Well, it is what we're all thinking is it not?"

"Yes, dear lady, it is. The question now remains as to how we go. Have you any ideas on that subject?

"Actually ... that's where I come in," I answered breaking my own silence. "You see, I have a plan."

"A crazy one!" Henri burst out.

"Henri is probably right, but it's the only way I can think of to beard a lioness in her den."

"A lioness?" Linh repeated. Does that mean you may know who the murderer is?"

"It does ... at least I think I do ... just a gut feeling ... got no proof. I'm sure the police have honed in on their suspect now, but need to get more proof in order to convict. Circumstantial evidence and my gut won't cut it."

"And that's where her 'ladies' and I come in." Henri added for good measure.

" 'Ladies', who are these ladies of whom you speak?" Lien's curiosity peaked.

"They are my belly dance students. I teach a class at the Senior Center. You should try it sometime. My ladies range from fifty-five through eighty years old. They are absolutely amazing! Several of them could give *Dancing With The Stars* a run for their money."

Lien giggled that tinkling laugh of hers. "Belly dancing … what do you think Linh? Should I take up the belly dance in my old age?"

Smiling affectionately at her mother, Linh replied. "My dear mother, one could never call you old, and it is good to see you laugh again after all we have been through. As for the belly dance, maybe you should try it when our period of mourning has ended. You need to make new friends—we both do. This hiding in our house every day in a perpetual state of mourning, is not healthy for you, nor me, if I am being honest with myself. We must welcome life back into our home."

"You are very wise my daughter and we shall do just that. But first there is much to be done, if we are to know any peace. We must seek justice for my husband and your father."

"That's the spirit, Lien!" Henri boomed out heartily.

"What is this crazy plan of which you speak and how can we help?"

Taking a deep breath I explained what I had in mind. By the time I had finished, Lien and her daughter were on board—much to Henri's chagrin.

"OMG!" She wailed, comically, her head in her hands. "Now I have to deal with three crazy ladies instead of one! I'm tempted to call Lieutenant Kai and turn you all in. He'd straighten you out real quick!"

"Calm down Henri. You know you wouldn't do that."

"What makes you so sure?"

"How long have we known each other?"

"Too long! And I still think you're nuts!"

"Yes, but now we have safety in numbers. Isn't that what you wanted?"

"I suppose so. Much as I hate to admit it. I'll still be there anytime you need me—nuts or not."

Reaching over I gave her a hug. "Thanks, Hen, you're a dear."

"I believe this is where it is time for a huddle, as they call it in football," Linh said. Henri and I laughed as poor Lien looked confused.

"Please. What is a 'huddle' and why must we enter into one?"

"A huddle is when a group of people crowd into a tight circle together to discuss their next strategy. Remember, you have seen it when you watched the football games with Papa Sterling."

"Oh." She giggled. "Yes, now I remember. So we are to put our heads together in a symbolic huddle, in order to come up with ideas as to how we may help the police—without getting arrested for interfering with an investigation. Have I got that right?"

"You have." I smiled.

"So what is your plan, Miss Esme?

"Please it's just Esme. I don't go in for formalities."

"Alright 'just Esme'," she teased. "Please explain."

"OK, I'll try. You already know that Harry had been informed of your death. Several years after returning home and being discharged from the Veterans Hospital, here in Connecticut, he married on the rebound—meaning that he had just come out of one relationship and was very vulnerable. Harry was still recuperating and in a great deal of pain. He was forced to check into the hospital periodically for further PT … that's Physical Therapy. As you can imagine he must have been very lonely as well—a prime target for anyone wanting to take advantage of the situation. That is exactly what happened. As far as we know, Harry met Gerda Grant when she worked with him as a Paraprofessional Physical Technician. I imagine he became dependent on her and she managed to worm her way into his affection. Gerda already had two very young children from a previous marriage. You met the daughter yesterday, Ms. Shelby Grant Browne or just Shelby Grant as she was formerly known. Harry adopted both children. However, Mrs Grant had bigger plans for herself and the kids. After ten years of marriage she divorced Harry and married a wealthy widower, with a son of his own. To make a long story short, the children never saw Harry again."

"Until Shelby turned up here in Leicester." Henri added. "She swooped in and like her mother before her took over. Poor Harry didn't stand a chance!"

"Somehow, Shelby inveigled him into making her his prime beneficiary. Harry, believing that you were dead, complied with her wishes."

"But what happened to her mother? Didn't she even bother to make an effort to remain in touch with her own children?"

"Please let me take it from here …," Henri pressed.

"Oh, alright."

"Mrs Stevens, as she was now known, became estranged from them. Her third husband had suffered a massive heart attack and died, leaving the bulk of his estate to his son. Gerda, herself, was given a very comfortable pension and inherited a large home in Beverly Hills, as well. However, this is where it gets good, her son and daughter were left with nothing but token sums. Needless to say, this did not sit well with her children, who now had to fend for themselves. To add insult to injury, Mama Bear decided not to share—so much for motherly devotion."

"This last of course is only speculation, you understand." I added.

"Hence the estrangement," Linh murmured. "Yes, I see. And you feel that losing the fatted calf, as they say, would give rise for one to search for another."

"Exactly!" Henri crowed triumphantly. "Like mother like daughter."

"But what of the son? Does he not figure into this scenario as well?"

"I'll take it from here," I told Henri. "First of all, I should explain that most of the information I have gleaned comes from surfing the web. It's amazing what you can find online and in the cloud these days." The ladies nodded in agreement. "So when I started searching for suspects and motives, I immediately checked out the most likely candidates. Two of his Senior Center acquaintances stood out. However, they were already being vetted by the police. That's when I happened upon all the info about Gerda and her brood. When I looked up the two kids, I noticed that there was more on brother, Richard, than Shelby. Turns out he had absolutely no reason to maintain contact with his mother or sister—even less to seek out his stepfather. You see, although husband number three had never officially adopted them, he did take care of the kids' needs. Stevens even sent them to top-notch universities and trade schools. Turns out, Richard attended USCSD—that's University of Southern California, San Diego campus. He ended up getting a high paying job as the CEO of a Research Facility studying oceanography in San Diego. I looked up the place. Trust me. That man does not need the money! Shelby, not being as academically motivated, chose the trade school route. She became a Paraprofessional Herbalist and worked in one of the VA's rehab centers. Ironically, that's where she reconnected with Harry—quite by accident, actually. The rest we can only surmise."

Lien had been listening intently all through my narrative. She now added her own thoughts.

"What you are telling us is that this Shelby, whom we had the dubious pleasure of meeting at the funeral, is a very likely, how do you say it, candidate, for the murder of my Harry. The police have not been able to prove it as yet, so you want to obtain that proof for them. Am I correct?"

"You are."

"I must admit, you are playing at a very dangerous game, indeed."

"So I've been told numerous times, by numerous people—including Henri, here."

"Then why do you persist?"

"For the same reason as you. To get justice for Harry."

"But you are of no relation to him, and as you yourself have stated, you hardly even knew him. Why do you care so much?"

"For several reasons. The first being, that I literally tripped over his poor dead body. Secondly—and Henri would agree with me on this one ... now that we've met and bonded, I want to help you gain closure so that you can get on with your lives. You deserve to be happy. That's it in a nutshell."

"I am touched that you feel so strongly about our situation, but I would not have you put your own life in jeopardy and those around you. However, we are both honor bound to assist you in any way we can."

"Please tell us. What can my mother and I do to help?"

"I think the best thing for you to do is pay a visit to the executor in charge of Harry's will. Produce your credentials and make a case for acquiring information on the disposition of his will.

"Also, find out who else inherits in the event of Shelby's death. Tell the executor that under the circumstances, you are thinking about contesting the will. I must warn you however, that if that woman finds out what you are up to and thinks you want a piece of the action, you may be placing your own lives in danger—perhaps even more so than me. If she's killed once to get her hands on Harry's fortune, Shelby Grant Browne won't hesitate to eliminate any potential competition."

Chapter 17

CAREFULLY choosing my outfit ahead of time (I get like that when it comes to funerals and condolence calls) for my visit to Shelby's home, I worried about how it would play out. As usual, my permanent support staff of one, Mrs. Henrietta Hirshfeld, had finally agreed to come with me, after much wheedling, albeit grudgingly. Only after I had promised her that the rest of the crew was planning on making an appearance did she consent. Having taken care of that piece of business, I dressed in my usual uniform of leggings and a tunic, finished off by one of my numerous hip belts. Kissing my boys goodbye, I drove over to the Senior Center for my class and our next group meeting.

All the ladies had been contacted regarding this. I could almost imagine Melisande drooling when I had called to remind her of our meeting. When I mentioned Henri's and my visit to Lien and Linh, her exact words were, "I'm positively salivating! Been wondering when you were planning on calling in the troops. Maybe we'll finally be able to latch into something we can sink our teeth into." Our resident Miss Marple enjoyed nothing better than a good old-fashioned snoop, and I'd just given her cause for one.

"Well consider yourself called upon," I had laughed.

Melisande was one of the first to arrive. Bursting into the auditorium, she breathlessly called out, "Let's get started with class already. I'm raring to go and in snoop mode in the bargain." This elicited another round of laughter from me and the others present.

"Glad to hear my super sleuth is 'raring to go'. Hope you put as much energy into your shimmying today as you have with your sleuthing."

As I was setting up my music and laying out the scarves and hip belts,

Rosemary, Marina and Jayne joined us, with Flor bringing up the rear. Rosemary's ears perked up on hearing the word snoop.

"And about time too," she exclaimed. "We've all been sitting around twiddling our thumbs. It's time for action. So what's next?"

Grinning, I answered. "What's next is our class. Gather your stuff, grab a bottle of water and get ready to roll. There'll be plenty of time for discussion after class."

This last was greeted by groans from the impatient and a chorus of cheers interspersed with Middle Eastern dance yells from the movers and the shakers. We got down to the business of dancing for the next hour, taking a well-earned water break halfway through; during which time I announced the imminent arrival of Lien and Linh Sterling(née Browne).

"By the way, our newest members, Harry's first wife and daughter, Lien and Linh, are due to join us any time now, so please make them feel welcome."

This announcement was followed by excited hush; a ripple of anticipation running through the group. Next everyone began to talk at once. I held my hands up for silence.

"Ladies, please! I know you're excited, but it's time to get back to dancing."

Back to dancing we went. Good thing the killer shimmy was coming up—that would give them all a chance to work off their excess energy! Next came veil work to our two favorites—"Malaguena" and "Aziza" from *An Oriental Bouquet*. Our routine, "Rachel," an oldie but goodie, sung by Shoshana Damari followed. Finally, we ended with our usual meditative creative movement cool down—this one to the tune of "Somewhere Over The Rainbow" in honor of Lien, who had just walked in, followed by daughter Linh. I motioned for them to throw off their coats and join us, which they did, shyly at first and then full throttle—the excitement of our group being highly infectious.

The music ended, everyone clapping and cheering as they put away their dance paraphernalia. They practically bowled over our two newcomers in a show of welcome. Once again, I held my hands up for silence, "Ladies, please! I know that you all want to welcome our newbies, but take it easy. They're not used to quite so effusive a display."

"In other words, back off and let the poor things catch their breath will ya?" Leave it to dear Henrietta Hirshfeld and her bullhorn voice to bring everyone back down to earth. Lien bowed modestly. "My daughter and I thank you for your so very generous welcome. We are overwhelmed!"

"We also want to thank you for all your efforts into finding my poor father's murderer and allowing us to join you." Linh added.

"Well, ladies, now that we've welcomed Lien and Linh into the fold, I believe it's time to get down to business."

"Yeah and about time too!" Rosemary exclaimed.

Charlotte Rae warbled: "My, this is so excitin'."

At which point a chorus of ladies humorously sang out in return, "And you haven't been this excited since your pappy agreed to let you marry your Yankee boy!" This in turn brought on a round of mass hysterics. The laughter finally subsided enough for me to continue.

"Now, you all know that earlier this week, Henri and I paid a condolence call to Lien and Linh," I said, nodding to the mother and daughter. "We had a delightful tea and very illuminating discussion. We are thrilled that these lovely ladies have joined in our unified search for the truth behind poor Harry Browne's murder."

"And …," Henri added, pausing for effect. "In case several of you haven't figured it out yet," Henri pointedly looked at Charlotte Rae, then continued. "Since they have now joined our little investigative group, Lien and Linh have been eliminated from our suspect list. Obviously, they are very committed to finding out the truth as to why Harry was killed."

"Well, that brings us back to our main, but not only suspect, Ms. Shelby Grant Browne."

"That's right. She officially went back to her adopted name after her stepfather's death. Interesting …," Marina commented quietly.

"I thought so. And with all of us working together, we'll catch her out yet. However, we need to continue our research."

"Yes. It is imperative that we find out a great deal more about Shelby, before we make any moves regarding her connection to this case."

"Thanks, Marina. Couldn't have put it better myself. Furthermore, we still need to look into anyone else who may have had a reason to want Harry out of the way for good. We can't afford to put all our eggs in one basket, if you'll pardon the cliché. Seems like I'm full of them these days," I continued thoughtfully.

"Remember. Just because Shelby managed to have herself declared sole beneficiary, that does not necessarily make her a murderer."

"Nope. Just a very greedy b#*@!." Henri mouthed off.

"Henri …!"

"True on both counts." Flor added.

"Before we move ahead on that front, we need to be absolutely sure there are no other suspects hiding in the woodwork. Speaking of which, has anyone seen or heard from either Norton or Adolf?"

"No!" exclaimed Rosemary. "It's like they've both disappeared into thin air."

"Ro is right. No one's seen or heard from them since this whole thing started. Not since we heard that report that they headed somewhere out west." said Marina.

"Yeah!" Arne exclaimed. "They up and disappeared right around the time Harry was found. Remember? The police were trying to locate them, so they could check on their alibis among other things."

"OK! We need to do some follow-up on that dubious duo, just in case. Remember, they were inordinately interested in those coins. Now that we've found out how valuable they are, it's just possible that it all comes down to greed on the part of Norton and Adolf. Nothing would surprise me when it comes to those two. Speaking of which, I think it's time we pursue that avenue and I know just the person who can do it—Chuck Shackleton! I'm going to grab him right after his bridge game."

Just as I was steeling myself to field more questions, we had a most welcome break in the form of Chuck Shackleton, himself. Nonchalantly ambling through the auditorium, he stopped. "Greetings ladies. Just taking a break between rubbers," he said doffing an imaginary cap. "Hope I'm not interrupting anything important."

His comment drew a few nervous giggles from those present and quite a few gulps as well. Seeing their reaction he quickly amended his statement.

"Bridge rubbers …."

More giggles followed with several loud guffaws from who else but Henri, Mel and Flor. At this point I found it necessary to jump in … talk about perfect timing!

"Hey there Chuck, you must be psychic! We were just talking about you."

"Oh, yes? Anything interesting?"

"As a matter of fact, we need some advice that you are best equipped to give us regarding certain events of the past few weeks."

"I'm guessing you need more info on our friends, Betz and Jones. Right?"

"Right. They're still MIA."

"And you were hoping I could help you find out where they are?"

"Uhh … yes. Any chance we can meet after your final rubber?"

The ladies erupted into laughter!

"Ladies please! As usual, you're worse than my high school students …."

"Yeah!" Henri and Flor yelled out almost the same time.

Rosemary snorted. "That's because we're older and have had more time to perfect it." That sent the rest of my crew into gales of laughter. Fortunately the whole repartee had flown over Chuck's head. At that moment he had suddenly spotted Lien. I felt like I was witnessing a boomer version of *West Side Story*. An instant *frisson* rose up between the two. The air positively hummed with anticipation as all eyes turned to them! Forgetting what he'd been about to say, Chuck changed gears.

"Who, may I ask is this lovely lady?" Taking Lien's tiny pale hand in his great big tanned ones, he turned to me. She stood there giggling like a young girl on her first date. I proceeded to make the introductions.

"Chuck, I'd like you to meet our newest member, Ms. Lien Browne Sterling and her daughter, Linh. Ladies, this is Charles Shackleton—just call him Chuck."

Chuck's eyebrow shot up almost two inches, when he heard Harry's name.

"Browne? Not 'The' Harrold Browne?"

"The very same," I answered, trying to control the laughter threatening to escape me.

"Then you must be the little lady I've been hearing so much about." Nodding as he still held her hand, Lien blushed delicately.

"Yes, Harry was my husband. We were parted during the Vietnam Conflict. My daughter and I have been searching for him a very long time. That is how we came to be here. Sadly, too late."

"I am so sorry for your loss. It must have been very difficult for you and your daughter …, but your name is Sterling. Did you marry again?" Practically holding his breath, he waited for Lien's answer.

"No. I never remarried. Sterling is the name of the very kindly old gentleman who took us in. Having no children of his own, he formally adopted me and became grandfather to my daughter, Linh."

On hearing this, Chuck let out a barely audible puff of relief. "So it is just the two of you?"

"That is so—just the two of us. Papa Sterling died several years ago, but has left us comfortably off."

"Maybe I can take you both out sometime? You know ... take a tour around our beautiful little city. Lots to check out."

"I should like that very much," Lien replied, furiously blushing as Chuck finally released her hand. Controlling her laughter during the whole exchange between her mother and Chuck, Linh sat back beaming. I could almost read her thoughts. Turning to me, she winked, whispering "It looks like mama has found her—how do you say it in Hebrew? *Bashert?*"

"That's right ..., and it's called Kismet in Arabic! You sure learn fast my dear. I hope I'm not jumping the gun by adding a great big *Mazel Tov* to you all! That's 'good luck' in Hebrew. We could use some good news these days."

"Well, I'd better get moving and let you ladies continue with your meeting." Chuck reluctantly took his eyes off Lien. Walking over to Linh, who was still trying to stifle her laughter, Chuck shook her hand. "Very nice to meet you Miss Sterling." Eyes twinkling with mischief, she replied. "You as well Mr. Shackleton, but please call me Linh. I have a feeling we will be seeing a great deal of each other in the future."

Turning a lovely shade of pink, Chuck replied. "That would be great. And please call me Chuck. Everyone else does."

"That's right, Chuck," Rosemary teased as the rest of the girls exhibited signs of breaking into another major giggle fest. Of course, friend Henri felt obliged to add her two cents as usual. A wicked gleam in her eyes, she declared. "Sometimes we even call him 'Chucky' or 'Chuckles'."

That did it! Chuck took off at a gallop. Heading for the cafeteria, he managed to wave goodbye, with at least a modicum of dignity. Just before he disappeared into the cafeteria, I shouted to his receding back: "Hey Chuck! Don't forget to check back in with me after your last round of cards. I really need to talk to you."

"Will do." He shouted back, barely turning around.

As soon as poor Chuck had gone, the whole room burst into laughter—much to the chagrin of poor little Lien, who sat there in a daze, holding her hand close to her flushed face. The rest of the meeting continued uneventfully for the most part. Henri and I brought the group up to date on our impending visit with Shelby Browne.

"Henri and I have already contacted Shelby. We are planning on stopping over tomorrow to pay our respects."

Arne snickered. "And bring her one of your delicious kugels by way of admittance, huh?"

"Naturally." I grinned.

"I guess the rest of us should pay her a visit as well," Flor said.

"I think it would be a good idea. After all, we don't want her to become suspicious of our motives."

"Heaven forfend!" groaned Henri.

I continued, ignoring her outburst, "And we certainly don't want any of you to put yourselves in danger. Just keep it short and impersonal."

Our Miss Marple added, "In other words just extend condolences and make small talk. Most of all, get out of there fast!"

"Right! That is the plan." I replied.

Marina finished for me. "And if by chance she lets her guard down and does say something relevant, pretend not to notice, but report it to Lieutenant Kai or Officer O'Reilly ASAP. Remember, no more sleuthing!" That seemed a good note to end on. I called the meeting to a close.

"OK, ladies. We've had quite a workout today."

"In more ways than one. Let's go feed our faces!" Henri again.

"I'm all for that," said Flor.

"First ones there please grab a table for eleven," added Rosemary, counting heads. "Boy our numbers are getting larger by the week. Must be all the excitement."

"Yeah, that's it," Henri remarked snarkily.

Turning to Lien and Linh, Henri continued. "You are joining us aren't you?"

"We would not miss it for the world! It is almost like a party." smiled Linh, still bubbling with laughter from the sight of her mother being courted. "Come mother. Our food awaits." Linking arms, they picked up coats and hats and followed the rest of the group across the street to Sophia's.

As usual, Flor and Henri stayed behind to help me pick up. Piling veils and belts in bags, we stowed them behind the curtain in the corner of the stage. That done, Henri and Flor grabbed their coats, hats and dance bags. Waving goodbye they headed toward the lobby.

"Don't forget to save me a seat." I called out.

"Don't take too long or we may be finished before you even start!" Henri shouted back. I heard her cackling as the door closed behind her.

Now that I had the room to myself, I took a deep cleansing breath. Time to consult our resident expert on the great Southwest. As if on cue, Chuck himself ambled back into the auditorium.

"OK kiddo. What can I do you for? You mentioned needing some more information on the dirty duo."

"Well, it's like this, Chuck. Something's been gnawing away at my brain."

"Let me guess … the convenient disappearance of Betz and Jones. Been wondering about that myself, since you got me involved in this little investigation of yours. What exactly are you looking for that you think I can help? Actually, to tell the truth, after meeting Lien and her daughter, now I'm more interested than ever in helping you all to scope out the truth behind Harry's murder, if for no other reason than to give Lien and her daughter closure."

Stifling the urge to laugh, I continued. "So I noticed." The next moment, I sobered, remembering my own mission.

"That's exactly how I feel, Chuck. It's what I've been trying to explain to everyone when they tell me to back off! Oops, there I go, off on another tangent. Getting back to business. Since you seem to know a lot about the Southwest and have a number of connections, I was hoping that perhaps you could help us find out more about those bad boys." I paused, gnawing on my lip. "How the heck can they have so thoroughly disappeared? That's where you come in." I said, pausing to catch my breath. "Do you think you can discover their whereabouts?"

"I'm sure the police have already tracked them down. Probably the first thing they did after interviewing everybody here. Remember, I had a long talk with that big detective myself, after you sicced him on me. Seems like a smart guy. Knows what he's doing." Chuck added.

"I realize that, but they're not about to share that info with us, are they? Especially after telling me to butt out in no uncertain terms!"

Chuck grinned. "Got that right. But, why the urgent need to find out? Can't you just let the police handle it? Why do you want me to cover the same territory? It's not as if Harry was a good friend of yours. You said yourself, you hardly knew him."

"Look, Chuck. I may not have known him well, but ... and here I go again, sounding like a defective CD. By now it's public knowledge that I became personally involved when I literally tripped over Harry's poor dead body. I've been haunted by the sight ever since." I took a deep breath and continued. "I want justice for him. I want justice for poor Lien, who lost her husband for the second time and Linh, who never even got to meet her father! I want to be able to sleep again without visions of murderers and their victims haunting my dreams. That's what I want and why I won't back down!"

"OK, OK. Calm down little lady." Chuck reached out and patted me on the shoulder. "No need to give yourself a minor heart attack. Of course, I'll help in any way I can."

"Thanks, Chuck. Sorry about that outburst. Been having several of those lately. I just get so worked up when I think about it."

"So I noticed. What exactly would you like me to do?"

"I'd like you to try to find out where those other two are. Could they have had anything to do with Harry's murder, not to mention absconding with the missing coins?"

"What's the deal with those coins anyway?" Chuck asked. "Having seen them myself, I know they're very old and in damn good condition, considering. Probably worth a pretty penny. But why all the fuss? What's so special about those particular coins?"

"I guess you didn't get a really close look."

"Nope. Old coins not really my thing."

"Well, they are Jayne Hathaway's thing. You see, Jayne and Marina are the ones who first realized what several of those coins were and their significance. Since Harry was always showing them around, it was only a matter of time before others with a more sinister motive figured it out as well."

"Others being Jones and Betz, I take it?"

"Got it in one."

"Agreed. I definitely wouldn't put it past either of those two to come up with a plan to grab them for themselves—but murder? Norton may be a big ol' blowhard, but a murderer? To tell you the truth, I don't think he'd have the stomach for it."

"What about that sleazebag, Adolf Betz ...? Pardon the expression, but that little 'Hitler' really gives me the creeps! His name suits him to a tee."

"Betz is a whole different story. I wouldn't be surprised at anything that little worm is capable of. Certainly wouldn't turn my back on him in a dark alley!"

I shivered. "Me neither!"

"Let's get back to those coins. I assume they are worth a bundle?"

"They are."

"Kindly enlighten me."

"Sorry. I should have explained sooner. According to the girls' research they are extremely rare, uncirculated editions of 1838 Victoria Regina coins. They were lost, probably stolen, on the way to Australia for distribution."

Chuck let out a long, low whistle. "No wonder everyone's after those babies. Must be worth a fortune, possibly even priceless!"

"Yes, they are, and there are quite a few more where they came from. We think Harry might have left a stash where he found them ... unless of course, he did the intelligent thing and put them in his safe deposit box."

"And you think that's what those two frauds were trying to find out?"

"Possibly even worse. We're wondering if they had anything to do with his death. Obviously from what you just said about Betz, you think it's a possibility too."

"Got that right. That guy's capable of anything! OK. Say I locate either one or both of those clowns. What then?"

"Good old Chuck. You always get right to the point. I'd like you to quietly check with your acquaintances—both business and otherwise. Ask them if they've seen or heard from either of those two. Find out if any of the coins have gone on the market; if so, where and when? That sort of thing. Most important of all, can you check with your sources to see if any old mines have been tampered with lately? Stuff like that?"

"Done and done little lady. I'll get back to you as soon as I hear anything."

"Thanks, Chuck! I knew we could count on you! Now that's taken care of, it's one more thing off my mind. Well, I'm off to meet the girls. They'll be wondering where I disappeared to." Laughing, I grabbed my things and headed for the door, waving as I went.

Chapter 18

Less than a week later, I received a call from Chuck.

"Hi Esme. Got that information you asked for. How 'bout meeting with Lien, Linh and me for lunch—on me of course?"

Laughing, I replied. "With an invitation like that, how could I refuse! Where and when?"

"Today, one-thirty. That new Vietnamese restaurant on Main that Linh's been raving about."

"You mean Pho? Been wanting to check that out for ages! See you in a few ...."

Hanging up, I shuffled over to my walk-in closet, pulled out some warm leggings, my favorite navy blue tunic and gray leather boots. Checking my minimal makeup and whipping my fine, flyaway hair into some semblance of order, I was ready to take off.

I still had several hours before I needed to leave, so I decided to call Henri and bring her up to date. As usual, Henri practically answered on the first ring. I swear, when she's not busy rushing around all over town, that woman must post herself in the window facing mine and wait for me to buzz.

And I thought I had a sixth sense ....

"Hi Esme. What's up? Any news on the Southwestern front?"

"Yes. I just got a call from Chuck. Says he's got some info for us. He's taking Lien, Linh and me out to lunch at that new restaurant, Pho ... and no, before you protest, I cannot bring you along. I was tempted to ask if I could, but figured that would be downright rude, since Chuck's already treating the three of us."

"Oh, alright," Henri grumbled, like a sulky child who's been left out of a treat. "But you'd better call me as soon as you get back!"

"Do you one better than that," I laughed. "Call Jayne and Marina. The three of you can stop over for Vietnamese coffee and a pastry as soon as you see me pull into my garage. I'll bring you all up to date then."

"You've got yourself a deal, lady! And make that Vietnamese tea please. See you in a few."

"You got it!" Still laughing, I hung up.

Two hours later I was sitting in Pho with Chuck and his ladies. Orders placed, the waiter returned with our coffees. We sat back in the comfortably padded booth, sipping our drinks in companionable silence, as we awaited our food. We had ordered the sampler, featuring a little taste of everything—the main dish being Pho of course (that's Vietnamese for soup). Mine was vegetarian with tofu, Chuck's beef, Lien choosing chicken while her daughter opted for shrimp. There were also plates of Vietnamese salads, noodle and my favorite—fresh rolls.

We dug in ravenously, as the dishes were set out one after another. Ending with mango sticky rice, the four of us sat back, pleasantly full. Time for that talk. Chuck dove right into his disquisition.

"I'll make this as brief as I can, ladies," he said, as he began ticking off each point on his fingers.

"Number one. Jones and Betz were definitely in Arizona around the time of Harry's death—a little town called Atsa Chooli. It means Eagle Mountain in Navajo. My fire department buddies heard about it from one of their Navajo counterparts. Sent me pictures. Got 'em right here. Thought you'd want to check them out."

"You'd better believe we do!" I burst out, avidly watching as Chuck reached into the pocket of his parka and pulled them out. He passed them around for us to look over.

"As you can tell, the town is almost deserted. Place emptied out when the local silver mine went bust. Only a handful of Navajos and die-hard Arizonans stuck it out. The mine itself's been out of commission for decades now—not safe. However." Chuck paused theatrically. "However, my friends went and looked the mine over themselves. It was completely roped off with danger signs all around it. Naturally that didn't stop my guys. They're firefighters. What they did is cut through to one of the safer sections. By the way, it had already been broken into. There were footprints everywhere. The guys heard later that the police from back East had been round as well."

I sighed. "I should have known Lieutenant Kai and his minions wouldn't waste any time checking out our information."

"Hey! That's a good thing, right? Remember, it's their job to catch the bad guys. Isn't that what we all want?"

This time it was my turn to blush from embarrassment—emphasis on the ass which I was currently being.

"Of course you're right!" I said covering my burning face with my hands. "I don't know what's gotten into me ... what kind of idiotic game I've been playing at."

Lien reached over, gently patting my hand. "Please do not distress yourself, Esme. You have been under a great deal of stress, as have we all. Everyone has a breaking point. Perhaps this is yours."

I took her hand as I reached for a tissue in my pocket. "Thanks! You are very wise my friend. And yes I do understand." Pulling myself together I turned back to Chuck. "Sorry for the interruption, big guy. Please continue."

"Okay. Number two. When they checked out the cave, they found signs of recent digging. They also found what looked like a rather large blood stain."

We all gasped at this disclosure. "Did I hear you correctly? Blood? Could your friends tell if it had been there a while?"

"They could. According to the guy who arranged that little expedition, the blood appeared to be only a few weeks old at most." We gasped again. My hands flew to my mouth as I gave voice to what we were all thinking.

"Oh my God!" I cried. "Do you think it was one of those two?"

"Could be. Would be one hell of a coincidence if not. By the way, that leads me to point number three—a telling piece of info. It appears that only one of those two was spotted afterwards. Adolf Betz. He was seen getting on a bus headed out of town. Nothing more was seen or heard of regarding Norton Jones. Furthermore, one of my colleagues checked the airlines as well as the buses leaving Arizona. He hadn't been on any one of them."

"Well that tears it!" I exclaimed. "Looks like not one, but two murders ... will it never end?"

"Sorry kiddo. I was afraid it would turn out to be something like that."

"So where's Adolf? And what exactly happened to Norton?"

"Betz is probably keeping a low profile in some sleazy hideaway. Remember, he'd be the first person the police would go after under the circumstances. As for Jones, I heard the police are still searching for his remains."

I gasped! "I sure hope they find him soon."

"I'll let you know if anything else turns up, regarding that SOB, Betz."

"Yes, please do. I'd be willing to bet that he may turn out to be the key to finding out who actually murdered Harry—assuming of course, that Betz, himself is not the murderer."

"I wouldn't want to take you up on that bet, since odds are, you're right. By the way, there is one additional piece of information I know you'll want to hear. Those coins you asked me to look for? Apparently, the police sent out a description of the missing coins to all dealers in a thirty-mile radius of the mine. A number of them turned up in an antique coins and gold shop in a nearby town. Reputable dealer. Called the police as soon as he heard that they were vital evidence in a murder investigation. Guess the good Lieutenant has them in his evidence locker by now."

I was completely blown away. "Wow, I am impressed! I knew you were good, but not this good. No wonder you're such a past master at bridge!" I winked, laughing. "Remind me never to take you on in any game of wits."

Now that we'd taken care of business, we finished our coffees, packed up what was left of the food and stood up to leave. I hugged Lien and Linh then shook hands with Chuck.

"Thank you. Thank you. Thank you! You've gone way over and above the call of duty. Name your poison … oops poor choice of words … name your favorite dessert and it's yours. Anytime I can help you, don't hesitate to call."

Warmly shaking my hand, Chuck replied. "Don't worry kiddo, it was my pleasure … been getting a little bored since I retired. This certainly gave me a lift. Just let me know if you'd ever like me to do some more sleuthing in the future."

"Heaven forfend!"

Chuck laughed. "Knowing you, anything's possible." Giggling, Lien and her daughter nodded in agreement.

"OMG, it's unanimous! Do I really have that effect on everybody?"

"Probably," Chuck smirked. "But it's one of those things that make you, you."

"Thanks! I think. OK wiseguy, if that's the way you feel, I just may take you up on your offer—hopefully not for a very long time!" I groaned as the others laughed. "Well, I'd better get a move on. There are several very anxious ladies waiting for me at home. Speaking of which, I promised to bring them back some Pho goodies." Slipping into my coat and taking up my hat and gloves, I walked with them to the door and then returned to collect my takeout order.

As expected, Henri, Marina and Jayne were all peeking through the window as I drove up, I pressed the button to my garage door and quickly pulled in, the door closing behind me. Grabbing the goodies I threw open my car door and climbed out making a beeline for the house. No sooner had I placed the stuff on the counter and hung up my things, then the doorbell rang. The gang had arrived.

I let them in, took their coats and led them into our cozy kitchen. Once they were all seated, I quickly set out plates and cups and placed my purchases in the middle of the table.

"Dig in girls while I tell you a little story … "

Chapter 19

A ND so it was, that with no small degree of trepidation, I found myself dressing for what was supposed to be a friendly condolence call. Armed with another of my special kugels—this one pineapple, I psyched myself up to beard the lioness in her den. Waving goodbye to my two boys I headed downstairs.

"Be careful and don't say or do anything to make her suspicious." Paul called out.

Gee, hadn't I already heard that from Jeannie ... or was it Marina? I'd had so many warnings thrown at me, that I couldn't even recall who said what anymore. "Don't worry, I'll be the soul of discretion!" I yelled back.

"Yeah. Right ...." His last words echoed in my ears as I shut the door.

I picked up Henri and we drove over to Shelby's house. It turned out to be a large, ultra modern, detached condo located in the swankier part of town. Why was I not surprised? It was obvious she had followed in her upwardly mobile mother's footsteps. Taking advantage of her stepfather's largess, Shelby had recently moved into the place, equipped with all the bells and whistles: professional landscaping, a large indoor/outdoor patio the length of the house, and even a tiny goldfish pond.

Shelby answered the door, wearing a tight black sweater, red patent leather belt, black jeggings and fuzzy little black mules with red satin bows. She reminded me of a black widow spider.

The inside of her house was as impressive as the facade. We passed through a long hall. A large open kitchen was on our left and the living room on our right. The kitchen contained all the latest appliances, such as, stainless steel stove, refrigerator, dishwasher and a double sink. The counters were the latest black granite, including a generous island in the middle of the kitchen, which was equipped with yet another sink and several electrical sockets on the side of the golden oak cabinets. The floors were also golden oak. The overall impression was that of a home straight out of *Architectural Digest.*

I was impressed!

Shelby led us into the open living room coldly decorated in various shades of white, with slashes of black and red here and there—a white leather sofa and love seat sat on either side of the white brick fireplace. A white velveteen overstuffed chair and ottoman sat under a large picture window.

"Thanks for this kugel. Smells delish. Please, have a seat. Make yourselves comfortable, while I cut up this yummy looking kugel and brew us some of the special coffee you brought, or would you prefer tea?"

"Please don't go out of your way," I said. "Tea will be just fine."

"Great! How do you take it?"

"Straight, no extras," Henri chimed in.

"You are ladies after my own heart," Shelby smiled. "That's the way I like it."

We sat down rather gingerly waiting, afraid that we might do something to mess up that pristine white furniture or scuff the fluffy white throw rug under our feet with our shoes. I was almost tempted to remove them altogether and leave my shoes by the door, but then paranoia took over. What if we had to make a quick exit? Was this a mistake or what?! Oh well, here we were, stuck visiting in the home of a possible murderess. Couldn't do anything about it now. Just tread carefully and watch my mouth. Reality dawned. I finally realized that everyone had been right when they'd warned me against such a deadly game plan. Boy, was this one of the most harebrained ideas I had ever come up with—hopefully not a fatal one ....

While I had been agonizing over my profound stupidity, Shelby returned with a tray full of top shelf goodies from companies whose outlets I couldn't even afford to walk into let alone patronize. All this on a para's wages? I thought not. However, as the heiress to a tidy fortune? Definitely! I stole a glance at Henri and could tell she was thinking the same thing.

Sitting back, I turned on the charm. "This is such a lovely spread, Shelby! It really wasn't necessary for you to put yourself out for us. We're supposed to make things easier for you in your time of mourning. You shouldn't feel you have to feed us."

"Nonsense, it's the least I can do! You've both been so thoughtful. Besides, I rarely have any company. It's nice to sit down and visit with you—especially, since you were friends of my dear father."

At this point Shelby slipped a very expensive silk handkerchief out from the inside of her sleeve and dabbed at an invisible tear. Then, pulling herself up removed two delicate Mikasa plates, silver forks and spoons from the tray. Placing each set on hand woven white linen mats resting on the black lacquered cocktail table she leaned forward and set the loaded tray of goodies in front of us. In the background we heard the sound of a teapot whistling. Excusing herself, she stood up.

"That'll be the tea. I'll be right back."

"Gotta admit, that young woman sure knows how to lay out a good spread"

Boy, I'm going to gain five pounds with all the condolence calls and stuff!" Henri snorted.

"Let's hope that's all she lays out ... " I mumbled under my breath.

"What?" Henri asked, her mouth full.

Changing tack I added, "Nothing, nothing ... it is quite a presentation. That's for sure! She does seem pretty nice and down to earth despite this set up. Maybe we're barking up the wrong tree. Oops. There I go again with the clichés. What is with me? Oh. Here she comes again. Would you check out that dragon teapot? I'd kill for one of those!" Realizing what I had just said, I almost choked on the delicate Belgian chocolate wafer I'd been scarfing down.

"Would you get a grip already? You're rambling on and on." Henri hissed under her breath. "Remember this was your crazy idea, not mine. Just sit there and watch your mouth. Here, shove a cookie in it. That'll shut you up!—at least for a few minutes. By the way, you weren't wrong. That bit with the crying into her silk handkerchief was a tad over the top to say the least."

Henri's words hit me like a smack in the face.

"Yes, but who spurred me on to undertake this investigation in the first place?" I hissed back. "You did! Aided and abetted by our dancing ladies."

"Guilty as charged." Henri admitted, "But I've been having second thoughts. This whole investigation thing is beginning to get out of hand and I'm concerned for your safety."

"Ya think?" I snapped. "That's what the powers that be have been telling us all along. My own husband has been jumping down my throat! I'm not sure how much more I can take." As I continued my rant, I could feel my blood pressure steadily rising. If I didn't calm down soon, not only would I give myself away, I'd probably have a mini heart attack to boot. Wouldn't that go over big ....

Making a Herculean effort to relax I finished my cookie and leaned back against the sofa just as Shelby approached, pushing an ultra modern glass and steel tray table. She handed us each a matching Mikasa mug in shades of black, white and gray, then placed one for herself on the end table next to her, also glass and steel. First she poured the tea into our cups and then her own.

"Hope you like Prince of Wales Earl Grey. It's my fave—when I'm not drinking coffee that is."

"Love it!" Henri and I declared.

"Especially Prince of Wales! Ever try Lady Grey?" I asked.

"No. Actually, that's one I haven't checked out yet. Is it good?"

"It's absolutely delish! I'll have to give you some."

"Very thoughtful of you. Matter of fact, that's how I ran into my dear stepfather again. We met while I was working in the Vet Hospital, when Harry came in for a checkup. I didn't recognize him at first. It had been so many years since we lost touch. Later, we ran into each other again during one of those health fairs they offer at your Senior Center. He mentioned a little of his history. It suddenly dawned on me, that this was my beloved stepdad. I could see in his eyes that it dawned on him at the same time. He asked if I'd like to join him for a cup of coffee. He loved his 'cup o' joe', as he called it ... said that's how the guys in his platoon referred to it ... because it was plain and simple and down to earth in a time of chaos."

"Yep. That sounds like Harry alright. Always self-effacing." Henri agreed.

Here was my chance to bait the hook. Showtime!

"Except when he was showing off those coins of his." I added.

Henri took over. "Yeah. Did you know that he actually told people he had a cache of them safely stashed away?"

Shelby feigned a look of surprise—priceless!

"No. I had no idea. What kind of coins?"

"Oh ... " Henri paused nonchalantly. "Just some newly minted, uncirculated Victoria Regina coins. He talked about them incessantly. Showed them around to anyone who'd listen, didn't he, Esme?"

"Yes. I'm afraid so. He carried them loosely in his pockets. You mean he never shared any of his wilder stories with you?" I asked, wide-eyed. Two can play that game and I'm a past master.

Shelby blinked several times, then decided to pull the poor little orphan act, breaking out her still dry hanky once more.

"No. We rarely spoke of monetary matters. We were just so happy to have found each other again."

Oh my aching teeth! Shelby was slinging the syrupy sentiment around so heavily that I thought I'd have a major sugar attack. However, I managed to play my own part in this theater of the absurd with surprising panache, as did Henri.

Reaching out I gave Shelby a motherly pat. "This whole ordeal must have put a great deal of strain on you, but you seem to be bearing up like a trouper."

Not to be outdone, Henri nodded sagely in agreement. Then she made her move to extricate us from what was becoming one very uncomfortable situation! Replacing the tea things on the tray, Henri grabbed one last goody, this one a ginger scone, complete with Devonshire cream. She wasn't about to pass that up after this debacle. Next, Henri conspicuously checked her watch.

"Oh my goodness, will you look at the time?" She declared in her most un-Henri-like voice. "It's been such a lovely visit that we almost forgot the time." Then she turned on me. Esme! Why didn't you remind me, that we have to leave! You know that Doc D. gets really ticked when I'm late for an appointment—Oops, please excuse the language, Shelby. My eye doctor is not a patient man. Office is always packed."

Talk about pouring it on, but I wasn't about to complain.

Taking my cue, I mumbled. "Oh, I am so sorry! We were having such a nice visit, I forgot to check my Fitbit. But you know Hen," I paused—very effectively I thought. Playing my part to the hilt, I continued. "I shouldn't have to remind you. It's your appointment, not mine," I scolded.

Following Henri's lead, I replaced my own tea things on the tray and rose to take my leave. Shelby was caught completely off guard by our sudden retreat. Pasting a smile on her expertly made up face, Shelby stood up as well. All I wanted to do at that moment was head out the door, jump into the car, step on the gas and get the heck out of there! Go home to a nice, hot, cleansing bath.

With all that racing through my mind, I made straight for the entrance. Grabbing my coat and hat I said goodbye; Henri close behind me. Shelby accompanied us to the front door. An odd look in her cold green eyes made me shudder inside. Graciously thanking us for our thoughtful visit and gifts, she shook hands and opened the door. The look on her face as she was closing the door gave me pause. Remembering that last look as we left that coolly impersonal house, I felt a chill run up and down my spine—and it wasn't even a cold day! As a matter of fact it was one of those lovely mid-winter, fifty degree days when the sun was so warm it burned large slushy holes in the snow below. Henri and I silently exchanged glances as we climbed into my car. I could tell she felt it too.

Once we were safely ensconced in my car, Henri finally let loose, declaring, "It'll be a cold day in the Big H before I ever set foot in that house again!" I just nodded mutely, as I clicked my seat belt, turned the key and pulled out of her driveway. We were safely out of her clutches—weren't we?

So why did I have this feeling like someone had just walked on my grave ...?

Chapter 20

SEVERAL days after that disquieting visit with Shelby, I had my answer. It was the following Thursday. Still edgy from our visit, I exhibited a rarely seen sober side during class. The music was less riotous, my demeanor lacking in its usual animation. Even the breakneck shimmies I was known for were lacking in energy. Of course, my ladies took notice and when we finally finished with "Music of the Night," which I found highly apropos under the circumstances, they all surrounded me, concern on their faces. The most concerned of whom were Lien, who had happily joined our little coterie, literally jumping in with both feet, and our honorary member—Linh. After giving the two of them a welcoming hug, I waved everyone else away saying, "I'm fine. Just having an off day. That visit with Shelby really did me in."

"I'll second that! That woman is a real piece of work. You gals better be very careful if and when you pay her a visit. As a matter of fact, just hand over the goodies and head for the hills."

I couldn't help but chuckle. At this point I felt obliged to run interference. Henri on her soapbox is quite a sight to see.

"Come on Hen, it wasn't that bad. She was very polite, and you said yourself that she laid out a good spread."

"That she did. Though I'm not sure it was worth the weird vibes I got from her."

"Not even scones with clotted cream?"

"OK, maybe those, but I still couldn't wait to get out of there and I know you felt it too."

Shuddering at the memory, I answered. "Alright, I admit that it was definitely not a visit I'd want to repeat. That said, if you haven't called on her yet—Don't! Besides, enough of us have already got that covered."

Rosemary and Flor both breathed a sigh of relief.

"Guess that takes care of us, Flor."

"You better believe it!" Flor replied. "That's one visit I wasn't looking forward to paying!"

Of course, in Mel's case, my comment was like throwing down the gauntlet. Our resident Miss Marple wasn't about to let any bad vibes stop her from checking out a potential perp.

"Well, I'm still going. Gotta check this broad out for myself—bad vibes or not!"

"OK." Marina put in. "Just be careful. Listen. Don't talk."

It was time to switch the direction our conversation was headed. "I just want to add that you've all done a wonderful job talking to people, checking on stuff, etc. But I think it's time for all of us to take a step back and let the police get on with it. Now that's taken care of, I'd say it's time we close up shop and hit Sophia's. I don't know about you girls, but I'm ready for some nice, warm comfort food! How about you?"

"Ah sure am!" chirped Charlotte Rae.

"Well, you don't have to ask me twice," said Henri. "Come on gals, let's get this show on the road before Sophia's gets too busy."

"Right behind you," Rosemary called out.

Flor brought up the rear as we headed *en masse* out the door, waving to Diane and Joanna as we left.

We were just crossing the street when I received an urgent call from my husband. Let me tell you that my husband doesn't usually do urgent, so I knew that something was very wrong on the home front. Paul had let Streak out to do his business and gotten involved with some household chores of his own while the little guy was still out. When he finally called Streak to come in, the pup was nowhere in sight. We have a very high, sturdy, predator proof, chain link fence, so Paul knew that it couldn't be our resident coyotes. Grabbing his jacket and hat, Paul had headed out to look for him. There isn't much room to wander in our yard, so Paul figured the poor little guy had gotten stuck in some bushes again. Unfortunately, that had happened before, his old eyes not being what they used to be. Paul did his usual patrol of the grounds. He noticed that our gate was unlatched and partially open. That's when he put in the SOS to me.

"Streak is missing. I checked all around his usual spots. Then noticed that someone had unlatched the gate."

As I listened, I felt like I was in danger of a full-blown anxiety attack.

"Turns out our neighbor's son, Amir, saw a classmate get off his bike, open the gate and coax the dog out with a big old bone. You know our Streak—give him a treat and he's yours for life. So the kid grabbed him, shoved him into a box or something on the front of the bike and took off."

"Oh no!" I cried. "I had this really weird feeling after I left Shelby's house, but I never thought she'd stoop so low as to kidnap a dog. Ooh, how stupid can I be! If she did murder her own stepfather, she's capable of anything!"

"Calm down, Esme. She may have nothing to do with Streak's disappearance. Maybe it's another of those pranks the kids down the block decided to pull."

"I don't think so! Their mother was ready to rip 'em a new one after the first time. I doubt very much they would try something worse. No! Everyone was right," I whimpered. "I should have stayed out of stuff I know nothing about. They all warned me. If I could find information on Shelby, what's to stop her from using the same technique on me." I managed to pull it together and continued, "Listen, this is no time for any more I told you so's and feeling sorry for myself. You need to call Lieutenant Kai right now! He was expecting her to pull something like this. I'm on my way. Be there in ten minutes. Love you. Bye."

* * *

By the time I got home, Paul had already contacted Lieutenant Kai and given him the information on our neighbor. Bordering on hysterics I asked, "What did the lieutenant say when you told him?"

"He told me to sit tight and he'd get back to us as soon as he had more info."

Pacing back and forth, I kept jumping every time I thought I heard the phone.

After what seemed like hours, Lieutenant Kai finally called. I picked up on the first ring. "Hello Mrs Fine, just wanted to let you both know that based on the information your husband passed along earlier today, we've spoken to your neighbor, Amir. He identified the young man who took your dog as Kevin Dean. Amir also told us that Kevin lives several streets away and often delivers newspapers in the neighborhood. Amir said Kevin's a nice kid—not the kind who gets into trouble. That's why he didn't think twice about the incident until he heard your husband calling for the dog."

"Thanks for the update, Lieutenant! So, did you manage to track down this kid—Kevin? Does he have my dog?"

"We have located the young man in question and contacted his mother. She informed us that he was still out on his rounds and approximately where we can find him. She's also given us written permission to collect the boy and bring him down to the station for an informal interview."

"Well, that's a relief. So what's next?"

"Under the circumstances, since the dog in question belongs to you and ... " he continued pointedly. "Given your recent history concerning a potential murder suspect, we felt there might be a possible connection. Therefore, you may meet us down at the Police Station and quietly sit in on the conversation, as long as you do not ... I repeat—do not interfere with our interview! I hope I've made myself perfectly clear, Mrs. Fine."

"Perfectly, Lieutenant. Thank you so much! I'll be right there."

Bestowing a quick kiss on the hubby, I raced toward my car. I was just about to jump in when I felt a strong warm hand on my shoulder. Paul. Gently removing the keys from my trembling hand he opened the passenger door for me and walked around to the driver's side.

"You're not in any condition to drive yourself. I'll drop you off at the station and pick you up—unless the lieutenant himself decides to detain you or drop you back home."

Grinning nervously, I slapped him lightly the shoulder, then gratefully climbed, into the car.

"Thanks dear, you always come through for me in a pinch!"

* * *

As I entered the recently renovated building, I spotted Lieutenant Kai leading the terrified boy to one of the interview rooms.

Why, he's just a kid, I thought to myself as I followed after them. He can't be more than twelve years old. How on earth did kids like him get roped into doing something so stupid or even dangerous? If he hadn't taken my dog, I almost would have felt sorry for him.

Lieutenant Kai motioned through the glass enclosure for me to enter. Taking a seat near the door of the small room I sat back and listened.

"Some lady gave me five bucks to grab the dog. She said it was a joke. Just wanted to give her friend a scare. Told me the other lady wouldn't mind. They pulled pranks on each other all the time. If I succeeded she'd give me another fiver."

"What did this lady look like, Kevin?" Lieutenant Kai asked the young man as he cowered in front of the large detective.

Kevin continued. "Tall. Skinny. Big dark glasses and a big brown hat— one of those floppy things like my mom wears. The lady had it pulled way down over her face."

"That could be Shelby." I hissed, turning to the Lieutenant.

Glaring at me, Kai paused mid-interview. He returned his attention to Kevin. "Excuse us a moment, Kevin."

A stony expression on his small brown eyes, Kai took me aside. "Mrs. Fine, as you may recall, the condition of your continued presence at this interview was that you would maintain silence here. Watch and listen— nothing more! If you utter one more word, I will have you removed. Have I made myself perfectly clear?"

"Crystal! I stammered, head bowed.

Good! Now, if I may continue? Remember, you are only here because it is your dog who has been taken."

"Sorry, sorry. I'm just so worried."

"I understand." Lieutenant Kai answered in a gentler tone, as if talking to a child. "If you'll just let me do my job we'll get him back. Now may I continue?" He turned back to Kevin. "That's very observant of you, Kevin. Can you remember what the lady was wearing?"

"Yeah. She wore dark sweats. Had long bony fingers too … with these long red nails … kind of like a witch. I almost decided to pass on the deal, but ten dollars is ten dollars. Get a lot of chips and stuff for that."

"So you grabbed the dog. Then what did you do?"

"I did what she told me to—dropped the little guy off in an abandoned warehouse other side of town."

"Can you take us there? It's urgent! The woman is a person of interest in a murder inquiry."

"Ya mean she's a suspect? I sure don't want any part o' that! Yeah, I'll show you."

"Thanks. We'll take my car. It's faster. You can throw your bike in the trunk."

Once again I caught that terrified look in the boy's eyes—as if he was afraid he'd be hauled off to prison any minute now.

"Don't worry, Kevin, You can sit up front in the passenger seat. That way no one will think you're in trouble. Anyone who sees you will just figure you're on a ride-along. OK?"

"Wow! You got one of them souped up cars like on TV?" He asked as they approached the lieutenant's cruiser.

Kai laughed, "Yes we do. Ready?"

"Sure!"

"Then hop in and don't forget your seat belt."

Kai turned to me. "I'm guessing you want to come along as well, Mrs. Fine."

"Damn right I do! Excuse me, I mean 'darn' .... Well, what are we waiting for? I want to get my dog back before that b#*@! poisons him too," I muttered under my breath, so as not to freak out poor Kevin.

Rolling his eyes, Kai opened the back door for me. I climbed in as he went around to the driver's side. Strapping on his own belt, He started his car and took off at a breakneck pace; blue lights flashing. I held on for dear life praying all the way that we'd get there in time.

A few minutes later, Kai pulled into the now darkening parking lot of a small, rectangular, metal roofed, warehouse with scarred, oxidized, aluminum siding. Somewhere in the distance I heard the desperate barking of a dog—my dog. We all got out of the car and headed toward the building. Kevin pointed to a spot toward the back of the building. There was a heavy padlocked metal door. Kai grabbed the pair of metal cutters he had taken from the trunk of his car and made short work of the lock. I dashed in the direction of the now frenzied barking. Lieutenant Kai and the boy following close behind. At the end of a long, muddy gray paneled hall we found the door behind which poor little Streak could be heard panting between hysterical barks. Kai loped in front of me, surprisingly fast for such a big guy. He made short shrift of the wooden door, smashing it open with two kicks of his steel toed shoes. Out dashed Streak right into my arms, frantically licking me.

"How's my little guy," I crooned, hugging his quivering little body close to my own. As I cuddled my poor dog, I quickly put in a call to give Paul the good news.

"Hi dear. We found Streak. He seems to be fine. Not hurt. Just dirty and extremely freaked out. We're on our way home now. Gotta drop the young man off first. See you in a few …."

"Well Mrs. Fine, fortunately for you, we got here in time. No harm done. All that remains at the moment is to decide the fate of this young man. Will you be pressing charges?"

A heartfelt sigh issued from the boy.

I looked at him and back at Lieutenant Kai.

"Seems to me, he's learned his lesson, so I won't be pressing charges—this time."

"I agree."

"However … I believe you owe me some restitution Kevin—that's payback, by the way—for what you put me and my dog through."

"Anything miss! Just tell me what I gotta do. I don't hold with no kidnapping of animals or nothin' else."

"Let me see," I said, keeping the poor kid in suspense. "I think we'll start by having you do some dog sitting and general care-taking of Streak. You can feed him, walk him and clean up after his messes."

"OK miss. You got it. Thanks for not pressing charges. My mother woulda' killed me. Might even of sent me to my dad! No way I could deal with that!"

The Lieutenant turned aside to hide the smile I saw hovering on his lips.

"Good! That's settled then. You can start now by making friends with Streak. And getting him to trust you again. By the way, treats work."

"Thank you miss. Thank you! Don't worry, I promise I won't let you down."

"You'd better not," warned Lieutenant Kai. "Remember, we have a nice warm cell waiting for you if you do."

Kevin looked like he'd rather be anywhere but there.

"Yes, Sir. Got it!"

"Oh, one more thing," the Lieutenant continued gruffly, "we'll need you to work with our facial recognition artist in order to get an actual picture of the person who approached you."

Kevin visibly perked up. "Solid! You mean you're gonna pass the picture around to find out if anybody else seen her?"

Kai, pulled a serious face. "Yes, Kevin. That is the procedure in cases such as this."

"Wow! Just like in the movies. Wait'll I tell my friends!"

Kai coughed. "Are you sure you're going to want to share your part in this?"

Looking down at the ground, Kevin scuffed his sneaker back and forth. "Uhh, maybe not." Brightening up somewhat, he continued. "But it's still exciting! Boy, maybe I'll become a cop some day. Try to help people, like you mister."

Kai smiled, patting the boy's shoulder. "Maybe you will, young man. Maybe you will."

Kevin turned bright red and burst forth with a smile as bright as the sun.

"Gee thanks, mister, 'scuse me, I mean, Lieutenant."

"Good! Now let's get you home to your mother, and Mrs. F. and her dog back to her husband."

We all piled back into the car. Lieutenant Kai headed for our respective homes. He dropped Kevin off first. Pulling Kevin's bike out of the trunk, he passed it over to him, as his mother stood by and watched, arms folded over her ample bosom. A stern, no nonsense look on her face, she met Kevin at the door. I knew he was in for it. Once again I felt kind of sorry for the poor kid. He had a good scold coming, but I hoped that was all he'd get.

Speaking of scolding … from the steely look in the lieutenant's eyes I got the feeling that I was in for it myself. Sure enough he lambasted me big time.

"Well Mrs. Fine. Luckily for the both of you, we were able to get your dog back in one piece. I hope you've learned your lesson as well as that young man we've just dropped off. How many times have I warned you to steer clear and let the police do their job? You and your ladies have repeatedly refused to listen. Remember, next time it could be you or one of them. Is that what you want—to be responsible for their deaths?"

"You're frightening me, Lieutenant."

"I mean to. I repeat, THIS IS NOT A GAME! Lives are at stake. There is a cold-blooded murderer out there who will stop at nothing. This time it was almost your dog. Next time it could very possibly be you."

"But, all I want to do is help." I stammered.

"You can help by letting me know if anything else crops up relating to the murder. That is all! Understood?"

"Yes Lieutenant. Understood. I'll do my best to keep out of it."

"I certainly hope so," he replied. "Well, here we are at your door."

The lieutenant pulled into our driveway, turned off the engine and got out of his car. He came round to let me out just as Paul raised the garage door.

"Thanks for returning my wife and dog, Lieutenant—although I'm tempted to let you keep her and I'll take the dog," he snorted.

Kai let loose with one of his deep throaty laughs. "No thank you, Mr. Fine. She's all yours!" He climbed into his car. I smacked Paul in the arm with my free hand and rewarded Kai with a dirty look. Paul, Streak and I headed into the garage. Lieutenant Kai backed down the driveway, the sound of his laughter echoing through the quiet night.

Henri had been watching through her window, ready to pounce as soon as she saw Lieutenant Kai take off. I had just settled poor Streak in his bed with a doggy treat and his special stuffed toy, when the phone rang. I dashed over to pick it up before it went to voice mail. The first words out of her mouth were: "How's the mutt—I mean your little precious? Did he manage to take a bite out of his captor?"

"Watch it Henri. He may be a mutt, but he's my mutt. He's fine, except for some dirt and the need of a good meal. No, he did not take a bite out of the kid who grabbed him. I actually felt sorry for him. No, not my dog, although that goes without saying. I meant the kid. He really is just an innocent. Someone took unfair advantage of that fact. After the lecture from Lieutenant Kai and seeing his mom's reaction, I don't think we'll have to worry about that young man ever becoming a career criminal. His mom looked like she was ready to take a belt to him. At the very least that poor kid will probably be grounded for a month of Sundays. But the good news is, that after meeting the good lieutenant, he's now thinking of becoming a police officer when he grows up. How's that for a complete 180?"

"Well what d'ya know … but enough of the kid. Just tell me what happened."

I proceeded to do just that ….

* * *

"So where do we go from here? Obviously, we're getting close or whoever it was wouldn't have put the grab on your dog"

"I realize that, as does Lieutenant Kai. However, he warned me off BIG time and in no uncertain terms."

" 'You could be next' he said, 'or one of your ladies'. Really put the scare into me!"

"So, what else is new? It's not like you've ever listened before. Why now?"

"Why now? What if this deranged person decides to go after one of you—just because he or she might be concerned that you know something?" Shaking my head I continued. "I wouldn't want that on my conscience."

"Look. We're all big girls. Been around a long time. I should think we would know what we're doing by now and what we're facing. Besides, don't you want to see that b#*@! caught and tried?"

"If it was her … " I countered.

"How much more proof do you need? You said yourself, the kid described her to a tee."

"Yes, but she was well covered up—in that getup it could have been anyone. The cops need more proof than that. Besides, Lieutenant Kai's pretty much on the ball. For all we know he might have already taken care of that."

Henri back-pedaled. "Well, what about Harry? Don't you want justice for him? What about that big galoot, Norton? He may have been a big old blowhard, but he didn't deserve to go that way either. And while we're at it. What about that cocky little creep, Adolf Betz, who seems to have disappeared into thin air? Seems to me that the cops could use a little help."

"Operative word being 'little', Hen. Lieutenant Kai specifically told me to back off. Just let the police know if anything crops up. That's it! Besides, aren't you the one who's been suggesting that we do just that, in your own 'subtle' way—especially after our unnerving 'visit' with Shelby? Why the sudden change of heart?"

Henri hesitated for a long time before answering—another first for her.

"Why? You want to know why? Because I'm ticked off that's why! First of all, because Harry was murdered. Next, because your dog was pup-napped. And now, everybody's on pins and needles not knowing what's going to happen next. I guess what I'm trying to say is, at last I understand what you meant by needing closure. I need closure!" Having finally run out of steam, I could almost picture her wilting.

"Oh my dear old friend, I was so busy obsessing over everything that I never stopped to think how all this has impacted you."

"And I'm sorry I lost it", she mumbled. "The whole thing's beginning to get to me. I feel so helpless—and you know how I loathe the feeling of not being in control!" Suddenly Henri switched gears. "Look, it's been a long, very trying day for everyone—especially you! You must be beat. How 'bout we discuss this further after we've both had a chance to grab some rest?"

"Now that sounds like a very sensible prescription for our mental and physical health! Right now all I want to do is soak in a long hot bath and then jump into bed. Why don't I call you in the morning?"

"Sounds good. Sleep well."

I smiled into the phone. "You too. Nite, nite."

Hanging up, I threw off my clothes, grabbed a towel and headed for my Jacuzzi, which Paul had already thoughtfully turned on. After soaking for a while I dried off, got into my night clothes and fell into bed, exhausted by the day's events. The last thing I heard as I drifted off was a door softly opening and closing again, followed by a warm little body jumping onto the bed and cuddling up beside me. I was out for the count.

Chapter 21

THE next thing I knew, it was late morning, the sun shining through the curtains and Streak still lying beside me curled up in a furry little ball. Checking my bedside clock, I almost knocked the poor pup off the bed as I sat up abruptly—twelve o'clock. I had slept half the day away! Gently pushing Streak aside, I climbed out of bed, padded over to my husband's office and planted a kiss on his lovely bald pate.

"How are you doing after your misadventure? Did you sleep alright?"

"As a matter of fact I did. First decent sleep I've had since this whole thing started. I must have been truly wasted. Last thing I heard was you letting the lil' guy into the room. Nothing after that. Although ... now that you mention it, I did have some rather strange dreams."

Paul smiled. "More little old men with rheumy eyes?"

"Heaven forfend! No, this was like a sort of fractured montage—all bits and pieces flying around trying to form a whole. And at the center of it was a blurred image of a woman, who I can only imagine, must be one of his daughters."

"What do you mean, daughters? I thought he only had one—a stepdaughter."

"Don't you remember? I told you about the young wife, who was thought dead and got left behind when they shipped Harry home from Nam?"

"Oh yeah. I do recall something of the sort. But what's this about another daughter? You never said anything about her."

"I'm sure I told you. He had a little girl by that young woman, but never knew. In fact, it was only recently that Lien and her daughter, Linh, finally located him. Right before he was killed."

"No. You never told me about it. Remember, you have a habit of thinking you've told me something, but not always doing so."

"Or maybe you don't always listen," I retorted, smacking him gently on his head.

"Look, why don't you just tell me now, and we'll call it a draw?"

"Oh, alright," I pouted, and proceeded to explain the Vietnam connection.

I had just finished bringing Paul up to date when the phone rang. Checking the caller ID, I showed the name to Paul. Shelby. Vehemently shaking his head he mouthed, "Don't answer it!" Paying no attention, I pressed speaker. Probably calling to schedule that coffee date we had discussed during our visit. No. More like checking to see how her attempt at frightening me off had gone. Little did the b#*@! know that our dog was safe and sound; currently sitting at my feet.

"Hi Esme, this is Shelby Browne." Interesting, now that she was in line to inherit, she'd not only taken back Harry's name, but dropped the Grant. "I just wanted to thank you for your thoughtful visit and that delicious noodle pudding. I was wondering if you were available for that coffee date we talked about when you stopped by?"

From the corner of my eye I could see Paul vigorously shaking his head and wildly—for him, gesturing at me to decline the invitation. Ignoring him, I accepted. We decided on the when and where and I hung up. Paul was livid! Grabbing me by the shoulders he exploded. "Are crazy?! Are you deliberately looking to commit *harakiri*? Because that's what you'll be doing if you meet with that nutjob. Haven't you been listening to anything Lieutenant Kai or I have said?"

"What?" I uttered petulantly. "How dangerous can it be sitting in a public place having a cup of coffee or tea?"

"How dangerous?" He sputtered. "Try insanely dangerous. You've seen all those shows where women have been roofied or drugged in some other way. We're dealing with a possible murderer here."

"Oh come on, Paul." I laughed nervously. "Those are all TV shows. That doesn't happen in real life."

"Doesn't it? How about we call and ask your lieutenant friend the percentage?" Paul started to pick up the phone. I gently pulled his hand away.

"I tell you what, Shelby has never met you right? You didn't attend the funeral, and you hardly leave the house when you're in the middle of designing one of your computer programs. Why don't you go to the coffee house either a little before or after I show up? You can look for one of your gourmet roasts and maybe grab a donut or something while you're at it. Then you'll be on hand to bail me out in case anything happens. Which I doubt it will."

"What if one of your friends spots me? Then what?"

"It's a big barn of a place. All you have to do is maintain a low profile. Keep your baseball cap on like most every other guy there. Grab a table behind one of those humongous support beams. You'll be all set."

"You said yourself this is not a TV show, but you're sounding more and more like the heroine of some low budget mystery flick by the minute." He wasn't smiling. I could tell Paul was torn. He didn't want me to go, but he knew what a stubborn fool I could be at times. Almost against his better judgment, he reluctantly agreed to my foolhardy plan. Little did I realize that he had a plan of his own ....

Chapter 22

ADOLF Betz had gone on a drinking binge in celebration of his new-found wealth. Tequila shots were the order of the day and here in Arizona the choice of brands was varied and plentiful. Unfortunately, Betz had forgotten just how deadly tequila could be … how smoothly it went down until suddenly—BAM! It hit like the kick of an irate donkey. Such was the case with the arrogant Mr. Adolf Betz, after he'd abandoned the lemon and salt and started seriously chugging.

"Who needs vodka when ya got this stuff?" he crooned to himself, clutching the bottle close to his chest. "This is the way to go! Sure, it'll knock you on your ass, when you've had a snoot full," he snickered, "but it feels great going down."

With that he took another deep swig and slowly slid off the beat up puce green overstuffed chair he'd been sitting on. He'd almost run out and it was too late to pick up another bottle. Time to hunker down for the night. Between the drinking and the events of the day Betz had overextended himself and was starting to feel the effects of his little treasure hunting excursion.

Wildly swinging the practically empty bottle around, he lurched toward the chair. The only chair in the tiny room, it had seen a lot of similar action through the years. If chairs could talk, this one would have much to say. Tripping on a frayed piece of carpet, he landed with a thud.

"I'm getting too old for this crap," Betz grunted. "But it sure as hell was worth it! I'm rich, rich, RICH! And best of all, I don't even have to split it with that big tub o' lard. Idiot thought he was so smart. Some people are incredibly gullible. Beats me how they manage to hang in for so long with all that stupidity. Think they got all the answers ....

"Well they can't put one over on me." Betz sat up straight, puffing out his scrawny chest. "No one. I mean—NO ONE gets the best of Adolf Betz! Hey! I made a rhyme ...." He slapped his knee, giggling inanely. "Yeah. Everything's all set now. Just gotta take care of that greedy b#*@! and collect the rest of what's comin' to me. Then easy street here I come ...!" he crowed.

Still snickering, Betz unsteadily pulled himself up to his full five-foot four inches. He staggered over to the beat up twin bed, with its torn and stained faux Naugahyde headboard, also puce green. Sitting on the edge of the lumpy mattress, Betz could hear the creaky protest of the worn out old springs as they gave way under his own welter weight frame.

He sat there for a time, just surveying his surroundings: the dim overhead fixture—cracked and decorated with the desiccated remains of long dead insects; tacky curtains of fifty years ago with their chintzy acetate lining, matching bedspread with now murky shades of yet more puce. Shaking his head, sparse ponytail pathetically swinging back and forth, Betz stripped down to faded boxers and greasy sleeveless undershirt and tossed his torn jeans, bolo tie and fringed shirt onto the chair. Peeling off his socks and adding them to the pile, he was suddenly overwhelmed by the combination of booze and too much exertion. He hadn't seen that much action since his early boxing days. Been a world champ back in the day, but nobody remembered that now. Nobody gave a damn! He'd been reduced to bragging about his prowess, bullying and insulting everyone in sight. And what did it get him? Nothing. *Nada ....*

"I'm getting too old for this ... " he muttered to himself again, the full force of the tequila beginning to take hold, as he took yet another swig from the bottle still clutched in his hand. "Empty," he grunted, turning the bottle upside down and tipping it into his mouth to grab the last dregs. "Time was when I could put away a ton of this stuff and then go out and crack heads. Guess that time is long gone." He took one last belt.

Feeling logy and not a little nauseous, Betz got up and headed for the closet sized bathroom. He turned on the tap. Running his hands under the lukewarm water, he shook them out, then shoved a not too clean finger under it as the water trickled out. He began to brush his teeth. Next he splashed his face and dried himself off with a threadbare towel, which had been hanging forlornly on the dented towel holder. Taking one last look at himself, Betz sucked in his aging gut and struck a boxing pose. Smirking, he strutted in front of the filmy mirror, murmuring, "Still got it ain't ya. Sure, a little flab here and there, but what can you expect from a guy pushing seventy-something …."

Cackling dementedly, reminiscent of a victorious hyena, Betz smiled a toothy grin; then began to gag. Wobbling unsteadily, becoming more nauseated by the minute, he staggered toward the bed. Throwing the covers back he was just about to climb in, when he heard a knock at the door. "Who the hell is visiting this time of night! Probably some idiot too drunk to find his own door … " he snarled. Cursing, Betz padded over in his bare feet to answer it, first peering out through the grimy window. He opened the door.

"Oh. It's you …."

Chapter 23

"Oh my God! You're kidding, Chuck! Your guys actually found the missing link, or should I say—skunk?"

Chuck laughed. "They did. And you should say 'skunk', although I could think of a few stronger descriptors."

We were sitting in our second favorite fast food joint. Located just a few doors down from the Robert W. Remington Town Hall. It was the favorite hangout of town workers when they wanted to take a break, or grab a quick cuppa and a delicious homemade muffin or pastry.

Chuck had called me earlier that morning to give me the news. Here I was an hour later anxiously awaiting his explanation. I had called Henri as soon as Chuck rang off, but she'd already taken off for parts unknown. Speaking of which, I was about to hear to what parts unknown Norton had disappeared. Talk about irony. I absentmindedly stirred my mint cocoa, as he relayed the information gleaned from his connections.

"Let's start at the beginning. You understand, I'm acquainted with fire department workers all over the country. It's like a fraternity of sorts. We're all brothers, and some sisters," He grinned. "We take care of each other. The guys in Sedona have a great relationship with the Police Department there and they hear things; added to the fact that the Fire Department has a great bunch of EMTs.

"It seems that just around the time Norton and Betz showed up in the high country, give or take a few days, there was an emergency ambulance call at one of those sleazy pay-by-the-hour motels out in the boonies. It appeared that some guy had drunk himself into a stupor and was found in a coma the next morning by the local cleaning woman. He was lying in a pool of his own vomit, an empty bottle of tequila on the floor beside him and another almost full clutched to his chest. The EMTs rushed him to the hospital and discovered a gash on his lower left arm as well as swelling of the face and throat. The cops were called in, since the circumstances were suspicious. Almost immediately the doctors suspected aconite. They pumped his stomach, cleaned and dressed his wounds and did everything they could to undo the damage, but he was pretty far gone by the time they had reached him."

"How horrible!" I cried. "I wouldn't wish that on my worst enemy. Didn't they also put him on oxygen? I heard that stuff causes breathing difficulties as well. Probably from the swelling in the throat."

"As I told you, they tried everything. You realize that the first thing the EMT guys do, is put the patient on oxygen. Especially where swelling is concerned. As luck would have it, one of my buddies was on call when the call came through. When they entered the room my buddy immediately recognized Betz as the guy I'd been asking about. He phoned me as soon as he got back to the station."

"Do they know what happened to him? Who was responsible? As if I can't guess …."

"Well, here's the thing. When interviewed, the manager and several guests in nearby rooms remembered seeing a tall, skinny girl with a stoop slinking into his room and then leaving again a few minutes later."

My eyes widened. It couldn't be, could it? "What was she wearing?" I asked, practically holding my breath.

"I was just getting to that. She was wearing big dark glasses and a big floppy brown hat pulled down over her face and dark sweats. Her hair was long and stringy, like a cheap wig. She was also described as having 'long bony fingers, with these long red nails'. Sound familiar?"

"You bet it does! That's almost word for word the same description given by that kid, Kevin, who was bribed to snatch my dog after being assured that it was a trick being played by a friend. That can't be a coincidence. We've got to tell the police right away, so they can send a picture."

"Already been done, kiddo. Trust me. Those guys know their business. Want any more info you'll have to ask them directly. But you know what they'll say."

"Yeah, I know. Just smile and nod and tell me it's being taken care of, and they'll let me know as soon as they have any definite information."

"That's right, little lady. My advice? Let them do their job in peace, and put your significant energy to use elsewhere. You've done all you can for now."

"Have I? I'm not so sure ...."

"You have. Now it's time for you to leave it to the professionals. Time and again, they've proven they know what they're doing. Please! Trust me on this."

"I guess you're right, Chuck. That's what everyone from the police on, down to my own husband, keeps telling me. My ladies and I should stick to belly dancing and mind our own business. But this is my business," I sobbed. "You weren't there. I was ...."

* * *

When I got home I headed straight to my husband's office. The whole gruesome tale came spilling out—kind of like the vomit I pictured when Chuck reported the latest discovery made by his friendly connections.

Betz might have been a vile piece of work and possibly even a murderer; but the picture of that man writhing in pain, was indelibly etched in my brain—right next to poor dead Harrold Browne.

* * *

That night I couldn't fall asleep. When I finally did, more nightmares assaulted my poor overloaded brain. No more weird little creatures. This time Betz himself paid me a visit—one I happily could have lived without. There he was writhing in agony, spittle running down a mouth twisted, stomach distended; his whole body swollen by the poison invading it. Positively revolting!

I sat up trying to dispel the vision. Groggily Paul turned and enveloped me in his strong arms; cradling me as if a baby. "Another bad dream?"

"Yeah," I sobbed, hiccuping. "The worst! This time it was Betz. Slowly, painfully dying in that motel room. I felt like I was there, watching the whole thing. It was absolutely horrible!"

Hugging me closer, Paul murmured, "It's alright now. There's no one else here but you and me. As he said this a small wet nose protruded from underneath the covers and began to lick my tear stained face. Laughing despite myself, I pulled the lil' guy toward me.

Patting the dog, Paul grinned. "And let's not forget Streak."

I laughed again. "I'm better now, thanks to you two."

"Good. Think you can get back to sleep? Want me to bring you a glass of water—or maybe something a little stronger?"

"No, I just want to crash." I kissed him and, cuddling Streak, I rolled over on my side. Soon I was out like the proverbial light.

Chapter 24

Thursday afternoon. Another week had gone by and once more it was again time for Bellyrobics class. I was still reeling from the ordeal of my dog's kidnapping, not to mention the further revelations Chuck had socked me with regarding the attempted murder of Adolf Betz by the same disguised woman! I was too tired and way too stressed out to deal with anything, let alone get psyched up for class. However, as every good teacher and performer knows—the show must go on. And so it was that I managed to drag myself out of my warm, comfy, cozy bed and get ready to take on the day.

No sooner had I arrived, when once again I was surrounded by my ladies. They had gotten the lowdown from Henri and Flor about the dog-napping of poor Streak.

"Don't worry girls, I'm alright. It's just that the consequences resulting from our snooping have now literally hit home. As I tried to tell you last week, Lieutenant Kai and all the other naysayers were right. This has definitely been a dangerous game we've been playing. Last week, I found out just how dangerous it can be. You've already heard that my dog was taken. What you might not have heard is that Lieutenant Kai thinks it was a warning for me to back off." This announcement was followed by a chorus of groans and shocked outcries.

"Fortunately, a very observant young neighbor witnessed the whole incident and had the presence of mind to tell Lieutenant Kai, when he and Officer O'Reilly answered the call. They've now almost conclusively identified the person behind the dog-napping. However, the police are keeping the name of the perpetrator and the witness under wraps until they have tied up all the loose ends."

"What loose ends?" Flor called out.

"I'll bet the loose ends are the murder of Harry and Norton!" Mel said.

"That may or may not be. Either way, I'm not at liberty to comment at this time. Remember, anyone who would go to the extreme of kidnapping a dog on top of committing murder, would not hesitate to strike again. I'm just lucky that we found the little guy before it was too late! At this point the murderer or murderers have absolutely nothing to lose, and I don't want to put anyone else in harm's way. That being said I'm calling a moratorium on anymore sleuthing from any of you!"

"And what about you?" Marina asked archly.

"That includes me as well." I answered, mentally crossing my fingers and adding a "pooh, pooh" for good measure.

Henri gave me one of her "yeah right" looks. Hey, two could play that game, I thought, as I answered her with an innocent wide-eyed look. Of course, she wasn't buying any of it. Have I already mentioned that the woman knows me too well?

Chapter 25

I had agreed to meet Shelby at 2 o'clock, after the lunch rush at Flo's Coffee Hut in downtown Leicester. A landmark building, Flo's had been around as long as I could remember—at least sixty years. Wedged in between Jo Ah Korean Restaurant, another one of my faves, and an antiques mall, Flo's had a weathered gray brick facade. Inside was the classic etched metal ceiling which was supported by a number of beams spread throughout the building. Over-stuffed sofas, and an eclectic variety of tables and chairs were strewn throughout the space. The walls were a very pale gray, almost white. They were decorated with all manner of coffee themed posters and sculptures. One whole wall was devoted to coffee pots, mugs and other paraphernalia, both contemporary and vintage.

I entered the building and waved to various acquaintances. Paul had already made himself comfortable behind one of the pillars, his head buried in his laptop. Catching his eye, I went and placed my order for an old favorite, Lady Grey Tea, just enough bite for a winter day, and a mocha almond biscotti. Might as well indulge while I waited. Yum! I took my goodies over to a corner table in the window nook at the front of the coffeehouse. There I could wait for Shelby and engage in the time honored pastime of watching people as they came and went.

I hadn't been there more than five minutes when Shelby entered, dressed to kill. Oops, wrong choice of words. She wore a hunter green car coat with a red and black Tartan scarf and a red beret to match. Thigh high black leather boots over black leather leggings completed the outfit. I waved to her and she slithered over, undulating as she went. Would've made a great belly dancer with those moves. She removed her coat and placed it on the back of the chair, revealing a black angora tunic.

"So glad you had time to meet with your busy schedule and all," she purred, like a cat who'd just trapped a mouse and was playing with it. I got the feeling that I was the mouse. Out of the corner of my eye, I sought out my husband. Still, there and still working on his laptop. I gave an inward sigh of relief and sat back to enjoy my tea.

"I see you've already settled in. I'll just grab myself a cup of coffee and join you. Then we can get to know each other better."

As Shelby went to over to place her order, I caught Paul's eye once again. I could barely make out the warning he mouthed, as Shelby headed back to the table.

"Isn't this nice," she said. "Good company and a warm drink on a cold winter's day."

"Yes. I just love this place! You never know who you're going to run into. I often come here with one or more of my students after class."

"That's right. You teach at the Senior Center where dad used to hang out. I believe you said you teach belly dancing. Boy, would I love to take your class, if I was older!" she continued, doing a little figure eight in her seat."

"I can see that you'd be a natural." I replied. "You should check out my regular adult class sometime."

"Maybe I will someday—if you're still teaching, that is …."

Gulp.

All of a sudden, Shelby's face took on a solemn expression.

"Are you alright?" I asked.

"Yes, I'm fine. I just remembered that you also mentioned being the one who found poor dad when you and your students were heading up to class. It must have been terrible for you!" She closed her eyes and shivered. Boy, either I was much mistaken to suspect her or she was one heck of an actor—and believe me, I've met quite a few in my day.

Time for the first test. Patting her slim, long fingered hand, with blood-red nails to match, I replied, "It was absolutely horrible! You see, I literally tripped over your poor dead father as I was going up the stairs. I'll remember those staring eyes and pained expression the rest of my life. I still have nightmares about it." As I finished my narrative, Shelby noticeably flinched. Did I detect a slight note of guilt and possibly even a little regret in that gesture? I certainly hoped so. Even a narcissist like her might have a conscience. After all, she didn't actually hurt my dog, though I'll probably never know what she might have done if we hadn't rescued my little guy in time. Now it was my turn to shiver, but I had to see this charade through to the end. Hopefully not mine.

"Enough about me, Shelby. How are you holding up after your ordeal? I know how close you became when you and Harry finally reconnected. It must have been quite a shock for you when you found out he had a whole other family—and in the middle of the funeral yet. I don't know how you managed to stay calm." I could see that last jab had gotten to her. Those scarlet nailed fingers of hers, clenched so hard, they left marks on the inside of her palms.

"Yes. Quite a shock. You see, my mother never mentioned that dad had been married before. I had no idea that I had an older sister!" Just as Shelby was about to continue, we were accosted by Charlotte Rae and Arne, who had entered and were heading our way. They had already conveyed their condolences to Shelby at the luncheon, so introductions weren't necessary. Having heard about Streak during dance class, they came rushing over to envelop me in a group hug.

"We are so glad you got your po' lil' doggie back unharmed!" declared Charlotte Rae. "Ah sure hope they find who did it."

"As do I." I heaved a sigh. Shelby wasn't the only accomplished actress in this burg.

Arne echoed the sentiment. "Yeah. It's a sad day when a little dog is not even safe in his own yard. Don't you agree?" she asked turning to Shelby.

The look on Shelby's perfectly made up, peaches and cream complexion, was absolutely priceless! A mixture of emotions flashed across her face like one of those old time flickers, as she almost tipped over her coffee cup. Then opening wide, her large green cat's eyes, she replied. "Yes. It must be a terrible feeling, wondering, worrying about your poor little dog."

"Well we ought to be going. We'll leave you to your conversation. Nice to meet you again under happier circumstances, Shelby," Arne said.

"Yes, mighty nice to see you again, Miss Shelby," Charlotte Rae drawled.

"A pleasure to see you as well."

I said goodbye to the ladies and they headed over to the counter. After polishing off the rest of my biscotti, I reached for my tea and took a long sip, but by now it had cooled off and tasted a little bitter, the bergamot scented leaves had probably floated to the bottom of the mug.

"Sorry for the interruption, Shelby. My ladies can be a bit overwhelming at times."

"Think nothing of it. I can tell they really love you."

"Well, it's a mutual admiration society. They are quite amazing for their age."

"But, what's this about your dog? I believe you mentioned that you have a little terrier-cross. Did something happen to him?"

"Someone must have left the gate ajar by accident and the little guy made his escape. They finally found him and he's back home now. Safe and sound."

"Oh. That's good. It would be such a pity if he had fallen into the wrong hands. You know there are some ruthless people out there. They kidnap dogs and use them for practice training dogs in the illegal dog fight trade."

I flinched ever so slightly. "Well, as they say, all's well that ends well and our little guy is home sleeping it off with his daddy. Speaking of which," I consulted my Fitbit, "it's getting late and I'd better get a move on. Got another class to teach tonight."

"Why don't you stay a few minutes and finish your tea?"

"That's OK. I'll just take it with me. I've got to make a quick stop at the library and I can toss the cup out when I'm done." I stood up, suddenly feeling a little woozy. "Didn't get much sleep last night and sometimes I get a little logy by this time of day. The fresh air will take care of that." I put on my coat, wrapped my scarf around my neck and slapped my hat on my head. Grabbing gloves and tea, I said goodbye and headed for the door, Shelby's eyes following my progress as I stepped out into the brisk winter air. Still feeling quite dizzy, I managed to make it across the busy street. Suddenly my legs gave out from under me ....

Chapter 26

I woke up in a cold sweat. Those pesky little rheumy-eyed nightmare creatures were giving me the heebie-jeebies again. Only this time, they morphed into cackling little green-eyed witches, sporting Tartan plaid and scarlet red claws. Shelby! Suddenly, I remembered. Charlotte Rae and Arne had grabbed my attention. After they left, I finished my biscotti, planning on washing it down with my tea. The tea that had gone cold and developed a slightly bitter taste. I thought that was just the bergamot collecting at the bottom. Shelby had managed to spike my tea, with what I could only assume were some very potent tranquilizers. Thank goodness for my overly sensitive taste buds, or they might be scraping me off the pavement by now! Lying there, my thoughts all in a jumble, slowly opening my eyes, I looked up, my head swimming. Closed my eyes again, hoping the dizziness would subside.

Suddenly I felt a giant shadow towering over me, blocking the sunlight. Through my half closed eyes I could see Lieutenant Kai accompanied by Junior. Where had they come from? Opening my eyes a little wider I found myself surrounded by worried faces, not the least of whom were Henri and my own dear Paul. Hoarsely whispering his name I tried to get up, but found myself gently being pushed back down after another set of hands placed a pillow under my head and wrapped me in a warm fuzzy white blanket. By now Paul had found his way to one side of me while Henri commandeered the other.

"I told you this was a crazy stupid idea," she muttered gruffly in a voice that could barely conceal her emotions. Paul stroked my sodden locks and kissed my forehead, deep concern in his beautiful blue-gray eyes. Trying to keep it light he said, "So much for having your back; Here you are flat on it in the middle of the street. Told you your cockeyed plan wouldn't work." Taking my hand in one of his warm, strong ones, he continued stroking my hair, with the other.

"Yeah, you were right—as usual." I murmured weakly. "I think, I've finally learned my lesson."

"I hope you mean that. Although knowing you, I wouldn't count on it. But this isn't the time for a discussion. You need to get whatever crap that b#*@! hit you with out of your system and concentrate on recuperating. You've given us all quite a scare. Listen, Rich and the EMTs are on the way. Think you can stay put?"

"And awake!" Henri growled.

"And awake!" My husband echoed. Try not to drop off til they get here."

"I'll try. Somehow, I don't think I have a choice, do I?"

"Ya think?" he smirked, mimicking me.

In the background I heard the sound of engines roaring, horns blaring, as our old friend Rich and his trusty crew pulled up. Still holding tightly to my hand, Paul stepped back to let them through. Van doors opened and the crew burst out through the back of the vehicle, dragging a stretcher with them. Rich led the way. Kneeling, he checked my pulse. Lifting first the left lid, then the right, he shone a light in each of my eyes. Then he stepped aside as two techs gently lifted me onto the stretcher. Talk about embarrassing. Good thing I was wearing pants and my decent undies.

In my fuzzy brain, I still recalled Mom pooh poohing as she told me: "Always make sure you're wearing clean underwear when you go out. You never know when you may have an accident." Talk about one heck of an understatement! If only my dear, departed Mom could see me now. She would have had a minor angina attack! Giggling idiotically, I murmured under my breath, "I took your advice mommy." The techs covered me up once again and tied me to the stretcher. They wheeled it over to the ambulance, Paul still maintaining his grip. I slid open my eyes. There was that large shadow again, accompanied by a much smaller, thinner one. Lieutenant Kai, leaned towards me as they prepared to settle me in.

"That was very brave, but extremely foolish of you, Mrs. Fine."

"Please, call me Esme" I said, remembering my manners despite the predicament I was in. Besides, I could already feel a little of the dizziness dissipating as I spoke.

"Very well … Esme. If we hadn't been on hand, you'd have probably joined Mr Browne in the hereafter. Good thing we were warned ahead of time what you were up to."

"I bristled, glaring at my darling duplicitous husband. "You told them what I had planned, didn't you?"

"Yes. I did. You think I'm crazy too? And with good reason as it turns out."

At this point, Lieutenant Kai, stepped in. "Actually, Mrs Fine … Esme. Your husband was not the first to warn us of your ill-advised plan." He pointed to Henri. "It seems your partner in crime, if you'll pardon the expression, was feeling rather … how shall I put it?"

"Crazy! Guilty! Try whacked out crazy guilty!" Henri brayed over the noise of the crowd. "Yes, I told him your whole lunatic plan—including the part where we even recruited poor Lien and her daughter to do some detecting. And you know what? I'd do it again!" Continuing her tirade, "I'd do it all again, because I love you for all your craziness. We all do," she said pointing to the others. "That's just who you are. But I'm getting the signal from Rich Isaacs and the Big Guy, that it's time to get you to the hospital." Our friend Rich approached Paul as he climbed up beside me. "I'm sorry, Paul. You know you're not supposed to ride along in the back, unless the patient has special needs." Grabbing Paul's hand and holding on for dear life, I feebly snapped at our long time friend.

"Listen, Rich, you know me how long now? I think you'll agree that I am a person with special needs and right now I needs my husband. I'm having a hard enough time keeping it together," Finally running out of steam I sank back into the confines of the stretcher and closed my eyes. Paul winked at Rich, who shrugged his defeat. Smiling he said. "OK. You win. Take a seat next to your wife."

"Thanks, Rich!" I smiled, eyes still closed, death grip on Paul easing up a bit. Rich climbed up beside us. His partner did one last check, having ascertained from my behavior, that I was in no immediate danger. Shutting the back doors of the ambulance, his partner signaled to the driver to take off, which she did at a more sedate pace, red and blue lights blinking away. His partner remained behind to speak with Lieutenant Kai.

I could hear Henri's voice echoing above the crowd and pictured her waving wildly, along with Charlotte Rae, Arne and the rest of my lovely ladies, who had joined the throng. You'd think we were going on a nice long trip, rather than a not so nice trip to the hospital.

It had been quite a day, and I was totally spent, thanks to a little help from that evil witch, Shelby. I took a deep revitalizing breath. Well at least we've got her dead to rights this time. That b#*@! was going to be going away for a very long time .... And my crew and I had helped!

As we sped off, I turned to Paul. "Got a tissue, dear? My mascara's running."

Chapter 27

O N a warm spring day with the sun shining down, we all gathered together in the Senior Center's cozy library for the final chapter of the murder, which had been dubbed, "The Body in the Basement." Lieutenant Kai was there accompanied by his trusty young assistant, Officer James O'Reilly (AKA: Junior). The Lieutenant had kindly agreed to bring us up to date on the events of the past few weeks, in recognition of the important role my ladies and other cohorts had played in capturing a cold, calculating murderer.

He began by stating that this had been one of the strangest cases he'd ever come across.

"This case has had more twists and turns and false leads than an old English maze. However, thanks to your help—and often, interference, we have been able to catch the murderer of Harrold Browne and accessory to the murder of Norton Jones." An audible gasp rose from the group, mine among the loudest. Lieutenant Kai grinned, looking right at me.

"Surprised, Mrs. Fine? That's one you didn't expect, did you?"

Laughing self-consciously, I graciously responded. "You've got me there, Lieutenant. I certainly didn't see that one coming, although to be honest, I kind of wondered why the murderer changed his or her MO for that one. I never realized that they were working in tandem. Bravo Lieutenant! Please enlighten us."

"Thank you," he smiled. "With your permission I shall continue.

"As I have already stated, our perpetrator was the mastermind as well as accessory to Norton Jones' murder, although she didn't actually wield the hammer. However, she did try hard to help Adolf Betz meet his maker. Since he was already in a drunken stupor, she merely helped him along with a small but potentially lethal dose of aconite slipped into his bottle of tequila, while he was out of commission. She also rubbed some of the stuff into a cut on his hand for good measure. We'll probably learn more from her fellow accomplice, Betz, when and if he comes out of his coma."

"Boy, that was one busy little b#*@!!" Henri muttered loud enough for all to hear.

Lieutenant Kai soldiered on. "As you may have heard, Mr. Betz has already been arrested and taken into custody for blackmail, hindering an investigation, and murder—the murder of Mr. Norton Jones. Mr Jones' body was finally found by the local police. He'd been dumped in a mine trolley and pushed deep into the bowels of the mine. DNA samples were extracted from the vehicle and the victim's body. Several hairs were found which proved identical to those of Betz. The prevailing theory is that Betz was rather careless in his disposal of Jones. Obviously, Betz never expected the body to be found. Betz, himself, is currently under protective custody in the hospital." An announcement which was greeted by cheers and roars of approval from all those attending, myself included.

"So, the little worm finally got his comeuppance did he?" Henri crowed. "By the way, where does the swine fit in with the murder of Harry in the first place?"

"An excellent question, Mrs. Hirshfeld. It turns out that Mr. Betz actually caught our murderer in the act of slipping her stepfather a vial of capsules, telling him they were special vitamins. He didn't quite realize what he'd seen until he heard about Mr. Browne's murder. He put two and two together and decided to blackmail her. He already knew about the map and cache of coins. Inadvertently, he'd heard Harry telling Jones about it and realized that Grant probably knew as well. He wanted a share of the takings. Thought he could make a deal with Grant. That's when he sealed his own fate. She knew Betz couldn't be trusted. She also knew that Norton Jones would have to be taken out of the picture as well. So she pretended to make a deal with Betz to split everything 50/50 if he could hasten Norton's demise."

"No honor among thieves," Melisande hooted.

"Yeah! Bet she hauled ass and followed him to make sure!" shouted Flor.

"And you'd be right ladies. If you'll cast your minds back to the kidnapping of Mrs. Fine's dog, Streak, you may recall that we were given a good description of the woman involved. As you know she had disguised herself very well, so we could not get definitive ID on her. However, she made one very big mistake."

Somewhere in the background a small, sweet voice chimed in. Our newbie, Jayne. "Yes, she chose the wrong person to mess with."

Much to my chagrin, more roars of approval soared into the air as Lieutenant Kai raised his hands for silence.

"Thank you madam. Now, if you'll allow me, I'll let Officer O'Reilly explain, since it was his quick thinking that helped catch the murderer."

Officer Jimmy stepped forward. "Well it was like this. It occurred to me that the murderer was just arrogant enough to think that her disguise had served her well the first time, so she figured she'd use it again. I suggested that we show the composite picture to the police handling the attempted murder of Adolf Betz. They in turn showed it to the night manager and several people staying at the motel where he was holed up. They identified her as a woman who was seen sneaking into his room and leaving a few minutes later."

"Bam! Shouted Henri. "That'll learn the b#*@! to mess with the cops!"

"Uh. Thanks for the kudos," the lieutenant replied, as poor Jimmy backed off, breathing an audible sigh of relief. "I would appreciate it if you could control your enthusiasm until we have finished."

"Well, how about getting to it faster!" Henri barked. "None of us are getting any younger you know. Except maybe Officer O'Reilly over there," she added, as poor Jimmy turned an alarming shade of red. This was followed by an array of titters, giggles, several groans and more cheers. Poor Lieutenant Kai. I sure wouldn't want to play to this audience right now.

Shaking his head, Lieutenant Kai continued. "This whole case hinged on who had motive enough to want Mr. Browne permanently out of the picture and how the murder was accomplished. You all know that we already had the when. What remained was where and how. The where was easy. However, most baffling was the how. How did the murderer manage to have a solid alibi during the time of Mr. Browne's death?"

"And it almost worked too!" Flor, yelled out, unable to resist.

"Flor," I cautioned, "please let Lieutenant Kai finish. There'll be plenty of time for comments and further clarification later."

"Oh, alright. Sorry for the interruption, big guy," she grumbled sitting back. Coughing to conceal his laughter, Lieutenant Kai continued.

"Thank you, Mrs. Ruiz. As I was saying, we were somewhat stymied as to how Mr. Browne could make it to the stairs of the Senior Center before succumbing to the poison. This was cleared up when the medical examiner discovered remnants of a doctored capsule in Mr. Browne's system, which also contained traces of aloe, ground up apples seeds and peach pits."

"Boy, that b#*@! wasn't taking any chances," Henri muttered *sotto voce*.

Ignoring her comment, Kai continued. "That mixture, added to a capsule, would take time to melt before releasing its lethal contents. Time enough for the killer to make sure he/she had an iron clad alibi. When Officer O'Reilly searched Mr. Browne's apartment, he discovered a bottle of probiotic capsules in the medicine cabinet, several of which had also been tampered with. It was just a matter of time before Harrold would take the lethal dose. Furthermore, after a thorough search of the various suspects' homes, we found a few grains of ground up peach pit and several apple seeds stuck in the cracks of the floor under a kitchen counter. The murderer must have missed them when cleaning up. Unfortunately, her greed took over and she decided to speed things up. This was where she made her first mistake. She was seen, as we've already mentioned, by the unscrupulous Adolf Betz."

Henri, turned to the detectives. "Look, Lieutenant, we all know who committed these terrible crimes and basically why. Can you please cut to the chase and name some names? It might keep the confusion to a minimum."

"Alright," answered Lieutenant Kai. " I have already named the accomplice and murderer of Norton Jones. Since the newspapers have been having a field day with this story and the perpetrator of these crimes has already confessed, it will no longer prejudice the case if I mention her by name—Ms. Shelby Grant Browne.

"Let's begin with a quick summary of her background and how Ms. Browne came to cross paths with the victim and later, her co-conspirator. As you all know, Shelby Grant is Mr. Browne's stepdaughter. Her full name is Shelby Grant Browne. However, she had dropped the Browne when her mother left her second husband for a more well-heeled businessman, one Mr. Jared M. Stevens, taking her children with her. Having moved cross-country, the children completely lost touch with their stepfather. Until one day, quite by chance, Ms. Grant, as she was now called, ran into him while running a Vitamin and Health Food booth during the Healthy Living Fair at the Leicester Senior Center. At this point I should mention," pointedly glancing my way, "several of you had already figured out that Shelby, a Paraprofessional and herbalist, is very knowledgeable about poisons. She and Harry began to talk. Soon, Shelby put two and two together and realized that she was talking to her long-lost stepfather. Figuring that he was an easy mark, she told him who she was and began to insinuate herself into his life once more. Only this time, she had an ulterior motive. Harry had shown Ms. Grant his cache of coins shortly after they reconnected …."

"And don't y'all forget those lovely gemstones!" Leave it to our resident southern belle to remember that little tidbit ….

"Thank you, Ms. Knowles."

"That's 'Mrs', honey."

"Excuse me …," Kai coughed, "Mrs. Knowles. As I was about to add, Ms. Grant did not know where he kept his valuables. However, she had already pegged Mr. Browne as being something of a rich eccentric and figured that he probably just left them lying around his apartment. Being a rather shrewd and calculating young woman, Ms. Grant decided to take advantage of the situation and during one of her visits to Harry's place, she wheedled the old man into making her a gift of some of them. Thrilled to have her back in his life, Harry agreed."

"Unfortunately, Ms. Grant got greedy and decided she wanted it all. You see, she had discovered something that no one else was privy to—except of course, Harrold Browne's lawyer. Mr Browne had never changed his will. Shelby and her brother were still sole heirs to what turned out to be a rather sizable fortune."

An audible intake of breath was heard in the silence as everyone present took in the significance of this bombshell. Poor, shabby, little Harry Browne a millionaire? It was absolutely beyond comprehension.

Irrepressible, Henri broke in yet again. "What about the brother? Didn't she realize she'd have to share? And believe me, that woman does not like to share!"

"Good question, Mrs. Hirshfeld. We managed to contact the brother, Richard, who still goes by the name of Browne. He confirmed that there had been a permanent estrangement between Mrs. Stevens, AKA: Grant Browne, and her two offspring. He further stated that he had not seen or heard from either his mother or sister in years and had no desire to resume any relationship with them."

Kai nodded to Junior, who reached into his pocket, pulled out his trusty notepad and read. "His exact words were:"

> Those two are cut from the same defective cloth. They would stop at nothing to get what they want and I don't need that kind of bilge in my life. I have a beautiful wife, two great kids and a job that I love. I have no need for that poor old man's money. Shelby's welcome to it all and I hope she chokes on it!

Lieutenant Kai resumed the narrative. "Mr Richard Browne currently resides in Silicon Valley and is financially very sound. And before you ask, the younger Mr. Browne has no motive for wanting to do away with his stepfather. He didn't even know that he had been named in his will. Most important of all, Richard Browne has been nowhere in New England for the past two years, so it would have been almost impossible for him to doctor his stepfather's capsules. Getting back to the subject at hand, once again Ms. Grant took advantage of the situation, playing upon Mr. Browne's need for companionship, and in particular, that of a family member."

"More like preyed on." Henri snorted. "I always thought that young woman had the temperament and appearance of a barracuda."

"Henri, please let the lieutenant continue. You can comment when he's finished."

"Thank you, Mrs. Fine. Once we discovered Ms. Grant—now Grant-Browne's connection and subsequent involvement, the rest of the pieces fell into place.

"Any questions?"

"I have one!" I blurted out jumping up. "How long have your people been keeping tabs on me?"

Controlling the urge to smile, Lieutenant Kai replied. "Well, Mrs. Fine, knowing your propensity to play sleuth, one or more of our detectives have been keeping track of you on and off since this investigation began. We knew sooner or later you might get in over your head. And before you ream me out, I will admit that you and your ladies have been helpful, but you have also made it difficult for us to do our job and keep you out of trouble at the same time."

I sat back down, well and truly put in my place, a lovely shade of pink creeping up my face. This elicited a number of giggles, guffaws and one big cheer from my ladies.

"Well, if there are no other questions, I'll end on this note. Suffice to say, we now have Ms. Shelby Grant Browne dead to rights. It remains for the court and a jury to decide her fate."

At this point, Marina, who had quietly been listening in the back of the room, now stood up. All heads turned as she walked to the front.

"Actually, there is one more very important observation to come out of this tragedy," she paused taking a deep breath. An expectant silence engulfed the room as she slowly exhaled.

"As you all know, sadly, this murder has been dubbed 'The Body in the Basement' and stirred up many feelings. We have all heard about the gold coins that set the whole train of events in motion. However, there seems to be a larger implication and a lesson to be learned here. I can only quote what one desolate wife said when she hid a treasure map back in the mid nineteenth century. It was 'blood money' and she wanted nothing to do with it. She was right. One might even say the coins are cursed.

"How many lives were lost as those tainted coins slowly made their way into the pockets of Harrold Browne? Just about everyone that we know who has come into contact with those coins has died a violent death. First, it was the sailors; next, the stagecoach robbers. Even the innocent have met with an untimely end after coming in contact with them. Poor young Joe Bommarito wore one of the coins around his neck, a coin that his grandfather had given him to wear for good luck. The irony of it. Our own Harry died a horrible death all because of someone else's greed."

"That would be several 'someone else's' …," Rosemary added.

Marina paused to catch her breath. "And what of the perpetrator of all this, Shelby? She'll probably spend the rest of her life in prison. Who knows how many lives have been ruined or lost along the way? Lives that we know nothing about. I truly believe that this curse will not be broken until the coins are returned where they belong."

All at once the room erupted into wild applause as Marina returned to her seat.

Tears in my eyes, I rose and gave her a big hug. I thanked everyone for their help and support in solving this horrendous crime. Hand outstretched, I walked over to Lieutenant Kai. Grabbing his great paw I was about to shake it, changed my mind and gave the shocked Lieutenant a grateful hug. His jaw dropped, then suddenly he let loose with one of his booming laughs.

Waiting quietly in "the wings," my husband, Paul, approached, carrying little Streak in his arms. My pup had been granted a dispensation to the "no dogs allowed" rule because of the part he had played in the apprehension of the murderer of Harry Browne. Paul endowed me with a bear hug of his own, while the little guy smothered me in sloppy doggy kisses.

Epilogue

"ALL's well that ends well" wrote the Bard. Leicester is still the "City with Village Charm." The Senior Center is still the same, despite the excitement of several months ago. The members are back to doing their usual thing and the worst problem that has cropped up, since spring reared its lovely head, is that several of the garden club members had a set-to with the garden plot owners over one very desirable plot. Needless to say, Director Claudia has succeeded in negotiating the peace. Like Solomon, she has split the plot into two identical parcels; but unlike the wise King, this split has met with everybody's approval. My dear friend and boss, Tara at the Board of Ed., is still keeping me busy. Her wonderful assistant, Lisa, is still keeping me updated and on schedule with my many classes. And our Arne is officially keeping company with Thom.

Oh. I almost forgot one momentous piece of news! A big event has been scheduled to take place at the Senior Center early this summer. The wedding of the no longer hapless Lien Sterling (formerly Lien Browne), who now sports a stylish bob, and her very own Prince Charming—Chuck Shackleton! All of our members, their families and special friends have been invited. Special guest of honor is Lieutenant Ralph Kai and Officer James O' Reilly.

Guess who's giving away the bride?

But that's a story for another time ....

Esme's recipes

Grandma's Applesauce Kugel*

Ingredients
- 1 Package medium or wide noodles cooked al dente
- 4 Eggs
- 1/2 Cup Oil
- 2 cups Applesauce, unsweetened
- 1/2 Teaspoon Cinnamon

Topping
- 1 to 2 Tablespoons unsalted butter
- Cinnamon to taste

Directions
- Preheat oven to 350 degrees.
- Grease 9x13 glass casserole dish (I use olive oil spray, but real unsweetened melted butter also works)
- Combine noodles, eggs, oil, applesauce, raisins and cinnamon.
- Mix well. Pour into dish.

Topping
- Lightly mix butter and cinnamon together to achieve a crumbly texture.
- Spread over kugel.

Bake 45 Minutes.

* Note: For pareve (non-dairy) Kugel leave out butter or use vegan butter.

Serves 8 to 10

Esme's Healthier Noodle Kugel

Ingredients
- 1 Bag. Medium or wide noodles cooked al dente
- 4 Eggs
- 1/4 Lb. Melted butter
- 1/2 Lb. Cottage cheese (Small curd or country style)
- 1/2 Lb Cream cheese, Neufchatel or Part Skim Ricotta
- 1/2 Pint Greek Yogurt (may also use sour cream or combination of the two)
- 1/3 Cup Sugar
- 1 Teaspoon Vanilla
- 1/2 Teaspoon Lemon Juice

Topping
- 1 Cup Crushed Cornflakes, Kashi Mixed Grain Flakes or Special K
- 4 Tablespoons unsalted butter
- Cinnamon and sugar to taste

Directions
- Preheat oven to 350 degrees.
- Grease 9x13 glass casserole dish (I use olive oil spray, but real unsweetened melted butter also works).
- Combine all ingredients in blender or mixing bowl and beat until smooth.
- Mix in noodles. Pour into dish.

Topping
- Lightly mix butter, cinnamon, sugar and crumbs together to achieve a crumbly texture.
- Sprinkle on top of kugel.

Bake 45 minutes or until light golden brown on top.

Serves 8 to 10

Esme's Pineapple Kugel*

Ingredients
- 1 Package wide noodles cooked al dente
- 4 Eggs
- 1/2 Cup Oil
- 2 Cups crushed pineapple in own juice, drained (save 1/4 to 1/2 cup)
- 1/2 Teaspoon Cinnamon
- 1/2 to 3/4 Cup raisins (Your choice) Optional

Topping
- 1 to 2 Tablespoons unsalted butter
- Cinnamon to taste
- Optional: 1/2 Cup Kashi Mixed Grain Flakes, Special K or Corn Flakes. All crushed

Directions
- Preheat oven to 350 degrees.
- Grease 9x13 glass casserole dish (I use olive oil spray, but real unsweetened melted butter also works).
- Combine noodles, eggs, oil, pineapple, juice and cinnamon.
- Mix well. Pour into dish.

Topping
- Lightly mix butter, crumbs and cinnamon together to achieve a crumbly texture.
- Spread over kugel.

Bake 45 Minutes or until golden brown.

* Note: For pareve (non-dairy) use pareve/vegan blend instead of butter.

Serves 8 to 10.

Acknowledgments

Except for several people, who know who they are, the characters in my story are completely fictional, as is the story itself. The New England town Leicester, Connecticut exists only in my imagination. However, it is inspired by my own beautiful town of Manchester, Connecticut—the original "City with Village Charm."

Although the characters are fictional, the Vietnam skirmishes listed were not. Tragically, they actually occurred on the dates and times noted

I would like to thank my two devoted friends and editors for helping me whip this story into shape:

Debye Lurie who spent endless hours on the phone going through the story word by word.

Lynn Cohen who spent hours proof reading the galley and advising on the final manuscript.

Thanks also to Professor Steve (Tox Doc) Cohen, Toxicologist, for his advice on poisons and other toxic substances; and my good friend, Rick Berkman, who advised me on EMT protocol.

A big shout out and thanks to Tamara Womack-Speaks for her marvelous cover design! Thanks also to her terrific secretary, Liz Baerga-Dones, who was always there to help and keep me on target with all my classes.

Most of all, LOVE and THANKS to my very own Super-techie husband of almost fifty years, David Riedel, who took charge of the final edits as well as typesetting the book. Couldn't have pulled it off without you, dear.

Shimmy Shimmy Homicide has been a labor of love, a long time coming. I hope you have enjoyed reading it as much as I did writing it!

Stay tuned for: *Shimmied To Death.* The next in my Belly Dancing Boomer Mystery series.

And Keep Dancing!

Rima

Shimmied To Death Preview

Shimmied to Death A Belly Dancing Boomer Mystery By Rima Perlstein Riedel

L ATE summer at the Leicester Senior Center. Temperatures rising, and with them, tempers. Our members were just recuperating from an unexpected wedding; before that a rather messy set of murders. It wouldn't take much for the scales to tip either way ....

My name is Esmeralda Fine—Esme for short. Because of my background in Therapeutic Recreational Services, and as a long time Belly Dance Instructor, I'm affectionately referred to as the local *playlady*.

For some reason I often find myself in the wrong place at the wrong time. During the cold, dank months of winter, I had literally tripped over a dead body. With the help of my students and the unwilling support of a rather large, transplanted, Hawaiian homicide detective, named Ralph Kai and his young sidekick, James O' Reilly, I was instrumental in solving said murder.

They say that "every cloud has a silver lining." This definitely held true for the aftermath of the disturbing events of the past winter. As a direct result of the murders, a lovely couple met and married. Now, six months later, Lien and Chuck Shackleton returned from their extended honeymoon in Vietnam and surrounding parts, just in time for the latest Leicester Senior Center news. The town was preparing for a week-long celebration of the 200th Anniversary of Leicester's official incorporation as a Connecticut town. All town departments were to be involved.

Not to be outdone by the other departments, the Senior Center was going to sponsor a Multi-Cultural Fair—complete with a delectable array of ethnic foods, a fashion show, and other fun activities. The high point— special performances exhibiting the songs and dances from a variety of countries. Of course, I had been asked if my ladies would be interested in performing several middle eastern dances.

Interested? Talk about an understatement!

When I had told them, they were practically foaming at the mouth in their excitement. Needless to say, they literally jumped at the chance to be included in a once in a lifetime celebration. Having just gotten over what, for them, was an exciting—albeit rather frightening—experience, they were now champing at the bit in anticipation of their next adventure.

They were not going to be let down ....

During our usual Thursday morning belly dance class, we discussed what routines we would be presenting. Ideas flew through air like acrobats on the high wire. Finally, we agreed on one short routine to be presented by our newbies and another, longer one performed by the advanced students, led by two of my most exuberant and lovably loudest students—Henrietta Hirshfeld(Henri to her friends) and Flor Ruiz.

It was decided that I should do a short demo. As much as I had demurred, the group endured. Confronted by not one, but two forces of nature, I finally gave in ....

Henrietta, is a former New Yorker born and bred. She is not known for being terribly subtle and no one would ever refer to her as shy or retiring. Henri has been my neighbor and one of my dearest friends for close to twenty years. We've shared many a morning coffee together.

Equally outgoing and with definite opinions, Flor's been with me the longest, having followed me around from place to place during our forty some odd years of dancing together. One of my most loyal dance students and supporters, Flor has even gone so far as to promote my classes on social media and everywhere she goes.

When not busy proselytizing about politics and the state of the world, Flor has kept me informed regarding all belly dancing competitors. Believe it or not, like any other business, belly dancing can be a cut-throat profession. The competition can be stiff. I ought to know. As I've already mentioned, I've been in the business for over forty years! I'm not the oldest dancer out there, but I sure come close. Worked my way through college dancing and teaching and never stopped. But, I digress ....

My main nemesis, La Reina (The Queen), came on the scene like a bat out of hell, if you'll pardon the cliché. At least fifteen years younger (she'll never tell) and much hungrier, La Reina proceeded to make a name for herself. And boy did she live up to that name! That's how all the trouble started.

As I was saying, things can get pretty nasty out there and that's exactly what happened when La Reina signed on to perform at the Senior Center on the same night as my group was scheduled. She expected to have the honor of closing the show. However, because my students had been taking classes at the center for over twelve years, the honor went to us.

To say that The Queen was not amused would be a gross understatement. She was livid! I tried to reason with her, but she stormed off in a huff, vowing to get even if it was the last thing she did.

Days later, Flor phoned to update me on the kerfuffle that had followed La Reina's threats. "That *bruja* has been at it again!" Flor exclaimed breathlessly. "Accusing the PTBs of favoritism because you teach here. She's telling everyone that you made a deal with the program directors behind her back. Says that you don't even know how to teach!"

"Calm down Flor." I soothed. "No point getting all bent out of shape and lowering ourselves to her level. She's right about one thing, though. We have been given precedence over her group because our class is held at the Senior Center."

"I know that," but we have earned our place. That one's just out for the money and the publicity," Flor spit scornfully. You know she doesn't give a damn about her students. That's why they always come back to you."

"Flor, you are my biggest fan when it comes to belly dancing, but you and I both know that it's not the be-all and the end-all of our lives. Our ladies have become a family. We're always there for each other and always will be. Does it really matter whether we perform first, last or in between? We're in it for the fun and exercise. If it wasn't for all your hard work, I'd say the heck with it. Let her have her big finale."

Flor was positively fuming. I could almost imagine the smoke rising up.

"How can you say that? You deserve that honor. We deserve it. How would the girls feel if they got shoved aside after all their hard work?"

"Flor, please. You have to calm down. You're blowing this whole thing out of proportion. First of all, I never said we should back down. We just need to keep it in the proper perspective. If it means that much to you and the others, I'll just leave things the way they are. But remember," I warned, "Queenie can cause quite a problem for everyone, when thwarted. I just don't want her to ruin the show because of this. Tell you what, I'll bring it up at the next class ... or maybe even during lunch."

"Oh all right."

I could actually hear sulking ....

* * *

The night of the performance, La Reina was in rare form. You see, The Queen is a bit of a tippler. Known for her forays into the liquor cabinet before each performance, she was literally on a roll—pun intended. Angry that she had not gotten her way regarding order of appearance, the she-devil came at me scarlet claws unsheathed—what is it about that color that often brings out the worst in a woman?

Screaming like a banshee, and ready to do some major damage to my face, La Reina had to be held back by two of my favorite security guys— Felix and Ace. As they dragged her away to a safe distance I, being the classy woman I am, yelled out, "I hope you choke on your Uzo!"

Unfortunately, I chose the wrong time and place—as usual—to make this statement, since a number of people were on hand to hear my little outburst.

During what turned out to be her last performance, La Reina died from an overdose of a rather nasty caffeine cocktail slipped into her drink.

She had literally shimmied to death ....

About the Author

Rima Perlstein Riedel—Just call her Rima ....

A long time resident of Manchester, Connecticut—a city not unlike Leicester, Rima is the author of a number of short stories, novellas, and plays, written for and performed by her Manchester Youth/Senior Theater Troupe (MYST). Her stories and articles have been published in *Scholastic Scope* and *Noir At The Salad Bar* by Level Best Books.

In addition to her follow-on novel, *Shimmied To Death,* Rima is also working on the third novella in her speculative literature series, *POEtic Justice: The Poe Files.*

Shimmy Shimmy Homicide is written in loving homage to her many students who have shaken and shimmied through over forty years of dance classes!

Made in the USA
Middletown, DE
17 September 2021